T0114732

THE UNQUENCHABLE
FIRE

MICHAEL C. JONES

WESTBOW
PRESS®
A DIVISION OF THOMAS NELSON
& ZONDERVAN

WestBow Press books may be ordered through booksellers or by contacting:

WestBow Press
A Division of Thomas Nelson & Zondervan
1663 Liberty Drive
Bloomington, IN 47403
www.westbowpress.com
844-714-3454

Cover design by Jonathan Jones

Scripture quotations are taken from the Holy Bible, King James Version.

ISBN: 978-1-6642-9889-7 (sc)
ISBN: 978-1-6642-9890-3 (e)

Library of Congress Control Number: 2023908080

Print information available on the last page.

WestBow Press rev. date: 05/22/2023

ACKNOWLEDGEMENTS

First and foremost, I would like to thank my Lord and Savior Jesus Christ for saving me in 2004. Without Him, I am nothing!

Next, I would like to thank my wife Charlotte for her strength in Christ. Also her support in helping me to use this book as a way to deal with the PTSD that comes with having been in Fire Service.

I want to thank my children, Naomi, Zechariah, and Jonathan for all they do to keep me laughing and loving me despite my shortcomings.

Thank you to my friend and fellow brother in the Lord, Scott A. Smith for his contributions to this book including the use of his personal testimony.

And thank you to everyone at Westbow Press and their affiliates for helping to make my dream a reality.

FOREWORD

Mike Jones, the author of The Unquenchable Fire, has over 30 years of combined firefighter, EMS and medical experience, reaching from Northern California to Wisconsin. His hospital experience began right out of high school in 1987 where he served as a phlebotomist trainee and laboratory assistant. In 1988 and 1989 he ventured into ambulance service doing several ride alongs with two ambulance companies in California. It was during those ride alongs that Mike asked a lot of questions and got to know several of the paramedics very well. They shared with him the variety of different calls that they responded to. He later worked on hospital staff in Wisconsin, and also served as a firefighter there for several years.

Mike's writing experience also began early in his life, from creative writing classes in elementary school to writing and composition courses in high school and college. He studied drama in high school as well. This experience was developed even more later in his life when he wrote skits and plays through his local church. I was extremely surprised and impressed with his excellent writing skills, especially his attention to detail, which can only be described as meticulous. Not just concerning this project, but also his fire fighting and EMT experience, along with his detailed descriptions of the characters in this novel.

This experience is only topped by Mike's personal Christian testimony, not unlike many, including my own. His younger years dabbling in worldly pleasures, two failed marriages, and depression that led to thoughts of suicide. In 2001, he met the woman and mother of his future children, Charlotte. They married in 2002 and began a wonderful Christian family.

In 2004, Mike's life soon turned for the better when he met the love of his life, Jesus Christ, and was gloriously saved!

I met Mike and his family when I was asked to become the assistant Program Director and Evangelist at a Christian Camp in Whitewater Wisconsin in 2010. I worked alongside Mike and his family at that camp, and quickly grew fond of them, and struck a friendship that has lasted over 10 years.

When Mike asked me to proofread his manuscript for The Unquenchable Fire and write this forward, I immediately accepted. I'm so glad that I did. When I started reading the first few chapters of the book I was enthralled. I literally could not put it down. I know others who read this will feel the same way. I greatly admire Mike and his family for writing this book with the goal of trying to keep people out of the Unquenchable Fire. God bless you Mike and family, and anyone who may be reading this... To God be the glory! Amen

Scott A. Smith, Evangelist

"I indeed baptize you with water unto repentance: but he that cometh after me is mightier than I, whose shoes I am not worthy to bear: he shall baptize you with the Holy Ghost, and with fire: Whose fan is in his hand, and he will throughly purge his floor, and gather his wheat into the garner; but he will burn up the chaff with unquenchable fire."

MATTHEW 3:11-12 KJV

Original cover design by Jonathan Jones

CHAPTER 1

It is break of day in Gold City as the sun rises slowly over the morning haze. The birds are chirping at each other as they move from tree to tree in search of a morning meal. Rain storms have been passing across the city for the past few days, so the morning calm is a refreshing change. Suddenly, the quietness of the morning is broken by the sounds of a small plane spitting and sputtering over the tree line. The pilot desperately tries to control the plane as it veers back and forth, climbing and falling as it makes its way towards the airport landing strip just a short distance away. The pilot clings to the yoke of the plane, hoping he can keep his plane level and make it to safety. "Come on, come on!" he exclaims to himself, "Just a bit further, hold on, hold on!" From his viewpoint, the airport runway seems just inches away when in reality he is still one mile out. Unfortunately, the engine stops completely and the plane comes crashing down into the tree line behind the City Baseball Field.

As the plane is going down, it has caught the attention of an early morning jogger, who is taken back in suprise to be witnessing this first hand. Quickly, he reaches for his Cell Phone and dials 9-1-1. The phone rings three times, and then is answered by the Dispatcher. "9-1-1, what is your emergency?" The jogger quickly explains the situation to the voice on the other end. "Yeah hi, I was out for a morning jog along the trails next to the baseball fields, when I saw this plane crash into the tree line." The Dispatcher asks the caller a series of questions, to obtain as much informatiion as possible to give to the emergency personnel who will be responding to the crash. "Ok Sir, I need some information. Can you tell me your name?" He replies, "Benny, my name is Benny Greenfield." "Ok Benny, you are calling me from your cell phone at this number, so if we get disconnected we can call you back, right?" Benny replies most assertively, "Yes Ma'am, that's correct."

The dispatcher continues, "Is this a commercial jet, military plane, or private aircraft?" Benny replies, "No it's not anything big. It's like a small low wing aircraft, probably a Piper Cherokee Six." The Dispatcher is suprised by the jogger's description of the plane, "Benny, how is it you can give such a correct description?" To which Benny replies, "That's easy, I work at the airport." The dispatcher chuckles to herself a bit and continues, "Can you tell me if you could see how many people were on the plane?" Benny replies, "I believe there's only the pilot, but I am not sure on that." The dispatcher states, "Alright Benny, stay on the line with me while we get some help out there, Ok?" "Sure!" comes the reply as he is placed on hold.

The Dispatcher, trained in Fire and Emergency Medical Dispatch, begins to push a series of buttons which set off fire department station tones. She then pushes a red button and speaks into her headset, "Station One with Engine One, and Medic One, respond to the City Baseball Fields at the tree line, for a reported small aircraft down. Reporting party believes only one patient, possibly more. Dispatch repeating, Station One, Engine One, Medic One, aircraft down, tree line at the City Baseball Fields. Dispatch clear at Zero Five Forty-Five."

At the firehouse, the doors to the bays begin to rise. Firefighters are moving about inside, putting on gear and boarding trucks. Engines are started and emergency lights immediately come to life, in a mix of red and white. The engine rolls forward out of the bay as the ambulance follows close behind. Sirens begin to sound simultaneously as they alert any oncoming traffic of their entrance to the roadway, turning to the left as they depart the station.

In the passenger seat of the engine, Captain Becker reaches for the radio microphone to advise dispatch of their response. "Dispatch, Station One is in service with both units responding. Request Battalion One to the scene and a second engine from Middle Village." Dispatch replies, "Copy, you are in service. Will tone out Battalion One, and a second engine from Middle Village at Zero Five Fifty." Captain Becker returns the microphone to its holding clip, then turns to his crew to give instructions at scene. "Ropino, grab the keys from the cabinet. When we pull up, jump out and unlock the service road gate. Stillman, when we're on scene, take the foam line and be ready. Hawks, you're on the Pump Panel." After giving assignments to the engine crew, Captain Becker reaches for the radio microphone again. This time to give instructions to the ambulance crew. "Medic One from Engine One on Tach Channel Two, follow us in and stage just inside the gate. We will assess the scene and bring you in when needed. Park off to the side so the Middle Village crew can get by." Captain Becker pauses to await their reply. "Medic One copies, will stage inside gate to the side."

The engine rolls up to the gate as Ropino jumps out and quickly unlocks the padlock. He then pushes the gate aside and gets back into the engine, and they continue down the service road. Medic One then enters the open gate and rolls to a stop just inside as Captain Becker had instructed. Off to one side of course, so the responding engine from Middle Village can make entry. Meanwhile, Engine One comes to a stop about twenty yards from the wreckage. Each member of the team goes into action. Hawks switches the transmission over to the pumper, and takes his position at the control panel for water supply. Stillman goes for the number one hose crosslay from the engine's right side and approaches the crash scene. The hose is charged and ready to be used. Stillman opens the nozzle and begins to spray down the wreckage and the surrounding area to prevent any possible fire danger.

Captain Becker instructs Ropino to do a quick visual search around the crash site and look for any other possible patients. He also does a visual scan of his own to make agreement with what his firefighter may find. Firefighter Ropino returns immediately to the Captain and gives his report. "Visual search completed Captain. No additional victims located." WIth a slight sigh, Captain Becker is relieved to find out they are only dealing with one patient. "Ropino!" Captain Becker calls, "Get the extrication tools out and make ready to access the patient for the medics." Ropino nods in agreement and does as he is told. Captain Becker takes his portable radio to talk to the medics. "Engine One to Medic One on Tach Two." There is just a few seconds of silence before he hears a response. "Medic One here, go ahead Engine One." Captain Becker continues, "Go ahead and come on back to the crash site. I've got Ropino starting to cut the plane open for you to get your patient out. Just the pilot, no additional victims." "Medic One copies." comes the reply.

Back at the ambulance, Paramedic Schmidt shifts the rig into drive and heads back to the scene. He parks the ambulance next to the engine and Paramedic Ridge gets out of the passenger side. Lieutenant Kelly Ridge is a twelve year veteran with Gold City Fire Department. He is a very qualified and highly decorated Firefighter. He holds more awards and commendations than any other Firefighter/Paramedic in the station's history. His partner Rick Schmidt, has been with the fire department for only six years. They have worked together as paramedics for all six years Schmidt has been on the department. Lt. Ridge carries the medicine kit and heads directly to the plane. Schmidt follows behind him with the trauma bag. They leave the Cardiac Monitor in the ambulance for now.

They climb up on to what remains of the right wing just as Ropino opens the airplane door. Inside, between coils of wire, bent steering yokes and floor pedals is the semi concious patient. Lt. Ridge begins to remove the wire coils and loose debris out of the way to make access to his patient. He hands some of it out to his parnter, who tosses it aside. Lt. Ridge enters the plane, as the moving about as roused the pilot more from his semi-conscious state. As he begins his physical examination of his patient, he is met by some moans and groans of pain. With this, the pilot comes around and opens his eyes. He looks directly at Lt. Ridge and questions the situation. "What happened? I can't feel my right foot, and my head and chest really hurt." Lt. Ridge tries to keep his patient calm and reassure him. "Take it easy Sir, you've been in a bit of a plane crash. I think you are going to be fine. Please try to relax and stay calm. We will have you out of here shortly."

From outside the plane, Schmidt hands Lt. Ridge the cervical collar. He thanks his partner and turns back to his patient. "Ok Sir, I am going to place this collar around your neck. It will help to keep your head and neck still to prevent any further possible neck or spinal injuries." The patient gives a thumbs up as best as he can in agreement, following the instructions not to move. He applies the collar, then takes the Blood Pressure Cuff from

Schmidt who in turn gets out a pen and paper to record the patients vital signs. Lt. Ridge begins, "Respriations 30, Pulse 128, B/P 160 over 100." Schmidt quickly jots them down and awaits further instructions. "Rick, go back to the ambulance and set up an I.V. for me. A thousand bag of Lactated Ringers would be best." "Right Kelly!" Schmidt replies as he climbs down and heads back to the rig.

Lt. Ridge reaches for the radio microphone clipped to his shirt. "Medic One to Incident Command?" "Medic One this is Incident Command, go ahead." comes the reply. "Captain, we are ready to move the patient out. Do you have a crew available to help us out?" There is a brief pause. "Affirmative, the Middle Village crew is here and I will send them to help you." Lt. Ridge adds another request, "Message received, have them grab the backboard and towel roll from the ambulance on their way in." Captain Becker replies, "Copy Medic One, they'll be right there." As Captain Becker unkeys his radio microphone, dispatch breaks in, "Dispatch to Engine One, be advised, Battallion One cannot respond right now, but he will monitor the channel and respond if he feels it necessary." "Dispatch, Engine One copies, I will be Ballfield Command." Dispatch replies, "Copy Ballfield Command at zero six fifty-eight."

By this time, Lt. Ridge and the Middle Village crew have the patient on the backboard and out of the plane. The four man crew each take a corner of the board and walk to the back of the ambulance. Lt. Ridge follows close behind them, since he is ultimately responsible for the patient. At the back of the ambulance, Rick is waiting with the gurney. The Middle Village crew puts the backboard down on the gurney and the patient is strapped in for safety. Rick pushes a button at the foot of the gurney and it rises to the load position automatically. Lt. RIdge climbs into the back of the ambulance and readies the Medical Cabin for care and transport of his patient to the hospital. Rick closes the back doors and gets into the driver's seat and starts the rig. He rolls down the window and addresses the Middle Village crew, "You think one of you guys can back me out, please?" One of the four agrees as the remaining three return to their truck and back down the service road. In return for the backing assistance, Schmidt offers him a ride out to the service gate. The Fireman hops into the passenger seat and thanks Schmidt for his generosity.

Meanwhile, paramedic Ridge has been busy transferring his patient to the onboard oxygen, inserting an I.V. in the patient's right hand and watching the Cardiac Monitor. He begins to ask his patient a series of questions to help in his patient assessment. His patient has been groggy but still able to be responsive. Paramedic Ridge begins, "Sir, can you tell me your name please?" The patient takes a couple of breaths before speaking. "Tom, Tom Maxwell." he replies. "How old are you Mr. Maxwell?" Ridge asks. His patient expels a couple more breaths, "I'm fifty-four years young." Paramedic Ridge is impressed with his appearance for his age. "Well Mister Maxwell you look pretty healthy at Fifty-four. How long have you been flying planes?" "I have been flying for about thirty years now." He takes another breath and continues, "I learned how to fly in college, then got my first job as a Missionary Pilot." Ridge is quite taken back by that. "Wow, that's quite impressive. Are you married Mr. Maxwell?" "Yes I am! My wife is back home. Her name is Cheyenne. She couldn't make the trip with me this time." Lt. Ridge writes down his responses as his patient takes additional breaths. Lt. Ridge reassures him, "Not to worry, the hospital will contact her for you. Is there anyone locally that can be contacted?" Mr. Maxwell replies, "Well I am here for an Evangelism Crusade. I am an Evangelist brought here to lead the unsaved to The Lord. Are you saved young man?"

Lieutenant Ridge just looks at the patient with no espression on his face. More so to avoid answering the question, he excuses himself from the conversation to radio to update the ER. He picks up the headset, places it over his ear and speaks into the microphone, "Medic One to Gold City Base on Med Channel Five." He awaits a response. *Medic One this is G.C.H. Base on Med Channel Five, MICN Nelson, go ahead.* First, as protocol, he identifies the unit calling and begins his report. "Medic One, paramedic Ridge, paramedic Schmidt, be advised, we are enroute to your facility with a fifty-four year old male involved in a small aircraft accident, Break." When contacting Med Control, crews must say "break" after each transmission. *"Copy Medic One, do you have vital signs for me?"* MICN Nelson asks. "Affirmative, Vital Signs are Respirations 30, Pulse is 128, B/P 160 over 100. Patient is alert and oriented times three. He is on 02 via mask at 6 liters. Also have him on IV of 1000cc Lactated Ringers at TKO, break." MICN Nelson has been busy writing the information down and passing it on to the ER Staff. She comes back on the radio, *"Copy Medic One, no changes in treatment. Take another set of vitals prior to arrival. G.C.H. Control Clear SBK-38."* "Medic One copies, second set of vitals. ETA to your facility three minutes, Medic One Clear."

He takes off the headset and hangs it on the hook attached to the radio. He is then asked a series of questions by his patient. "I overheard you say your name was Ridge, right?" The paramedic looks a bit puzzled by the question, but answers his patient. "That's right, do I remind you of someone?" Tom Maxwell pauses a moment and then asks, "You're not by any chance related to Doctor David Ridge from Gold City Community Church?" Ridge fakes interest in the conversation, "Yeah so what, he's my dad." Tom Maxwell is quick to notice Kelly's sarcasm and continues, "I'm here as his guest speaker for the Crusade." Will you let him know my situation for me?" Paramedic Ridge really downplays that idea and continues with the sarcastic responses. "I am sure he'll be thrilled to find out his Crusade is postponed or even cancelled. I will tell you one thing Mr. Maxwell, my dad is a true Irishman and he has quite the temper for bad news. Besides Mr. Maxwell, I am bound by healthcare laws that forbid me giving out patient information like that. My dad and I haven't spoken to each other in years, so why should I start now?" Tom Maxwell is suprised by this and asks, "Well you do see him in church on Sundays when you are off shift don't you?"

Lieutenant Ridge has been as polite as he can be to his patient, but cannot take anymore of the probing questions his patient is asking, and finally asserts himself to regain control the conversation. "Mr. Maxwell, I haven't been to church since I graduated from high school. My dad and I are NOT on speaking terms. Quite frankly sir, my relationship with my dad is NONE of your business. Let's just deal with your care right now, Ok?" Tom Maxwell expresses a look of defeat, but turns the conversation back in his favor with one comment. "You're right Lieutenant, it isn't my business at all, but it is God's!" This comment triggers a defensive response with Kelly. "Mr. Maxwell, I made an agreement with God a long time ago, that I would stay out of his life if he stayed out of mine! It's worked out pretty well for me so far." Tom Maxwell looks directly at Kelly and replies, "You may have given up on God, but I'm sure he hasn't given up on you." Kelly expels a very obnoxious breath as the ambulance arrives at the hospital.

Ridge begins to disconnect the oxygen tubing and takes the IV bag from it's hook and lays it at Mr. Maxwell's head and prepares to move his patient. "Ok Mr. Maxwell, let's get you inside so the ER team can look at you." Tom Maxwell replies, "You mean so you don't have to deal with me anymore." Kelly casts a sarcastic smirk towards his patient as a way to quietly answer Tom Maxwell's comment. Just as he finishes his look, his partner, Rick Schmidt opens the rear doors of the ambulance. Rick releases the lock on the gurney and begins to pull it out. Lt. Ridge follows out at the head of the gurney as it locks into ther proper postition on the ground. Both paramedics enter the hospital with their patient. They are met by E.R. Charge Nurse Ashley. "Hey guys, we'll take him in Trauma Room Two." Schmidt and Ridge nod in agreement with her and roll the patient into the assigned room. They place the gurney next to the other bed and transfer the patient onto it. Two other staff members assist the Medics with this procedure.

The receiving nurse puts his IV on the pole and set up the Cardiac Monitor. One nurse begins to take a set of Vital Signs while the other connects the oxygen tubing to the supply port on the wall behind Mr. Maxwell's head. About this time, the on duty Physician, Dr. Rodgers enters the trauma suite. He turns to the paramedics and asks for a report. Ridge responds, "Patient is a 54 year old male victim of a small plane crash. Complaining of head and chest pain. Patient stated also that he could not feel his right foot. He is on a thousand bag of Lactated Ringers TKO. Initial Vitals at scene, B/P 168/100, Respirations 30, Pulse 128. We placed a cervical collar and loaded him in the ambulance and transported here." Dr. Rodgers thanks them for the report, "Alright men, thank you. Is there anything else I need to know?" Ridge expresses a feigned concern for this patient, "By the way Doc, I was beginning to get a little worried about the patient upon our arrival." Dr. Rodgers inquires, "Oh? and in what way?" Kelly continues, "Well, just before we got out of the rig here, he starts talking to me about Jesus. He seemed to really push it to the point that I was thinking maybe he was on something or some signs of shock or delerium." Dr. Rodgers replies, "Ok thanks, I'll check him out,"

Kelly and Rick leave the treatment area and head back to the ambulance. Schmidt turns to Ridge and asks, "So Kelly, shall we head back to quarters?" Ridge turns and replies, "Sounds like a good idea, but let's swing by the Golden Rings for breakfast." Both paramedics exit the Emergency Room and get back into the ambulance, with Rick driving and Kelly in the passenger seat. Rick starts the rig and exits the Ambulance Bay to the main road. Kelly picks up the radio microphone and calls dispatch. "Medic One to Dispatch, you can show us as available." He unkeys his microphone and awaits a response from the dispatcher. "Medic One, Dispatch copies you as available at zero seven thirty six." Inside the ambulance, Kelly and Rick discuss plans for after shift. Rick begins, "So Kelly, what do you have planned after our 48 is done?" Kelly answers, "I think I'll go home and get a little breakfast, then maybe a little reading, and play a little chess." Both men then look at each other and chuckle sarcastically. "No, after Breakfast, I'll go work out at the gym, come home, pop in a DVD or two. How about you, Rick?' "Oh, Annie has her Honey-do-list of jobs around the house to get done." Kelly begins to laugh, "You poor guy! I hope Sharon doesn't get like that with me." Rick returns the laugh, "Naw, she won't, she'll hire someone to do the work." Kelly agrees, "You got that right, Rick." Rick's chuckle changes to a grin and states, "Annie says we need more us time together. She heard or read something about how couples can improve their quality time by spending time with each other." Kelly looks at Rick with a stunned response, "Whoa, you have got to be kidding with me! Sharon and I have plenty of quality time." "Nope, I'm dead serious. Annie has been reading quite a few of those types of books lately." Rick replies. Kelly smirks at him and states, "Man, I am so happy to be single. No headaches, no worries, and no responsibility. Sharon and I see each other in many different ways."

The Medic Unit pulls into the resturant parking lot and heads for the drive thru. Rick places the order for both of them, receives his total, and pulls forward to the pick up window. While waiting at the window for their food, the two paramedics continue their conversation. Rick begins, "By the way, I heard some of your conversation with Mr. Maxwell on the way to the hospital." "Yeah so?" Kelly replies. "What a coincidence about knowing your Dad, huh?" Kelly responds, "I guess so, but I didn't see much to it." Rick looks at Kelly, "Hey partner, I was getting concerned he was going to bless a bottle of saline back there and baptize you right there in the back of the ambulance." Kelly chuckles out loud, "Ha ha Rick, very funny." Rick smiles back, "Hey, just looking after my partner." By this time the employee returns to the window and hands Rick their order. First the coffee and then the bag of food. Rick hands the coffee and food off to Kelly so he can divide it up while he drives away from the window. Kelly rummages through the bag and unwraps the breakfast sandwich for Rick and hands it back. Rick makes the turn back onto the road and takes his sandwich from Kelly.

Rick then takes a quick glance at Kelly as he bites into his sandwich, "Hey Kelly!" he asks, "Do you want me to close my eyes while I drive and bless the meal for you?" Both of them laugh together as they continue down the road. Rick again turns to Kelly and asks, "So, have you heard anything about the Captain's exam or the selection process yet?" Kelly replies, I should be hearing about that soon. There's supposed to be a test or interview date coming up this week if I remember correctly." Rick asks, "So if you get it, how is that going to work? I've never heard of two station captains on the same shift." Kelly just shrugs his shoulders and says, "You got me! All I know is their was a job posting for a Shift Captain and I applied for it. You know as well as I do, there's all that bureaucratic paperwork that they claim they have to do instead of just punching my name up on the computer and doing it all over the internet." Kelly finishes his sentence just as the ambulance pulls up to the Firehouse. The bay door opens and Rick backs the ambulance into it's spot inside. As Kelly gets out, he is greeted by Captain Becker who hands him an envelope and says, "Ridge! I think you might want to see this." Kelly takes the envelope, opens it and reads the letter.

"To Lieutenant Kelly Ridge from Gold City Hall.

This letter is to inform you that your application process is completed and we will be meeting with candidates for Fire Captain this coming Friday the 21st. Your appointment is scheduled for two o'clock in the afternoon in the City Council

Chambers. Please notify the City Administrator's Office of your receipt of this notice and confirmation of the scheduled appointment time. Thank you again for your interest and good luck.

Sincerely,
Clarence Vondersheim
City Administrator"

Kelly holds up the letter and calls out to Rick, "There it is partner! The answer I have been waiting for has arrived. Friday at two o'clock in the city council chambers." Rick stops and replies, "Well Congrats my friend. I am sure you will do great. If you'd excuse me, I need to restock the rig while you take care of the run report." Kelly smiles, and acknowledges the well wishes. He turns and heads for the report room.

CHAPTER 2

MEANWHILE AT THE RIDGE HOME, MAGGIE RIDGE APPROACHES THE TOP of the stairs. She looks down, over and around the full basket of laundry in her hands before stepping down the stairs. She pauses for a moment before descending to call out to her daughter. "Bethany me child, Momma's starting laundry soon. If ye need somethin' washed, please bring it down."

Margaret "Maggie" Ridge is the Matriarch of the family. She is a woman of Irish descent, full of integrity and a sincere devotion to her family's needs. She runs a very clean and orderly home. She is dedicated to her christian beliefs and strives to follow her biblical responsibilites as given in Ephesians 5 and Proverbs 31. She steps down off the stairs at the bottom. She turns to her left, and continues through the dining room and kitchen, arriving at the laundry room. She places the basket down on the washer and turns back to the kitchen. She opens the cupboard in front of her and removes a coffee cup. She closes the door and pours a piping hot cup of black coffee into the cup. She then picks up the cup and takes it down the hall to her husband's study.

She raises her fist to the door and gives two knocks, waiting for permission to enter. There is no response so she repeats her knocks. After another slight pause, she hears, "Come in!" from the other side of the door. She enters the study and is greeted by her husband, Dr. David Ridge. "Well Good Mornin' to you again me darlin' wife." in his gruff Irish brogue. Dr. Ridge is not a doctor of Medicine, but a doctor of Theology, with his Masters of Divinity degree. He is the Senior Pastor at Gold City Community Church. He spends a lot of his time in his study preparing his sermons when he is not at the church. He smiles at Maggie as she hands him the cup of coffee. He reaches up and graciously accepts her offering. Dr. Ridge proclaims, "Ah sure, it's a fine thing to be taken care of by the most precious woman on this planet. The Lord has surely blessed me with you Maggie. Precious indeed me Love." He turns back to his desk and puts the cup down on the coaster. Maggie looks down at his notes and then inquires, "So what glorious things from God's word is my wonderful minister husband preparing for his church?" David replies, "Ah me darlin', The Lord has a bounty of sermons for me to preach about. I just seem to be having trouble deciding on the right one." She looks directly into her husband's eyes and reassures him, "Now David, as long as we have known each other, you have never ever missed the mark when it comes to finding the right message." She gives him an affectionate embrace and whispers in his ear, "I love you very much David Ridge, and have total faith in The Lord that you will find the right one."

David gets that twinkle in his eyes that only Maggie can give him. They seperate from their embrace and David returns to his chair behind his desk. Maggie walks over to the loveseat just across from the desk and sits down. She notices the wrapped gift sitting on the side table next to David's reading chair and can't help but inquire. "I see you still keep your son's graduation gift in the same spot that he left it at." David looks up from his note making from verses, "Yes I do me love. I just can not put it away right yet." Maggie expresses that concerned wife and mother look on her face. "You, Me Husband, are still hoping that Kelly will come home and accept it some day." Sighing to himself and sensing defeat, "Yes Maggie I do! If he would just accept it, he would discover all the riches he really needs within it's pages." Maggie nods in agreement, "I agree me husband, the scriptures are full of references to true riches." "Aye Maggie, and it warns of the worldly ones too." David also adds, "God's Word is a treasure all it's own."

Just then, the phone rings and Maggie gets up to answer it. She picks up the receiver, "Good Day to you, Ridge residence, this is Maggie speaking." There is a pause as she listens to what the caller has to say. She asks if they can hold the line for a moment and brings the phone to her chest. She turns to her husband, "David, it's the hospital calling. The doctor says he was to ask specifically for Dr. Ridge." David gets up and walks over to Maggie as she hands him the phone. "Hello, this is Dr. Ridge. How can I be of assistance to you?" He listens intently as the voice on the other end gives him the information. David then replies, "Well thank you for calling and please tell him I will be there right away." There is another brief pause as he finishes the call and puts the phone back down on the receiver.

Immediately Maggie is curious about the call. "David, what is it? Is it about Kelly?" She continues, "I just feel like Kelly has been hurt! I need to go be with me son!" He makes it a point to reassure her, as he can clearly see that she is becoming more and more upset. "No me darlin' it's not about Kelly. I can assure you as his father and as your husband." He starts to pace the floor collecting the words in his mind, and then gives her the information he received. "Maggie me love, do you remember a few weeks ago when I arranged for Tom Maxwell from High Mountain Ministries to come and speak for the upcoming revival week at the church?" Maggie nods her head in agreement as David continues, "Well it seems that he flew up in his personal airplane early this morning. He had engine trouble and crashed it as he was approaching the airport. She looks astonished at David and blurts out, "Oh! That's terrible dear, Is he alright?" David replies, "Well from what the doctor said, he has several injuries and asked the Hospital to call me as soon as they could. He asked for me to come down to see him, so I must do that right away."

David turns and goes back to his desk. He cleans up his sermon notes and reference books before leaving. He cinches up his tie and reaches for his suit coat. Maggie comes around his desk and helps her husband finish putting himself together. She speaks very encouraging to David, "Well I do hope The Lord heals him from whatever injuries he has." David agrees with her, "Aye me darlin' I hope so too. The Revival was supposed to begin later this week. Now I'm not so sure if it will." He then returns the encouragement to Maggie, "Although, I am sure The Lord has it all in His plans for some good thing to come from it."

He leans over to kiss Maggie and be on his way. She follows him to the front door as he reaches for his keys on the entry table. Maggie opens the door for her husband. As he walks out, Maggie exclaims, "Please let me know how it goes me Love." David replies, "Aye Maggie, that I will, bye-bye for now." David turns and steps off the porch as Maggie closes the door behind him.

She turns around to continue her tasks and is met at the bottom of the stairs by her daughter. Bethany Ridge is the youngest of the Ridge children. She has red hair down to her shoulder blades. She is dressed in her hospital smock dress with a matching hair piece. she wears hose with anckle socks on and is in tennis shoes. She isn't a nurse, but is the Assistant Coordinator of Gold City Hospital's Ambassador Program. She helps to oversee the volunteers as well as heading up the clerical pool of staff trained to work in different units and departments. She holds up a full laundry basket and exclaims, "Here you go Momma, I'll take it back to the laundry room for you." Maggie smiles brightly at Bethany, "Thank you Bethany. I do appreciate having you around the house to help out." Bethany returns the smile, "Your welcome Momma. Besides, isn't obedience toward your parents very important in life?" Maggie's smile gets even bigger as she looks at her daughter. "Oh me precious child, it most certainly is." She reaches up and gently caresses Bethany's cheek and hair in a brushing motion. "I am so privileged to be blessed with you as me daughter. Your pretty smile and your positive outlook on life. There is a man out there somewhere that will be eternally blessed to have you for his bride." Bethany replies, "Thank you Momma, and his name is Jon Simon." Maggie asks her daughter, "Do you remember me child what we taught Kelly and you about obedience being three fold to the Godhead?" As they make their way back, Bethany recites the teaching, "Obedience to God means obedience to the scriptures, which means Obedience to your parents."

Maggie is pleased to hear Bethany's response, "It pleases me so when I see the fruits of our labors are evident in our children." Bethany grins at Momma and in a boastful manner exclaims, "Well, at least one of your children still does." Maggie quickly deflates her daughter with scripture, "Now child, whether you meant it good or bad remember what it says in Proverbs 16, verse 18!" Bethany's smirk diminishes quickly as she quotes the verse to Maggie, *Pride goeth before destruction and a haughty spirit before a fall. Proverbs 16:18."* Maggie confirms her daughter's recitation, "Exactly! We must not pass any kind of judgement on anyone including your brother Kelly." Bethany replies, "Yes Momma, I am sorry." Maggie takes a load of towels out of the dryer and places them on the folding table. She begins to fold them as Bethany separates the lights from the darks as the two continue their conversation. Bethany begins, "Momma, why doesn't Kelly ever come over and visit anymore?" Maggie expresses a forlorn look on her face as she explains, "Because your brother has found himself in the world of earthly pleasures." To this Bethany replies, "You mean like the story in the Bible about the The Prodical Son?" Maggie again confirms, "Exactly me young one." Bethany adds, "Well as that story turned out in the end, he returned home eventually." Maggie replies, "That is right Bethany. The Lord will send Kelly back home to us someday. It is not for us to say when, but it is up to Him." Maggie points towards heaven as she finishes her sentence. Bethany becomes discouraged and adds, "I just wish Daddy and Kelly will resolve their differences." Maggie looks at Bethany, "So do I Bethany, so do I."

The ladies finish sorting and folding the clothes. Bethany makes her way to the kitchen cupboard and takes out two cups. She pours the two cups of coffee as Maggie enters from the laundry room. Bethany hands her one of the cups and she takes a sip. Maggie moves to the dining table to sit down and continues the conversation. "So what does my little one have planned for the rest of the day?" Bethany sips her coffee and begins, "Well I need to work at the clinic this afternoon. It is a short shift from noon until five. I am covering for Kimberly today." Maggie replies, "Oh, does she need prayer for anything?" Bethany is quick to answer, "No Momma it's nothing like that. She took the afternoon off so she could finish up with her wedding plans." This comment spawns Maggie's curiousity, "Is our young lady a part of the happy day?" Bethany looks directly at her mother and replies, "Yes, but I am not part of the bridal party per say. I was asked to play piano for the wedding and provide background music at the reception. She did however agree to be a bridesmaid for me when Jon and I get married."

Maggie smiles, "Oh that is so beautiful when two people become one." Bethany looks at her Momma with reassuring eyes, "Now Momma I can hear the underlying message in that statement." Maggie replies with a stunned look on her face, "Is it that obvious me child?" To this Bethany replies, "Everything will work itself out Momma. Jon and I agreed that we would wait until he is finished with seminary before we would even consider marriage." Maggie asks, "Isn't he even done with his studies yet?" "No Momma, he still has about a year to go. I am really hoping the Daddy will take him on as an associate pastor so he can gain experience." "And then?" Maggie cuts in. Bethany continues, "And then, if this is what The Lord wants for us, we will make our official engagement public as the future Mr. and Mrs Jon Simon." Again Maggie cuts in, "Then you will marry and give us grandbabies to love and adore!"

They share a giggle as the phone begins to ring. Bethany goes over to the phone to answer it. She picks up the receiver, "Hello, Ridge Residence, this is Bethany speaking." She listens for a few seconds, "Oh hello Daddy. I will get Momma for you, please hold on." Bethany turns and hands the phone to Maggie. She speaks into the receiver, "Good Day me Husband. How can I be a blessing to you right now?" She listens eagerly as a devoted wife should as David begins, "Ah Maggie me love, I just stopped by the church for a moment and now I am on my way to the hospital." Maggie inquires, "Will you be back for lunch?" David replies, "Probably not me Darlin' and that is why I am calling you. Tom Maxwell and I have a lot to go over, so I might just get something from the hospital commissary." Maggie replies, "Thank you for calling me and letting me know." David replies, "You're welcome Maggie, bye bye." Maggie signs off the call, "Bye-bye me Husband, God Speed!" She hangs up the phone and continues with her duties as wife and mother.

As Maggie returns to her chair at the table, Bethany inquires about the phone call. "Momma, what's going on?" Maggie repiles, "Oh my child, remember the guest speaker Daddy had coming for the revival later this week?" Bethany replies, "Yes, Momma!" Maggie continues, "Well, he flew up early this morning in his private plane and crashed trying to land at the airport." Bethany has an astonished look on her face, "Oh Momma, that's terrible! Is he ok?" Maggie takes Bethany's hand, "He'll be alright me child. That's where your Dad is going right now, to the hospital to go over any changes of plans with him." Bethany's look of astonishment changes to focused listening, "Well, I do certainly hope that everything works out for the both of them." "I certainly do hope so, me daughter." Maggie replies.

Maggie looks at Bethany and returns to a previous conversation, "Now

Bethany, before all this melee about the guest speaker, we were talking about you and Jon." "Yes Momma, what else would you like to know?" Maggie starts to ask Bethany question after question as fast as she can, "Now does he plan to come and visit any time soon? When can your Dad and I have his folks over for dinner? When can we go shopping for your wedding dress?" Bethany quickly puts her hands up in a stopping gesture, "Whoa Momma, slow down with all the questions." Maggie reels herself back, "You're right dear, but sometimes your mother needs to know some answers. Bethany reassures her, "Don't worry Momma, when Jon and I are ready to move forward in our relationship, you and Daddy will be one of the first to know, I promise." Maggie is encouraged by Bethany's mature attitude about this matter. "Very well child, if that's the way you wish to have it, than I can accept the mature answer you gave." Bethany continues speaking in a euphoric state of daydreaming, "Oh Momma, I can just imagine the day when I become Mrs. Jon Simon, forever and ever. I love Jon so much that I yearn to be in his arms, but I know I have to wait for now."

As the two women continue their talking, the phone rings. Maggie jumps to her feet to answer it exclaiming, "Oh that might be your Dad needing me to fill a need for him, excuse me." Maggie answers the phone, "Hello, Ridge residence, Maggie Ridge speaking." There is a brief moment of silence followed by a moment of joy. "Oh, well isn't this a pleasant suprise! We were just speaking of you, one moment." Maggie places her hand over the mouth piece, "Oh Bethany, the phone is for you. I think you will want to take this." Bethany gets up and takes the receiver from her mother and places it to her ear, "Hello, this is Bethany." Maggie watches her daughter's face as though looking at a brand new sunrise enilghtening the hills "Oh Jon, you called me. I have been worrying about you so much. I really miss you and I long to see you again." Jon replies, I've missed you too Beth, quite a lot actually. I wanted to call you and tell you that our prayers might be answered soon. I may be able to come and visit you sooner than I had expected to." Bethany smiles even brighter, "Oh Jon, really?" Jon answeres emphatically, "Beth, I can almost guaruntee it, my Sweetheart. I can and will promise you that I will see you very, very soon and in person!"

Bethany is becoming so excited about Jon's news that she begins shaking with enthusiasm. "Oh, I am so excited to hear that Jon! You have made my day so much brighter." Jon exclaims, "Well Beth, if that's all it takes to excite you is me just telling you this news.." Bethany cuts him off, "Now Jon that's not playing fair." She begins to laugh as Jon smiles to himself about his future bride's giddiness as he continues, "Now I will call you again real soon with particulars about when and where I will be." Bethany has pulled back her enthusiasm, "Alright Jon, that sounds wonderful. I can't wait to hear from you again. Bye-bye Jon and God Speed!" She hangs up the phone and sighs to herself.

Bethany turns back toward the dining room table and notes a certain grin on Maggie's face. "Alright Momma, you knew this call was coming didn't you?" She throws a smirk of curiousity at Maggie as she finishes her sentence. Maggie is a bit suprised and taken back by her accusation. "Now child, what would make you say that?" Bethany replies, "Oh Momma, it just seemed like another one of your well planned schemes again." Maggie reassures her daughter, "I tell you me child, as God is my witness, this time I had no part in it." Bethany knows in her heart that whenever her mother uses the phrase, "As God is my witness" in her sentence, that she indeed had no part in the phone call from Jon.

Bethany now sits at the table and finishes her coffee time with her Momma. She feels a renewed sense of accomplishment even though it was a simple phone call. Maggie notices this on her face and compliments her on it, "Imagine that! Sometimes all it takes is a message from a loved one to set everything right." Bethany smiles at her Momma, "Yes Momma, that's all it takes." Bethany gets up from her chair and takes her cup to the sink. She turns back to Momma, "My cup is in the sink, I have to finish getting ready for work. See you tonight Momma, I love you." Momma replies, "Thank you Bethany, love you too." She walks her cup to the sink as well. As she stands at the sink washing out the coffee cups, she looks up towards the heavens and then bows her head and prays, *"Father in Heaven, I just wanted to say thank you for all the blessings you bestow on me. You gave me a loving and caring husband who fills my needs as best as he can. You give me a loving daughter who has not strayed from Your Word and wants to serve You in some capacity."* She pauses a moment before continuing,

"Lord, You have given me a son who I care for and love very much. I pray for him Father and I ask You, to please make a way clear for Kelly to realize his sin. Help him to find that he has been living a lie to himself, and please show him the way back to You. I thank you Father and I humbly ask this in the Name of Jesus, Amen." She takes a deep breath, opens her eyes and returns to her housework.

CHAPTER 3

BACK AT THE FIREHOUSE, PARAMEDICS SCHMIDT AND RIDGE HAVE returned from their run. The two men are busy doing their daily vehicle inspection of the medic unit. Kelly is inside the patient care area restocking and doing an inventory check of supplies. He is busy going through I.V. bags, breathing tubes and masks. After taking an inventory of each item, he places it back into it's correct compartment. He takes an occasional sip of his coffee. While Kelly is busy doing that, Rick is busy under the engine compartment hood. He is checking the belts for wear and making sure the oil, coolant, water and transmission levels are all at appropriate levels. This is a daily routine for all fire apparatus to be checked and maintained to deliver optimal performance in an emergency situation.

Rick finishes up with the engine checks and puts the hood down. He then proceeds to check each tire for proper tread depth and that they are inflated to the proper pressure. As he finishes his part of the checks, he comes around to the side door of the patient area. The door is open and he strikes up a conversation with Kelly. "So Kelly, we never did finish our conversation about the rest of your time off." Kelly stops what he is doing and responds to Rick. "Okay partner, what is it you want to know specifically about my time off?" Rick asserts himself and states, "I want to know if you and Sharon are going out again?" Without skipping a beat Kelly replies, "Of course we are! She's a great girl and we are just having a lot of fun spendig time together. We just can't decide sometimes where to go or what to do." Rick is taken back a bit by Kelly's response, "Wow, I have never heard you speak more positively about anybody like that than you do about Sharon." Kelly replies, "Thanks Rick for the positive reenforcement." Rick replies, "Hey, no problem Buddy, it was my pleasure to have introduced you both to each other."

Rick chuckles as he walks over to the mechanic's tool box and places a pair of pliers and a screwdriver into one of the drawers. Kelly's jaw drops in suprise and rebuts, "What? You never did that. We met on that nursing home transfer call eight years ago. Obviously two years before you were partnered with me. She was bringing food carts out and ringing a bell at the Nurses Station. She was going back for another cart from the kitchen. While I was doing the paperwork at the desk, I stuffed a rubber glove into the wide part if the bell and taped it in." Rick expresses that sarcastic smile of his, "I know Kelly. As you've said before that she made some comment about the proper use of a glove and you were sold on her just like that." Kelly reassures Rick, "Trust me partner, Sharon and I will be a couple for a long long time." Rick asks, "You really think that don't you Kelly?" "I sure do!" Kelly replies, "Not even God himself could end this relationship." Rick is quick to reply with a warning, "Watch it my friend, they said that about God not being able to sink the Titanic, and look what happened there!" Kelly fakes an insulted remark coupled with a sarcastic grin, "No worries, if there really WAS a God, he would have sank my Titanic a long time ago." Rick is taken back from Kelly's reply, "Wow! This coming from the son of a preacher." Kelly snipes back, "Well at least I am not a...."

Before he can finish his sentence, tones drop and station alarms sound. The voice of the dispatcher comes over the radio, *"Medic One respond mutual aid to Middle Village for a two car collision with airbag deployment. Second ambulance requested, Lincoln Avenue and Fifth Street. Repeating, Medic One respond Mutual Aid to Middle Village for a two car collision with airbag deployment at Lincoln Avenue and Fifth Street, time out zero nine forty seven."*

Kelly springs up from the jump seat and exits from the side door of the rig, and closes it behind him. He opend the passenger compartment door and jumps in. Rick closes the rear loading doors and makes his way to the driver's side. He opens the door, jumps in starting the rig with his right hand while closing his door with his left hand. Kelly turns on the emergency lights and reaches for the radio microphone, "Dispatch,

Medic One is in service to Middle Village. Dispatch replies, *"Copy Medic One, you're in service at zero nine fifty."* Rick shifts the ambulance into drive as Kelly sounds the siren as they roll into the street. Passing traffic immediately yields the right of way to them as they pick up speed and head for the call

They arrive on scene with Middle Village about five minutes after the dispatch. Kelly radios in their arrival, "Dispatch, Medic One, show us on scene with Middle Village." *"Copy Medic One, on scene at zero nine fifty-five."* Rick parks the ambulance right next to the Middle Village engine. Both paramedics jump out and head for the side compartment door. Kelly grabs the Trauma Bag and Med Kit. Rick grabs the portable oxygen tank and heart monitor if needed. Both of them walk toward the cars, and are met by the Middle Village Captain. "Hey guys, thanks for coming out to help!" Both paramedics acknowledge the greeting as the Captain continues, "Our guys are tending to both patients in vehicle one." He points to a blue Ford Taurus then continues with his report. "We need you guys to take care of the patient in vehicle two." He points to a red Pontiac Grand Am. "I have one of my guys watching him until you got here." Kelly asks, "Why, what's wrong with him?"

The Captain shrugs his shoulders a bit and adds, "He claims just a little chest pain and is refusing care. Something didn't seem right, so we asked for you to come take a look at him." The paramedics nod at the Captain and head for the Pontiac. Kelly takes the lead and Rick follows right behind him. They approach the Middle Village firefighter and get a quick report. Kelly inquires, "Hey Merv, whatcha got for us?" Merv stands and turns to make eye contact with Kelly. "This is Mr. Johnson. He's 74 years old and claims to be in tip top shape. He says his chest hurts and is refusing care. Maybe you guys can talk some sense into him. Something just doesn't seem right." Kelly replies, "Okay Merv, thanks we'll take it from here."

Merv nods and walks away as Kelly moves to the drivers side door and greets his patient. "Good Day Mr. Johnson, let's take a look at you and see how you are doing, Okay?" Mr. Johnson appears to be a very polite, distinguished and scholarly gentleman who is quite resistant to his care needs. "My good man, there's nothing wrong with me other than a little chest pain. I am quite fine, so if you will kindly get me one of those sign off forms, I won't take up anymore of your valuable time." Both Kelly and Rick look at each other as if they were signaling an impending doom to one another. Rick pipes up, "We just want to give you a quick exam and then we can go from there." Mr. Johnson starts to get more upset with the two paramedics. "Gentlemen please I..." Kelly cuts him off mid sentence, "Mr Johnson I'll tell you what. Please just walk with us over to the ambulance. We can check you, sign you off, and you can be on your way, Okay?"

Mr. Johnson is still quite adamant about going with the paramedics. After pondering their requests, he reluctantly agrees and walks over to the back of the ambulance. Kelly opens the back door of the ambulance first and climbs into the patient compartment. He moves some things around to accommodate Mr. Johnson. Rick invites their patient into the back of the ambulance with an open hand gesture. Mr. Johnson steps up on to the taliboard, stops, turns to Rick and states, "On second thought, I refuse. You two have been very patient with me and so kind." To this Rick replies, "Mr. Johnson, come on now. We have gotten you this far, so please let us finish checking you. I promise we will let you go after we are done." All of a sudden Mr. Johnson becomes very rude and biligerant to the paramedics. "Look, as I have already told you both, I AM FINE! I DO NOT NEED ANYTHING! I am a 74 year old man in tip top condition and I WILL NOT let you two..."

Before he can finish his sentence, he grabs at his chest and slumps down onto the gurney. Kelly calls out to Merv to come and assist the two paramedics. Lora, another firefighter from Middle Village is also summoned to help. Togther, Lora, Merv and Rick pick up Mr. Johnson's limp body as Kelly places the CPR board on the gurney. Then everyone works together to place the patient on the gurney face up to give care and treatment.

Rick jumps out and closes the doors behind him. Lora moves into the jumpseat at the head of the gurney. She pulls out the Ambu-bag and connects the attached oxygen tubing to the green nipple at the wall of the ambulance. She then turns a knob just above the nipple on to 12 liters of oxygen, and places the mask over Mr. Johnson's nose and mouth. He has become completely unresponsive and has stopped breathing. Merv is busy, next to Kelly on the bench seat setting up the I.V. bag and preparing it for giving the patient needed medications. Kelly has been busy opening the patient's shirt and placing the heart monitor pads on his chest. Kelly and Merv switch positions as Kelly reaches for the radio headset and removing it from its hook. He places the headset over his head and immediately calls the hospital ER. Rick has placed the ambulance into drive and heads for the hospital.

"Gold City Base, Medic One on Med Channel Five, how do you copy?" There is a long pause, but no response. Kelly repeats his call, "Gold City Base, Medic One on Med Channel Five, how do you copy?" This time the silence is broken by a voice at the other end. *"Medic One, this is Gold City Base, MICN Berry, go ahead with your traffic."* Kelly switches to voice activated mode on the headset and begins, "Medic One is en route to your facility with a 74 year old male involved in a head on car accident. We attempted treatment several times as patient was alert and oriented and continued to refuse care. During this time patient became more and more agitated and then collapsed onto gurney inside ambulance." Kelly breaks radio communication to take further orders from the Emergency Room. MICN Berry inquires more information about the patient. *"Medic One, E.R. Doctor wants to know if CPR was initiated?"* Kelly replies, "G.C.H. Base, Affirmative, however prior to our arrival on scene, responding Fire Personnel stated patient was complaining of chest pain on initial assessment." MICN Berry replies, *"Copy that Medic One, how are patients vital signs?"* Kelly replies, "Patient appears to be stabilizing, vital signs are as follows. Respirations 16, Heart Rate 78, B/P 160 over 90. Patient is breathing on his own. I do have additional manpower on board if patient were to code again."

There is a pause in radio traffic. MICN Berry comes back on the Med Channel, *"Medic One, what is your ETA?"* Kelly replies "We are about two minutes out." MICN Berry ends with one final radio call, *"In that case, we'll see you shortly. G.C.H. Base clear."* Kelly signs off as well, removes his headset, and returns it to its hook. Rick pulled into the ambulance bay, parks, and stops the engine.

Rick gets out and opens the back of the ambulance. They are met right away by the Trauma Team, led by Dr. Rodgers. They immediately receive the patient from the paramedics care as Merv, Lora, and Kelly bring out the gurney. Dr. Rodgers greets them very abruptly, "Thank you evryone, we'll take it from here!" The Trauma Team whisks the patient off and into the emergency room. As the two paramedics enter the Emergency Room from the Ambulance Bay, they are met by the voice on the other end of the radio. MICN Berry or better known by the medic crews as E.B. greets Kelly and Rick. "Morning Kelly, Morning Rick, thanks for passing off the patient to us." Kelly replies, "Sure thing E.B.." as they are joined by Merv, Lora in the hallway.

Curiosity has ovetaken the crew as Rick asks a question for the group, "So what was that all about E.B.? Dr. Rodgers doesn't usually meet us at the entrance doors." She smiles at the team and explains, "Oh that? That's something new that Dr. Rodgers wanted to try." Kelly replies with a puzzled look on his face. "Tell us please E.B., what the purpose of this is?" E.B. explains, "At random, Dr. Rodgers wanted to pick an ambulance run and see how we do timewise with an actual patient." Kelly expresses his sarcastic tone, "And this is supposed to improve services?" E.B. asserts herself, "Well according to him it's supposed to. Besides, he's already got the ok from the Hospital Chief Operations Officer. Wasn't too hard to do either when Rodgers is the Chief ER Doctor," Kelly looks at her with a puzzled look and another sarcastic tone, "Well, OK then. Rick and I will get our supplies for restocking the rig, and be on our way." They turn to leave and Rick adds, "Do we need to give Dr. Rodgers any kind of verbal report?" E.B. replies, "Nope, I think we're good. Besides, if we need any info we can just check the recording from the run tape." Kelly chimes in, OK, E.B. we'll see you later." Just as this is said, E.B. answers a phone call to ER. She smiles, waves and mouths, "Bye Guys!"

Rick excuses himself, "Hey Kelly, I need to make a phone call. I'll be just a minute." Kelly nods as they turn around and walk away from the ER desk. As they pass through the hallways, they are bumped into by a man who turns the corner at a hallway intersection. As he looks closer, he notices it is his own dad, Doctor David Ridge. Kelly shows no family emotion towards his dad as the two make eye contact. He treats him like any other human being. "Excuse me sir for bumping into you." Rick acknowledges Pastor Ridge with a polite smile and a head nod. Kelly, on the other hand, continues down the hallway towards the public phone banks.

Doctor Ridge on the other hand, stared intently into his son's eyes and saw nothing but a cold and angry look back at him. As his son and partner walk away, Doctor Ridge just stands there and stares at Kelly as he rounds the corner out of Doctor Ridge's view. A tear rolls down his cheek, as it still concerns him as to why Kelly is still so angry.

Doctor Ridge composes himself, turns and makes his way to the information desk. He is greeted by one of the hospital volunteers. "Good Day Sir, how may I help you today." Doctor Ridge offers a courteous smile and replies, "Yes, I am looking for the whereabouts of a Mr. Tom Maxwell? I received a call that he had been admitted here this morning." The volunteer inquires, "Are you a family member or friend?" Doctor Ridge replies, "I am Doctor Ridge from Gold City Community Church. I received a call that he was here and that I was to be visiting him."

The volunteer looks through some of her paperwork and then taps some of the keys on her computer. She looks up and states, "Yes, here it is. He is in room 315. What you need to do is go to those elevators and go up to Third Floor. Doctor Ridge thanks her and turns to the elevator and walks away. As the doors open, he steps inside and pushes the button for third floor. The doors close behind him and take him to his destination.

As Kelly and Rick make their way back to the ambulance, they switch sides with Kelly becoming the driver and Rick takes patient care in the passenger seat. They pull out of the bay and on to the main road. Rick grabs the radio microphone, "Dispatch, Medic One clear and returning to quarters." Dispatch replies, *"Copy Medic One returning to quarters at 10:40."* Rick replaces the microphone to its holder and turns to Kelly. "So, what was that all about with your Dad?" Kelly replies, "It's nothing really. Just father and son stuff." Rick looks at Kelly with more intensity and prods more out of Kelly. "Come on my friend, you and I have been the lead A-Shift paramedic for years now. That is one thing you have never told me about." Kelly tries to avoid the conversation again, "Oh come on Rick, that will just bore you to death." Rick begs him a third and final time, "Please Kelly, tell me what's going on with you and your Dad?"

Kelly gives in and leads with his own question to Rick. "Ok! ok!, do you want the long version or the shorter version?" To this Rick replies excitedly, "I'll take the long version because I like a good story." Kelly resets himself in the drivers seat and begins to explain it all to Rick. "When I was coming into my teen years, I was into car magazines. One day I was looking through a copy of Driving World and I came across the perfect car for me. I mean I wanted that car badly!" Rick replies, "So what did you do about it?" Kelly continues the story, "So, I went to my Dad and showed him the car expressing my deep desire to own that particular car. My Dad looked at it and blurted out that it was a $25,000 dollar car. He informed me that if I wanted it bad enough, I'd have to work for it." Rick shows more and more interest, even blurting out, "Man, I should have gotten some popcorn!" Kelly continues, "So, I did everything from paper routes to bussing tables and washing dishes in resturants. I scrimpt and saved a good chunk of money for that car. My Dad put it aside for me and told me he would give it to me at graduation from high school." Rick has become so absorbed in the story, he blurted out, "So you got your money for the car?"

Kelly rolls his eyes and tells him, "No! my dad refused to give me the money. Instead of handing me the cash, he gave me a box. When I opened it, there was no cash, just a bible inside the box." Rick exclaims, "Whoa! No Way!" Kelly finishes his story, "He said he felt that I needed that bible more and that all I desired was contained in this book and to trust all that is written in its pages." Rick is taken back by the story, "Man, I am sorry my friend." Kelly completes the story with one final comment. "That angered me so much that I threw the box down, went to my room, packed all my things and never went back."

By this time Kelly and Rick have returned to the firehouse. Kelly backs the ambulance into the bay and parks it. As they get out, they are met by Captain Becker. "Kelly, do you have a minute?" Kelly nods and replies, "Sure Cap, I am right behind you." Kelly follows Captain Becker into his office. Rick stays back at the ambulance and get it ready for the next call.

Captain Becker offers Kelly a seat and closes the door behind him. He looks at Kelly and states in an official capacity, "Lieutenant, I need a favor from you!" Kelly replies, "Certainly Captain, how can I help you?" The captain rises from his chair, "You see Ridge, my wife's father is very ill right now. He is in a hospital up North, and his prognosis is not good. I need to go up with her. I want you to be in charge of A-Shift rotation while

I am gone. Will you do it for me Ridge?" Kelly ponders the request for a moment and then agrees, "Sure Captain I'll do it." Captain Becker smiles at Kelly and states, "Thank you Lieutenant! Oh and one more thing. You will be in the Captain's seat on Engine One instead of the medic unit." Kelly smiles at the Captain and blurts out, "Thank you Sir. It will be good to get some basic fire skills in again!"

The Captain returns Kelly's smile and states, "If you were anyone else Ridge, you'd get inspection duty for life." Kelly replies, "Thank you Sir. Is there anything else I can do for you?" To this Captain Becker replies, "No Lieutenant, that will be all, dismissed."

Kelly gets up from the chair and exits the Captain's Office. He is quickly approached by Rick. "So what was that all about?" Kelly replies, "Captain Becker wants me to be in charge of the next A Shift rotation and I agreed to it." "That'll be fun." Rick replies, "I guess I will have to call you Lieutenant Ridge, instead of Kelly." Kelly puts his hand on Rick's shoulder, "Hey, it's only one rotation and it's not like I am going to another station." Rick understands and asks, "Can I pick my own partner for the ambulance?" Kelly looks at Rick and states, "No, but I will let you be senior paramedic for the shift." Rick argees favorably, "Fair enough partner, fair enough."

The two paramedics continue their day accomplishing tasks associated with the daily activities in Fire Service. Whether it's washing the ambulance, or testing of equipment, their is always something to do to fill in down time. Kelly goes over the duty roster for the next shift he is going to cover, while Rick picks up a book and a couple of magazines to read up on the latest techniques and methods involved in emergency care. Things remain quiet for the rest of the day, giving the crew time to catch up on training and various housekeeping tasks around the station until about 7:30 that evening.

CHAPTER 4

THE QUIET OF THE EVENING IS INTERRUPTED BY THE DROPPING OF STATION tones, followed by the dispatcher's voice over the radio. *"Gold City Medic One, unresponsive female, 1560 Magnolia Way. Repeating, Gold City Medic One, unresponsive female, 1560 Magnolia Way, time out 19:30."*

Rick heads to the driver's side of the ambulance and jumps in. As he starts the rig, Kelly opens the bay door and gets in on the passenger side. Kelly picks up the radio microphone and goes into service. "Dispatch, Medic One, we are in service." The dispatcher acknowledges their call. *"Copy Medic One, you are in service at 19:32."*

This particular call is not as far from the firehouse, just 5-6 blocks away. As they pull up to the house, Kelly notifies dispatch of their arrival and gets out before receiving a reply. He opens the side door and pulls out the trauma bag, oxygen, and heart monitor. Rick comes around from the back of the ambulance and picks up the heart moitor. Kelly picks up the trauma bag and oxygen. They proceed to the front door and notice it is open behind the screen door. They enter into the house and find an elderly woman sitting upright in a chair in the living room. Her mouth is dropped open and her eyes are closed. She has the appearance of someone who is sleeping.

Kelly kneels down next to the chair and places his hand on her shoulder. He calmly asks, "Ma'am, are you alright? Ma'am?" There is no response from his patient. He notices that the patient is not breathing and is absent of a heartbeat. He turns to Rick, "No response, looks like a full code. Initiate CPR." Rick stops setting up the heart monitor and helps

Kelly move the patient from the chair to the floor. Rick grabs the ambu-bag, attaches the mask and takes his position at the head. He delivers two simulated breaths into the patient, and notice they do not go in. He repositions her head and delivers two more breaths. He then hears air escaping from where it should not be, given he has had a tight seal around the mouth and nose with both attempts. Rick tries to deliver breaths a third time, but air is still escaping. He turns to Kelly, "I can't get air into her lungs."

Both paramedics begin a head to toe assessment and notices a small hole behind her left ear. He turns to his partner, "Hey Kelly, I found where the air escaped!" Kelly looks and confirms Rick's discovery. "Yup, looks like a bullet hole to me. I'd say from a .22 round." Both paramedics look at each other and freeze their positions as they realize the potential danger they are in. Slowly, Kelly reaches for his portable radio and puts it up to his mouth, depressing the transmit button. Using a very calm and quiet voice he calls, "Dispatch, Medic One, we have an unsecured crime scene here. Respond Law Enforcement NOW please!" Quickly dispatch replies, *"Confirming, you have a Code Five Silent, correct?"* Kelly wastes no time in answering, "Affirmative Dispatch, Code Five Silent and step it up please?" Dispatch replies, *"Copy that, Officers are en route to your twenty right now."*

Within two minutes, officers arrive at the house and enter through the front door. Kelly slowly gets up and turns towards the officers and says in a whisper, "Thanks for coming guys. It looks like we have a homicide victim here. We think the subject might still be in the house. Could you please do a walk through and check for us?" The two officers nod at Kelly, draw their guns and proceed to check the house. They do a full sweep of the house and find nothing. They return to the living room and inform the paramedics that they are safe. "Ok guys, the house is clear. You two can pack up and return to quarters. We'll take it from here."

Kelly and Rick nod in agreement, turn and pack up their equipment and exit the house. They get to the ambulance and begin to load their equipment. As they close doors and prepare to leave, the police duty Sargeant pulls up next to them and rolls down his window. He calls out to the paramedics, "Hey Ridge, Schmidt, you guys will never guess what happened a little while ago!" They both turn around and Kelly responds to the Sargeant's Commment, "Ok Sylvio, tell us what happened while we avoided the jaws of death. Donut shop in Middle Village burn down?" Sylvio explains, "No, even better. One of my men found a subject wearing dark clothing walking down the main road. No reflective colors, not even a flashlight on this guy." Kelly expresses disinterest in what Sylvio is saying and states, "Yeah ok, people do that all the time around here. We've even handled struck pedestrian calls on that stretch of road many many times."

Sylvio puts his hands up in a stopping gesture and continues, "Hold on a minute, I'm getting to the good part." Kelly interjects, "Sorry Sylvio, please continue with your story." Sylvio continues, "So my officer stops this guy and asks for ID. The guy reaches for his wallet and revealed a gun tucked into the waist of his pants." Kelly and Rick move closer to the squad car, gaining more interested in Sylvio's story as he continues, "My officer relieves the subject of his weapon. A recently fired .22 caliber pistol." Rick is really intrigued now, "So now you have a possible suspect?" The sargeant cannot contain himself any longer, "Even better! My officer arrests him on a weapons possession charge, and he immediately breaks down and admits to killing your patient inside that house."

Both paramedics are stunned by this outcome and Rick replies, "You have got to be kidding!" To which Sylvio collects himself and finishes the story, "No. Apparently the old lady was his grandma. He went to her house to demand money from her and she refused. So this kid, like 19 years old, puts the .22 behind her left ear and pulls the trigger. He panics, calls 9-1-1 for an unresponsive female, then flees the scene." Kelly is quite astounded by this, "What is this world really coming to?" Sylvio replies, "I don't know my friend, but it's a pretty cut and dry case for the D.A.'s Office. Have a nice evening gentlemen." Sylvio closes his window and drives away. Kelly and Rick just stare at each other for a very slow few seconds. They turn around and get into the ambulance. Kelly picks up the radio microphone from the dash and clears them from the scene.

As they head back to the firehouse, Rick starts up a conversation with Kelly. "Man oh man! I don't remember the last time I felt so close to death." Kelly looks up at Rick, "You mean the patient, or the fact it became a crime scene?" Rick replies, "I'm talking about the crime scene not being secure. I mean, that guy could have still been in there and taken us out before we knew what hit us!" Kelly tries to be encouraging, "I know, but those are some of the risks we take in fire service." Rick fires back, "Yeah, but that's not the way I wanna go. If I am going to die in the line of duty, then let it be in a fire." To this Kelly replies, "Now that is one thing that I do agree with you on partner."

At this point, Rick turns the conversation to a more deeper direction. "Hey Kelly, let me ask you, don't you ever worry about dying?" Kelly's response is quite certain, "Nope, I know that my life can end at any given moment, so I don't think about it!" Rick is taken back a bit by how callous Kelly is about death. "Wow, I'm really suprised by that answer." Kelly asks, "Why do you worry about it? Your a good Catholic. You believe in God and go to mass at Christmas and Easter. Hey you even go to confession once a week." Rick reluctantly answers but is cut off, "Well yes, but..." Kelly adds, "Good little Catholic boy has everything covered." Rick is a bit insulted and tries to turn the tables on Kelly. "What about you? You're a preacher's kid. Didn't he help you believe in God and show you how to live?" Kelly gives Rick a very assertive answer, "I tried all that stuff growing up until I decided it wasn't for me. So, I made a deal with God that if he leaves me alone then I will leave him alone. When I die, I will face my outcome as a man! It works out perfectly for both of us that way."

About this time they arrive back at the firehouse. Kelly reaches for the radio and notifies dispatch of their status. "Dispatch, Medic One, you can show us in quarters." Dispatch replies, *"Copy Medic One, you're in quarters at 2045."* Kelly returns the microphone to the dash clip as Rick shifts into park and pushes the garage door button clipped to the visor over his head.

As they get out of the ambulance, Kelly is met by Captain Becker who was waiting for him to return. "Glad to see my two best paramedics are safe. I heard what had happened at that call." Rick looks at the Captain, "That's nothing Cap! Wait until you read our run report." Rick excuses himself and heads to the report room to finish and file the paperwork for the call. Kelly proceeds to open the side door to resupply the ambulance for another run. Captain Becker places himself in the frame of the side door. "Kelly, I was waiting up for you to let you know that I spoke with my wife while you were on that call." Kelly stops what he is doing and looks up, "How's things with your Father-in-Law going Cap? Any changes?"

Captain Becker smiles at Kelly's questions, "Actually Kelly, I needed to update you on a few things before you take over tomorrow." Kelly pauses his work, "Sure Cap, what's up?'

Captain Becker begins, "She got a call from her sister that her dad made some improvement and is more stable. My Mother-in-Law is having a hard time with this whole situation." Kelly chimes in, "So you won't be going up North after all?" Captain Becker replies, "No, my wife left ahead of me earlier this evening. I am going to finish up some routine station paperwork in the morning and leave around noon to join her pending no other issues prevent me from leaving. I still need you to run the shift and handle calls on the engine." Kelly smiles brightly at the Captain, "You bet I will Captain. It will be good to get some time on the engine for a change of pace." Captain Becker looks directly at Kelly and replies, "It's also a chance for you to get more practice in that right seat acting Captain Ridge." Kelly puts his hands up and answers, "Hold on, that's not until tomorrow." The Captain just smiles and walks away saying nothing.

As Captain Becker is walking away, he turns back to Kelly and states, "Oh and Ridge, you better try and get a good night's rest. It will do you good seeing there's a lot of responsibility with being the Duty Officer." Kelly responds, "Will do Cap, and thanks for the advice." The Captain raises his hand up to acknowledge Kelly's response as he walks away. Kelly turns back to the ambulance and finishes up the restocking. The events of that last call keep echoing inside his head. He holds back an urge to call his mom about these events.

He closes the side door and makes his way to the kitchen before bed. He opens the refrigerator door and finds two plates of chocolate cake wrapped in plastic wrap. One with his name on it and the other with Rick's. He pulls his plate out and takes a few bites off the plate and puts it back in the fridge. He thought it was nice of the crew to leave a snack for both Rick and himself. He really wants to eat the entire piece, but something is going on in his head, and at this moment is unsure of what transpired tonight. He is so tempted to call his mom and seek some advice, however the probability of his dad picking up the phone at that time of night is high. The last thing he neeeds right now is his dad pestering him about God and religion.

Just as he gets ready to leave the kitchen area, Rick enters the kitchen from the day room door. He looks at Kelly, "So did you find anything good in the fridge?" Kelly looks up at Rick, "See for yourself." Rick goes over to the fridge and opens the door. He reaches in and pulls out the plate with his name on it and exclaims, "Awesome, all I need now is a big glass of milk to wash it down." Kelly moves over to the dining table and sits down. Rick pours himself that big glass of milk and sits down across from him.

Kelly sits there quietly for a few minutes while Rick makes that piece of cake a piece of history. Rick follows the last bite of cake with a large swig of his milk. Kelly looks up at Rick and asks, "You know partner, I was just keep thinking about that call tonight." Rick looks at Kelly, "I know it has been bugging me too. Every line of the report I was filling out was very chilling to me." Kelly remains silent in his chair, totally oblivious to Rick's comment. Rick has to touch Kelly's shoulder to get a response. "Hey partner, you still with me there?" Kelly looks up and responds, "Yeah sorry, I just had a moment of reality there about my life." Rick curiously asks, "You want to call your dad about it?" Kelly looks very sternly at Rick and blurts out, "Remember partner, I am in charge for our last shift tomorrow. I can make it very difficult for you!" Rick quickly replies, "Whoa! Hold on there my friend. I didn't mean to strike a chord with you." Kelly composes his temper, "Hey, I am sorry for snapping like that. I just can't remember when I have been that close to dying before."

Kelly turns the conversation back to Rick, "So what about you? What went through your mind tonight?" Rick pauses for a moment before answering, "I have no worries. I have been to Catachism and had Confirmation, so I know where I am going when I die." Kelly gives a smart aleck reply, "Yeah, but is St. Peter going to let you in or see if you remembered your key?" Rick replies, "Ha ha very funny!" Both paramedics look at each other briefly as Rick continues, "Every line in that report made my skin crawl tonight. I just can't believe that kid sent his own grandma to the morgue just for a few dollars." Kelly replies, "That part didn't really bother me as much as being that close to death and living to talk about it. Every other call we've been like that has had a secured scene."

Rick is in agreement with Kelly. "I definitely agree with you on that front, partner." Rick gets up, moves to the sink and washes his plate and fork. He then rinses these items off under the faucet and places them in the dish rack. He turns to Kelly and asks, "So, you about ready to hit the sack for the night?" Kelly gets up from his chair and goes to the sink. He follows suit as Rick did with his dishes and states, "Yeah, I am ready. You go on next to ahead, I'll be right there." Rick puts down the dish towel and heads off to the sleeping quarters. Kelly finishes his dishes and puts his hands down on the counter in front of the sink. He looks down at the sink, sighs heavily and brings his head up as if he was looking into a mirror. This whole call has made him feel uneasy. He tosses the dish towel over the dish rack and then turns for the door to the sleeping quarters.

He enters the sleeping quarters and makes his way to his bunk. Most of the rest of A Shift are in bed and already asleep. Kelly removes his uniform shirt and places over the back of the chair next to his bunk. He sits down on the bunk and opens the zipper on his duty boots and removes them. He then places the boots just down the bedside closer to the foot of the bed. He props his pillow up against the headboard then brings his legs up to a half sit/lay position. He turns on the bunk lamp and reaches for the sports magazine in the chair where he slung his shirt. Rick is in the bunk next to Kelly and notices his actions. Rick turns over facing Kelly, and says in a whisper as not to wake the others, "Can you imagine the look on Captain Becker's face when he reads the run report?" Kelly is in agreement, "I know, me too." Rick turns back over and exclaims "Good night partner, see you in the morning, pending we get a full night's sleep." Kelly replies, "G'night."

Kelly finds himself flipping aimlessly through the sports magazine in his hands. He pauses briefly for some advertisement or article that he may find interesting for the moment, then continues flipping through pages. He goes all the way to the back cover and closes the magazine. He sighs briefly and tosses it down on the chair. He slides himself down to a full laying position in his bunk amd stares in silence at the dimly lit ceiling, still thinking about how close he came to losing his life tonight. There was something really working his thoughts and racking his mind that he could not place. He finally comes to the conclusion that it was his own skills and training that gave him the will to survive this close call. He arrogantly reassures himself that it was all his years of experience and training that brought him back safely to the firehouse.

Kelly reaches for the lamp and turns it off. He settles into bed and hears Rick faintly begin to snore from his bunk. Kelly refluffs his pillows while lying there and snuggles his head into his fluffed head rest. Moments slow down in his head and his body begins to relax his muscles completely.

Just as he is about to enter the state of full sleep, station tones sound and the lights in the sleeping quarters go on. All members jump up and sit to the side of their bunks and begin dressing. Kelly and Rick also spring up and follow suit. The brief silence is broken by the dispatcher's voice. "Engine One, mutual aid to Middle Village. Commercial structure fire, 885 South Lincoln at Valley Automotive Group. Repeating, Engine One mutual aid to Middle Village. Commercial structure fire at 885 South Lincoln at Valley Automotive Group, time out 2200." Kelly and Rick settle back into bed as they were not called. The engine crew make their way out to the engine as Captain Becker joins them. He pushes the garage door open button as he passes in front of the engine and takes his place in the officer's seat and closes the door. Hawks fires up the engine and switches the light-bar to the on position. Ropino and Logan take their places in the rear jump-seats. Hawks shifts into drive and rolls the engine out while the Captain activates the sirens. The last thing the paramedics hear is the engine response over the radio.

CHAPTER 5

THE 6 A.M. ALARM SOUNDS ON KELLY'S CELL PHONE AT HIS BEDSIDE. HIS hand reaches over to the side table to shut it off. He then sits himself up on the side of his bunk, rubbing his eyes and coming to full awake mode. Rick has returned to his bunk from the shower. He acknowledges Kelly, "Good Morning Partner! Ready for the big day as Duty Officer for A Shift?" Kelly looks up at Rick and asks sarcastically, "How come you always wake up so upbeat and chipper every morning?" Rick sits on his bed and smiles back, "I don't know. I guess it was just how I was raised." To this Kelly replies, "Your Duty Officer will be ready to take charge after my shower and morning coffee."

Kelly goes over to his locker and pulls out a fresh uniform. He walks back to his bunk and grabs the uniform shirt from yesterday's shift and sets it in the dirty basket inside the locker. He removes a towel and his personal hygeine gear and heads for the shower. Meanwhile, Rick has gotten dressed and busy at his bunk putting fresh linens on and straightening up his area of the sleeping quarters. He sits in the chair next to his bunk and puts on his boots. Not too long after this, Kelly returns from the shower already dressed in everything but his uniform shirt.

He follows suit as Rick did and remakes his bunk, straightens up his space as well. He also puts on his boots and turns to Rick, "Are you sure your going to be able to handle the rig without my expertise to guide you for the next 24 hours?" Rick smiles and pats Kelly on the back, "Trust me partner, my shift just got a whole lot easier." Rick smiles at Kelly and walks past him heading for the living room of the station. Kelly grabs his uniform shirt and cell phone. He notices that there is a text message from his girlfriend Sharon. He smiles to himself and puts his phone in his pocket and continues into the living room as well.

Just as he steps into the living room he hears the bay doors go up and makes out the sound of the engine backing into quarters. Rick looks at Kelly, "This is going to be fun. The engine crew is getting back from an all nighter." Kelly waves the comment off with his hand as he goes over to the kitchen area. He grabs a mug from the cupboard and fills it with a piping hot cup of freshly brewed coffee. The entry door from the bay opens and Hawks enters followed by Captain Becker. Hawks makes his way to the computer in the report area as the Captain addresses his paramedics in a fun sarcastic way. "Well looky here! While us hard working heroes pull an all nighter, we are graced by two freshly uniformed recruits!" He chuckles to himself and then turns to head for his office and personal bunk in the officers quarters. He stops and turns to Kelly and Rick. "I have ordered the engine crew to sack out in their bunks for the next three hours and to catch up on some sleep." Kelly and Rick simply nod in agreement as the Captain continues, "The only time I want them up is to either use the bathroom or if tones drop, that's it!"

Rick replies, "Sure thing Cap! Anything else?" Captain Becker pauses for a moment rubbing his chin, "No, I think that just about covers it. You and Ridge find something useful to do for the next three hours, then we will do the offical shift change report then." Captain Becker then turns and continues to his office. Both of the paramedics look at each other briefly as Rick asks, "Got any ideas on what to do for the next few hours?" Kelly puts up his index finger, "Wait a minute." He pulls out his cell phone and sends a text to his girlfriend Sharon. He waits for a few minutes and receives a reply. He turns to Rick, "Come on partner, we're going out for breakfast." He goes out into the bay and opens the garage door. He gets in the drivers side and Rick jumps into the passenger side. As he starts the rig, he turns to Rick, "Since the Captain wants silence so the engine crew can get some sleep, I sent Sharon a text to swing by and pick Annie up, and meet us for breakfast at The Twist Cafe." Rick smiles at Kelly and replies, "OK, Let's do it." Rick grabs the radio microphone and calls into dispatch, "Dispatch, Medic One. We will be available by radio in response area."

There is a brief silence. *"Medic One Despatch copies, available in response area, time out 0700."*

The ambulance rolls out of the bay and onto the main road. It is a short drive from the fire station to the restaurant. Both paramedics get out of the ambulance and go inside the resturant. They get to their table and sit down just as Sharon and Annie arrive and enter the resturant. Sharon walks over to Kelly and gives him a big hug and a peck on the cheek. Annie makes her way over to Rick and embraces him in her arms and gives her husband a kiss on the lips. The two couples take their seats at the table and Sharon opens the conversation. "Good Morning! How are the two most awesome and hunky paramedics doing today?" Kelly pipes up, "Perfect as usual, because we have THE two most gorgeous women in Gold City for sigificant others." Rick raises his water glass and adds, "Cheers to that partner!" Kelly arrogantly throws in, "Of course they are in relationships with two of the most perfect men!" All four of them share a chuckle. The resturant waitress stops at their table and takes their order. She then turns and heads for the counter to begin their meal preparation.

Sharon looks starry eyed at Kelly, "So Mister Perfect, when are you going to make me a permanent part of your life?" Kelly chokes on the sip of water he just took from his glass. He then puts the glass down on the table and drops to his knees next to Sharon. "That's why I texted you earlier, because I wanted Rick and Annie to be my witnesses. Sharon, I love you very much. You have been a very important part of my life since we met eight years ago." He then pulls a small box from out of his pants pocket and opens it revealing a very expensive looking engagement ring. "Sharon Renfro, will you say yes and accept my invitation to be my wife?"

Immediately, Sharon blushes profusely as she is totally caught off guard despite her previous question to Kelly. Rick and Annie express their approval by a hushed golf clap as Sharon nods in agreement. "Yes Kelly, Yes I would be honored to share my life with the most handsome man in Gold City." Kelly gets up off his knees and meets Sharon at chair level. They embrace each other and share a small kiss. Rick is disappointed at the reserved response and exclaims. "Aw come on you two, make it count!" Sharon smiles deviously at Rick and Annie, "Oh don't worry you two, I'll show more appreciation on Kelly's next day off!" The four of them continue their conversation as their waitress brings them their food. The waitress tops off their coffee cups and returns to her other duties. They laugh and joke as they share each others company until those three radio alert beeps go off.

The voice of the dispatcher comes over their radios. *"Gold City Medic One, respond to Fifth and Main for a vehicle accident. Minor injuries, ambulance requested with probable sign off. Repeating, Medic One, ambulance request for a vehicle accident. Fifth and Main, time out 0815."* Kelly and Rick immediately spring up from their chairs. Each of them toss a twenty dollar bill on the table to cover the cost of breakfast. Kelly grabs his radio and responds while they make their way out of the resturant and to the ambulance. "Dispatch, Medic One responding from The Twist Cafe." Dispatch replies, *"Copy Medic One responding from The Twist Cafe at 0817."*

The two paramedics jump into the ambulance with Kelly driving and Rick as passenger. Kelly Starts the rig, flips on the emergency lights and rolls to the call in full code three response. Back inside the cafe, Sharon and Annie continue with their meal as though it was just the two of them. As Kelly and Rick roll to the call, Rick turns to Kelly, "Well it's about time you got the nerve up to pop the question to Sharon." Kelly smiles and glances quickly at Rick while driving, "Well, you know, that call last night really woke me up to what's important in my life." Rick looks awkwardly at Kelly, "So, Sharon is your most important asset, so to speak?" Kelly blurts out as they arrive on scene, "Nothing is as important as my Sharon." Rick picks up the radio microphone, "Dispatch, Medic One on scene."

Both paramedics jump out of the ambulance before they hear the dispatcher reply to them. They are approached by Sargeant Leo Minster from the County Sheriff's Department. "Thanks for coming guys. Two car fender bender. One guy sitting down was fine until we rolled up. Then all of a sudden his neck started hurting. I figured I better call for a medic unit to check him out." Rick thanks him and approaches his patient, "Hey I'm Rick from Gold City Fire Department, mind if I take a look at you?" The man gets up and walks toward Rick and Kelly and states a totally opposite story. "Yeah man, you can go. There's nothing wrong with me." Rick turns to Kelly, "Well partner, what do you think?" Kelly looks smugly back at Rick, "You're the patient care person, you tell me." Rick replies. "No obvious trauma. I say fill out a 22 RFMC, have him sign it and be on our way." Kelly pulls out the Refusal For Medical Care form and hands it to Rick. Rick takes down the man's name, address, age and reason for refusal and hands it to the patient to sign and date. Rick hands the man a copy of the form as paramedics excuse themselves and return to the ambulance. They wave at the Deputy, get into the ambulance and drive off. Rick picks up the radio microphone, "Dispatch, Medic One clearing the scene and returning to quarters. *"Medic One, Dispatch copies clear and return at 0902."*

As the two paramedics return to quarters, they continue their discussion. Rick asks, "So when are you two lovebirds getting hitched?" Kelly looks over at Rick briefly, "We have a date in mind but nothing definite. Somewhere between three to six months from now." Rick replies, "Well I hope you have a special place in the wedding party for your best friend?" Kelly smirks sarcastically at Rick and states, "Of course I do. We will need someone to attend to the guestbook!" Rick looks rather condescending at Kelly, "Oh well thanks for the special consideration."

About this time, they arrive at the firehouse and Kelly backs the ambulance into the Apparatus Bay. He shifts it into park and gets out, turning off the battery box knob under his seat and closes the door. Rick comes around the front of the ambulance and closes the bay door. Both men head into the day room and hear Captain Becker call for roll and morning briefing. The Captain acknowledges Kelly and Rick as they enter. "Ah gentlemen, you're right on time. Alright men, I have to leave town for the rest of the shift and Lieutenant Ridge will be Duty Officer in my absence. Please give him the same respect you would give me for this shift. Other than that, truck reports look great, and run reports are up to date, so thank you men for that." Captain Becker turns to Kelly, "Lieutenant Ridge, I hereby relinquish command to your able body and with that, Company dismissed!" Kelly turns around and heads out to the assignment board and writes out the apparatus assignment. The only change he makes is that Stillman will go on the ambulance with Rick, as Kelly stands there for a moment on what to do about that one firefighter needed for the engine crew. Captain Becker comes out of his office and solves Kelly's problem. "Ridge, Logan is here to work the engine crew with you, so your crew is covered." Kelly acknowledges the Captain, "Great Cap, thanks. Guess that takes care of the shift assignments."

Kelly goes over to his fire locker at the side wall and grabs his turnout coat and pants. He walks over to the engine and puts his gear next to it. He places his helmet in the space between the dashboard and windshield. Rick approaches Kelly, teasing him a bit about the change. He places his arm around Kelly and rests his hand on his shoulder looking at Medic One, "Don't you sweat a thing partner. I will take good care of our baby." Kelly once again answers him with that arrogant tone, "I know partner, but that medic unit is the second best thing that has ever happened to me. I know that rig more than any other piece of equipment over the last eight years."

As the paramedics turn and head back to the day room, tones drop. *"Gold City Engine One, respond mutual aid to Cherokee Hills for a commercial structure fire at 700 Nelson Road. Repeating, Gold City Engine One, respond mutual aid to Cherokee Hills for a commercial structure fire at 700 Nelson Road. Time out 0950."*

Kelly immediately turns around and heads for the engine. Hawks, Ropino and Logan join him as all four put on their gear for the call. Hawks jumps into the driver's seat and fires up the engine. Kelly climbs into the officers seat and closes his door. Ropino and Logan have taken their places in the rear jumpseats as well. Hawks flips on the emergency lights and drives out of the bay. Kelly activates the siren and radios their response, "Dispatch Engine One in service to Cherokee Hills." Kelly replaces the radio microphone in its holder. Dispatch acknowledges Kelly's transmission, however, Kelly is already absorbing himself in what to do upon arrival to scene at the call, and doesn't hear their response.

As the engine crew approach an upcoming intersection, Hawks slows the engine down to make a left turn onto Nelson Road and clear the intersection safely. As he makes his way through, the calm is broken by the silence when Ropino yells, "LOOK OUT!" At that moment, a stolen big rig tractor enters the intersection at a high rate of speed and slams into the side of the engine compartment between Kelly and Ropino. Pursuing police units come screeching to a halt at the intersection. They jump out of their squad cars to assist the mangled fire engine and crew. One of them approaches the big rig to check on the driver, only to find that he has broken his neck in the crash and is dead. Several officers approach the fire engine as one of them immediately calls it in, "2125, Gold City. Accident with injury, Gold City Engine One involved. Respond medical times two, Fire Battalion Chief and Car 99." Dispatch immediately replies, *"2125 10-4."* Right away Dispatch switches over to fire channel and activates station tones, *"Gold City Medic One, Battalion One, Middle Village Engines One and Two, Cherokee Hills Medic Four, traffic accident with Gold City Engine One involved. Intersection of Table and Mountain, time out 10:02."*

Stillman and Rick jump from the lounge chairs in the day room and run to the ambulance. They are joined by Captain Becker who jumps into the patient compartment and sits in the forward jumpseat. Stillman takes the driver's side and Rick goes to passenger for patient care. As they roll out of the station, Battalion One speeds past the firehouse enroute to the call.

Captain Becker states, "Looks like my heading north is postponed." Rick pipes up, "Guess not Cap! Sorry about that." Captain Becker turns to Stillman, "Step on it! No telling what we are headed for at this point, but we must remain calm no matter how bad it may be." Both paramedics agree, "Yes Sir."

As they approach the accident scene, all three men stare with a mix of shock and anger, coupled with the fear of facing the possibility of the deaths of their colleagues in the mangled fire engine. Captain Becker calls out, "Careful men, do your 360 walk around to check for hazards." They each take a third side of the rig and check for any obstacles or safety concerns. Just then the additional crews from Middle Village and Cherokee Hills arrive on scene. Each engine crew grabs their Jaws of Life and begin the task of cutting apart the engine so they could quickly access the injured firefighters.

This process seems like hours for the A shift team as they wait along side the Cherokee Hills Medics for clearance. With expertise, the fire crews make excellent time in cutting away at the engine. Both crews are given the ok and approach the wreckage to assess their patients and deliver care. Rick and Stillman rush to the rig and check Ropino and Kelly on the impact side as the Cherokee Hills crew attends to Hawks and Logan. Rick tells Stillman to attend to Ropino, while he takes care of Kelly. As he begins his assessment, he immediately notices that Kelly has what is called "Raccoon

Eyes", which is common with a Traumatic Brain Injury(TBI) from a blunt force strike to the head. As Rick assesses his vital signs, he notices that his breathing pattern is irregular and shallow. His pulse pressure is slow and weak. He has multiple facial injuries, as well as obvoius fractures based upon how his body is positioned. He is unresponsive but does have critical life threatening issues.

Stillman assesses that Ropino is in a similar state but is semi conscious, writhing about and moaning in obvious pain. Logan and Hawks took the least of the impact, but are still being checked and treated for spinal precautions. They both have numerous cuts and bruises on their faces and hands. Fortunately for the two firefighters in the back, their turnouts saved them from far worse injuries.

Rick calls out to Captain Becker and he approaches the engine. "Cap, please have a couple of firefighters grab the backboard and gurney from the medic unit." Captain Becker agrees and turns to summon the fire crews as Rick calls out again, "Hey Cap, I need you to set up an I.V. and get the heart monitor ready for us also please?" Captain Becker nods and turns towards Medic One. He jumps into the patient compartment and begins Rick's set ups. Sargeant Minster comes up to the rear doors of the ambulance, "Are you going to be ok Captain?" Becker looks at the Sargeant, "I'll manage, but is there any chance we can get a police escort to the ER? There's not enough time for Life Flight!"

Minster looks at the Captain, "Sure thing!" About this time the fire crews arrive at the back doors with Kelly and Ropino and load them individually into the ambulance. Captain Becker jumps out and takes the wheel of Medic One. Hawks and Logan are being loaded into the Cherokee Hills unit. Ambulance doors are closed as both units prepare to leave. Sargeant Minster jumps into his squad car and escorts both ambulances to Gold City Hospital E.R..

CHAPTER 6

THE EMERGENCY CREWS AT GOLD CITY HOSPITAL HAVE ALREADY BEEN on full alert, awaiting the patient's arrival. Both Medic One and Cherokee Hills Four arrive and enter the E.R. bay. Trauma crews immediatly take action and begin treatment of the accident victims. MICN Nurses Ashley and E.B. try to reassure Rick, Tiller and the Captain that they will do all they can to save their brothers.

As much as they want to be in the trauma rooms to assist, they know that they would become a distraction and become useless to the trauma teams. They each do their best to keep busy. Tiller and Captain Becker both decide to step outside and have a cigarette to help calm their nerves. Rick, on the other hand, reaches into his pants pocket and pulls out his rosary beads. He prays for his friends, "Blessed Mother Mary, Mother of Our Lord Jesus Christ, please protect Ropino and Kelly in there. Please ask your son to send an army of angels to protect and watch over them both. Please Blessed Mother, do not allow them to enter Heaven just yet." He pauses and clenches his rosary beads tighter as he continues, "I really hope you will let your son spare their lives, Kelly's especially." Rick drops his bead clenched fist to his hips, "Please Mother Mary hear my pretition as I pray this in the name of The Father, Your Son, and The Holy Spirit, Amen."

Meanwhile, as Tiller and Captain Becker are standing outside, Batallion One Chief Michael Brewer pulls up next to them. He rolls down his window and asks, "Any news on your men Captain?" Becker looks at his superior, "No Sir, we just arrived with them. Trauma Teams are working on them right now as we speak." Just as the Battalion Chief is about to speak, the news van from Channel 14 arrives in the parking lot. News Reporter Linda Barnett approaches the three men being followed by her cameraman. She calls out to get their attention, "Excuse me gentlemen, Linda Barnett Channel 14 News, Do you have a comment on the accident involving your firemen?" Chief Brewer exits his vehicle to make comment, "I am sorry, I have nothing I can tell you at this time. Please give us 1-2 hours to get the information you are looking for and we will have a press briefing at 1pm and let you know all the details as soon as we have them. This is a sensitive time right now for all of us in emergency services, and we simply ask you for some patience. Again we will have a press briefing at 1 pm. I have no more comment." Ms. Barnett nods in agreement and signals to her cameraman to stop recording.

Just then, Rick pops his head out the side door. "Captain, Tiller, oh and Chief Brewer, the ER Doctor would like to see us right now." Chief Brewer turns to Captain Becker, "Bill, you get the information on your crew, I'm going to head back to the accident scene and see what I can find out for the press conference. I will meet you back here about 12:30 to prepare for the news media." All three men nod in agreement as Chief Brewer gets back into his car and drives off.

The three men go back inside and meet with the ER Doctor in a private conference room. The Doctor greets them very seriouly and directly giving information on each member of the crew. He closes the door and begins, "Gentlemen, I am Dr. Rogers, Senior Emergency Room MD. Here's what I can tell you from least critical to most. Your driver broke his right wrist. He also has several cuts and bruises on his face and hands. The firefighter behind him, took alot of glass to his face and hands on impact and has back and neck pain. That rear passenger had the least injuries. Both of them will recover nicely I think. The second firefighter has a broken right leg as well as a right broken arm. Finally your officer in the front passenger seat has the worst of all of them. He has multiple injuries on his right side. We also believe he suffered some kind of blunt force head trauma as signs of raccoon eyes were present while examining him." This is quite a lot for them to hear as Rick blurts out, "So is Kelly going to make it or is he going to die?" Doctor Rogers look squarely at Rick, "Fella, I have him in CT and MRI right now. He more than likely will need to go to surgery and relieve any Inter Cranial Pressure that may be building on his brain. The next 24 hours will decide to outcome of your friend's survival rate."

Captain Becker asks, "Has the hospital notified family? Because I feel it is our job to do that coming from his brothers in fire service." Dr. Rogers replies, "If that's what you want to do, then go ahead. I will tell my staff not to call loved ones." All members of the fire department agree as Dr. Rogers excuses himself. Rick looks at Captain Becker, "Well Cap, how about if I take care of Kelly's family? Ropino is single and both his parents died in a train wreck five years ago so he has no family." Captain Becker replies, "That sounds good. I'll contact Hawk's family. Tiller, you take care of notifying Logan's wife."

Again all three nod in agreement. Captain Becker looks at his watch and notices that the press conference is only 30 minutes away. He pulls out his cell phone and auto dials Chief Brewer. The phone rings twice before Chief Brewer answers. "Hello, Battalion Chief Brewer speaking." Captain Becker begins, "Mike, it's Bill. Listen we need to notify family members about the accident before the press conference." Chief Brewer agrees, "Great, you handle that from your end. I have a few more things here at the accident scene to work out. Tell Ms. Barnett from Channel 14 News that we are postponing the conference to 2 p.m. Captain Becker agrees, "Will do Mike. Thanks and see you then, bye." Captain Becker ends his cell phone call and informs Ms. Barnett of the time change. She nods in agreement and steps away from the Captain, calling her station on her cell phone while one or two other news vans arrive, having heard the scanner in their newsroom.

Rick walks back over to the side door and lights another cigarette. He takes a few puffs and builds up his stamina and courage to break the news to Kelly's family. He then pulls out his cell phone and calls Gold City Community Church. The phone rings a few times before the church secretary answers, "Gold City Community Church, this is Lucy Doyle. How may I help you?" Rick takes a deep breath and then begins, "Yes, this is Rick Schmidt calling from Gold City Fire Department, I am looking for Dr. Ridge please?" There is a brief pause and Lucy returns to the phone, "I am sorry, but Dr. Ridge just left. Can I take a message for him?" Rick replies, "No, this is quite urgent regarding his son. Is there any way I can get his home number?" Lucy answers, "Can you hold for a moment while I get that for you. It won't take very long."

As Rick waits on hold, he notices Kelly's sister Bethany is approaching the ER door. He calls out to her just as Lucy returns to the phone with the phone number, "Here it is, are you ready Mr. Schmidt?" Rick replies, "Nevermind, his sister is right here. Thank you!" Rick hangs up his cell phone as Bethany approaches him, "Hey there brother's partner, you holding things down before Kelly comes back out?" Rick takes a deep breath and extinguishes his cigarette in the ashtray at the trash can. "Um, Beth, there's something I need to tell you." Bethany becomes interested and notices the News Van in the parking lot, "What? Did my brother save a handful of people again and the media is here to cover his heroic effort?" Rick swallows a big lump in his throat as Bethany sees the seriousness in Rick's eyes. "Beth, Kelly was on the engine today covering duty officer for Captain Becker. They were responding to a mutual aid call to Cherokee Hills. The engine turned left at an intersection and was T-Boned by a stolen big rig tractor. Kelly is in critial condition inside and facing emergency surgery."

Bethany is so horrified by this news that she can't say a word. Tears begin to form in her eyes as she struggles for words, "W-w-what?" Her breathing pattern changes as she tries in her mind to make sense of what Rick is telling her. "Wh-when? Why?" She sputters as she is trying to process this news. She finally comes around realizing what she has to do next. She asks, "Have you called my parents to tell them?" Rick replies, "I was in the process of doing that when I saw you. I was waiting for Lucy, the church secretary to get me their home number so I could." Bethany accepts a hug from Rick as she dries her tears, "Thanks Rick, I'll take care of that. Give me a few minutes and we can go back into the ER together." Rick nods and steps away from Bethany as she pulls out her cell phone and walks away.

Bethany dials her home phone number as Maggie answers after a few rings. "Hello, Ridge Residence, Maggie Ridge speaking. How may I be a blessinng to you today?" Immediately Bethany starts explaining things to her Momma. "Momma, it's Bethany. I need you and Daddy to come to the Hospital right away!" Maggie tries to calm her daughter down,

"Bethany did you have an accident? Are you ok?" Bethany assembles her words thoughtfully, "No Momma I am fine. But, it's Kelly. He's been in a terrible accident and is very critical here at the hospital."

Maggie asks, "Oh Bethany, he's not going to die is he?" Maggie becomes so emotional as David enters the room. Bethany tries to reassure her, "Momma, you taught me to trust in God and he would sustain me. Well, he will sustain us." Maggie reasserts herself as best as she can given the circumstances. "Yes my child, you are right. He certainly will." David approaches Maggie as he notices the very distraught look on her face. He whispers to her, "Maggie me love, what is it?" Maggie moves herself closer to her husband's shoulder and closes the call. "Alright Bethany, I will tell him and we will be right there. Thank you for calling, bye bye."

Again David asks in wife as she places the receiver on the hook. "Maggie me love, what's going on? You look like your whole world has crashed in on you." She looks up at him, fighting her tears as best she can, "Oh David, we must go to the hospital at once. Kelly has been in a horrible accident and we need to be there for him." David retains his stoic appearance, "At once me love, at once. Your son needs you." She looks very sternly at her husband and blurts out, "He's our son David, OURS!"

David grabs his suitcoat from the coat hook as Maggie reaches for her purse. They both exit the front door of the house and quickly make their way to the car. David remains a gentlman and opens the passenger side door for his wife. He closes it and goes to the driver's side. He enters, starts the car and they head off to the hospital as quickly and safely as posible.

Maggie turns to David and tells him, "I need to call Lucy at the church and get the prayer chain going." David nods in agreement as Maggie pulls out her phone and dials the church. "Hello Lucy, it's Maggie Ridge. I need you to activate the prayer chain. Kelly has been in a terrible accident and we need all the prayers the church can muster." She nods her head as Lucy takes the information down. Maggie finishes, "Thank you Lucy. We will let you know more as we get it. Goodbye." She hangs up her phone and turns to her husband and sighs, "Oh David!" David glances at her quickly, takes her hand and replies in a consoling tone, "There there me love. Our Savior Jesus Christ has it all under control."

Meanwhile back at the hospital, Chief Brewer has returned from the accident scene and goes into the ER. He finds Captain Becker, Tiller, and Schmidt in the main conference room along with Dr. Rogers. Chief Brewer asks, "Have all family members been notified of the incident?" Both Rick and Tiller nod in agreement, as Rick adds, "Kelly's family is on their way in as we speak." Captain Becker acknowledges notifying Hawk's wife and kids. Chief Brewer then asks, "So then we will proceed with the news conference once the Ridge family has arrived and has gotten to see Kelly."

About this time MICN Nurse E.B. knocks and enters the room, "Excuse me Gentlemen, but the Ridge family has arrived and they are insisting on speaking with all of you." Chief Brewer paces the room for a moment and then glances over to Captain Becker. He nods to his chief and E.B. closes the door and goes to get David, Maggie and Bethany from the lobby area.

There is a knock on the conference room door and then E.B. enters with Kelly's family right behind her. Dr. Ridge proceeds to pull out a chair for Maggie to sit down, but Maggie has other ideas though. She can see the hurt in Rick's eyes and immediately walks over to him and embraces him with a hug. There is a brief moment of silence while Maggie does this. She pulls back and looks into Rick's eyes and smiles ever so gently. Maggie turns away from Rick and goes over to where David is waiting for her to sit down. She sits down as Bethany sits to her left and David sits to her right.

Dr. Ridge then asks, "Alright gentlemen, we are here. Please give us all the details of what happened. Chief Brewer looks very directly into Dr. Ridge's eyes, "Ok Dr. Ridge, here's what we know. We wanted to tell you first before we have a press conference with the media." Dr. Ridge glances quickly at Maggie and Bethany, "Proceed please Chief." Before he starts Captain Becker cuts in, "I am sorry to interrupt you Chief, but maybe we should offer them something to drink like water or coffee." Chief Brewer agrees as the Captain motions to Tiller to get them each a beverage.

Chief Brewer begins, "At around 10 am this morning Engine One was dispatched mutual aid to Cherokee Hills for a commercial structure fire on Nelson Road. Lt. Ridge was given duty officer assignment due to Captain Becker having to leave town on a personal family matter." Dr. Ridge nods and motions the chief to continue. "As they were making a left turn onto Table Road from Mountain Boulevard a stolen big rig entered to intersection at a high rate of speed and T-boned the engine at the passenger compartment. Your son Kelly took the brunt of the collision. He is in critical condition as we speak and has been taken to surgery to relieve a fluid build up in his brain." Maggie can't help but blurt out, "Dear Lord in Heaven!" bringing her hands up to her mouth. Not to be using The Lord's name in vain at all, but prayerfully.

Dr. Ridge embraces his wife around the shoulder as Bethany moves in against her Momma from the other side. Chief Brewer continues, "We wanted to do the proper thing and inform all family members involved before we went to the news conference this afternoon." Dr. Ridge asks, "When will my wife and daughter be able to see him?" Maggie chides her husband, "David, what about you?" Dr. Ridge looks at Maggie and says, "That boy has wanted nothing to do with me for the last several years. I am not sure if I am ready to see him or if he even wishes to see me for that matter." Bethany jumps up from her chair and looks at her daddy, "Daddy, I respect you as my father, but I do not respect this attitue of ungratefulness you are expressing. Kelly is YOUR son and MY brother! Please Daddy, let your personal feelings go for now, please."

Dr. Ridge looks up at his daughter and touches her arm very gently, "You are right me daughter. Please forgive me ungrateful spirit. You too Maggie." Both women look at their family patriarch and acknowledge his apology. They all embrace each other. Dr. Ridge then turns to the four men, "I am sorry too gentlemen for my outburst. You may go ahead with your news conference. We will wait in here until you are done." Maggie turns to her husband with a suggestion, "David, why don't you go with them and say a few words on our behalf. Bethany and I will remain here." David ponders this for a few seconds and agrees, "Maybe you're right me love. I could ask for prayers publicly." Maggie smiles in approval.

The Chief, Captain, and Tiller excuse themselves as David joins them for the news conference. Rick asks if he could stay with the Ridge's until after the news conference. Both the Chief and Captain Becker nod in agreement and leave the main conference room and proceed to the press area for the briefing. Linda Barnett and her cameraman are all set up and ready to go for Channel 14 News. They have been joined by two other news stations as the story has hit the newswire.

Chief Brewer instructs the news media, "If you would please give us just a few more minutes? We are awaiting for Sargeant Minster to join us. He is the lead accident investigator and will be here soon." With that, he leans over to Captain Becker, "Please call the Sargeant and tell him we are ready to go forward with the press briefing." Captain Becker takes out his cell phone to call the Sargeant just as he pulls up in his squad car outside the ER doors.

He makes a few comments under his breath for only the fire officers to hear and then signals Chief Brewer to begin the conference. The four men take their place behind the microphones and wait for the signal to begin from the news crews. While they are waiting, the Chief turns to Dr. Ridge and explains, "I will go first, followed by Captain Brewer. Then Sergeant Minster will speak on behalf of Law Enforcement. After that, we will let you say a few words Dr. Ridge." Dr. Ridge just nods his head in agreement and says nothing.

CHAPTER 7

THE FOUR MEN WAIT PATIENTLY FOR THE SIGNAL FROM THE CAMERAS TO begin. They are given the ok and Chief Brewer steps forward to the cluster of microphones at the podium and begins, "Good Afternoon everyone. My name is Michael Brewer and I am Battalion Chief for Gold City Fire Department. With me today is Captain William Becker on duty Captain for the A shift. Also with us today is Sargeant Leo Minster from the County Sheriff's Department, as well as Dr. David Ridge, Pastor of Gold City Community Church." There is a prolonged pause as he gives the reporters time to write names down.

He continues, "At 9:50 am local time, Engine One was dispatched to a mutual aid call for a Commercial structure fire in Cherokee Hills Township just north of here. While attempting to make a left turn at the intersection of Table Road and Mountain Boulevard, Engine One was struck by a big rig tractor traveling at high speed and without any warning. By numerous eyewitness accounts, Engine One signaled approach to the intersection, slowed to the proper speed and begain executing a left turn correctly. It was at that time when the big rig truck entered the same intersection and struck Engine One at high speed. Engine One took severe damage to the right side of the passenger compartment between the officer's seat and the rear jumpseat. The four man crew suffered injuries from minor to very critical. They were treated on scene and transported here to Gold City Hospital to receive further skilled medical care."

He then turns the podium over to Captain Becker. He steps forward and begins, "Thank you Chief. As duty captain for A Shift, let me first express my deepest thoughts and prayers, concerns for my fire crew, as well as to their families involved." He pauses and takes a deep breath before continuing, "Each one of these men know the risks and consequences that goes with their jobs as firefighters. I feel strongly for them right now, because due to some personal matters, I did not ride the engine this time and had my paramedic Lieutenant take the officer's seat."

He continues, "Regardless of all that, these men are heroes and should be celebrated for that. This is truly a very sensitive time at the Fire Department as we have to put forward an alternate staffing plan to fill A Shift, which will continue to provide quality service to the residents of Gold City." The Captain takes another deep breath as he has become a little emotional. He pulls himself together and continues, "Right now, I will turn the podium over to Sargeant Minster, who will provide you with accident details and then I will come up and release the names of the firefighters involved in today's incident. After that, Dr. David Ridge will say a few words. Then, we will take a few questions and end the news conference." Captain Becker steps back as Sargeant Minster steps forward to the podium.

"Good Afternoon everyone. At 9:53 am, a big rig tractor was reported stolen from Down The Road Truck Stop at County Highway 68 and Interstate 76." He pauses briefly before continuing, "At 9:55 am, police spotted the stolen truck and attempted a traffic stop which then escalated to a high speed chase. The pursuit continued down Table Road and ended at 9:59 am when it collided with Engine One where Table Road intersects with Mountain Boulevard." Sargeant Minster looks up at the reporters briefly and then returns to his comments. "The driver of the big rig was pronounced dead at the scene." He takes a deep breath and continues, "He has been identified as Juan Carlos Guerra age 37. He was a wanted felon for drug possession and distribution charges as well as being involved with other various crimes in the area. He was better known on the streets and to the public as Jalisco Joe."

Sargeant Minster steps back from the podium as Captain Becker steps forward. "At this time I will release the names of the injured fire crew as families have been contacted already." He becomes a bit emotional as he reads the names, "First is Fire Apparatus Engineer Jay Hawks, 18 years of service. He suffered several cuts and abrasions to his face and hands, as well as a broken wrist. Next is Firefighter Markus Logan with 14 years of service. He suffered the least amount of injuries and was able to assist with the care of the other members before being taken in himself. He was moved to A shift to help staff the engine today. Next we have Firefighter Ronald Ropino, also with 14 years of service. He suffered a broken right arm and right leg, as well as several cuts and bruises. Finally, we have paramedic Lieutenant Kelly Ridge with 12 years of service. He took the brunt of the impact and is in the most critical condition. His injuries are severe and too numerous to mention. He is currently being treated as we speak."

Captain Becker puts away his notes and states, "At this time, I will turn the microphone over to Dr. David Ridge for comment. After that, I will take a few questions if you may have missed anything." He steps back as Dr. Ridge steps forward and begins, "A Blessed morning to all of you. Right now the Ridge Family is broken, because one of our members is fighting for his life inside the walls behind me. We ask that you would all give us our privacy, as well as that of the other injured men." He pauses briefly and continues, "As Senior Pastor of Gold City Community Church, I call on our church members to prayer for all of those involved, especially me son, Kelly." He starts to become emotional, but quickly regains his composure and finishes, "Thank you for coming out today and may The Lord bless us all."

Dr. Ridge steps back as Captain Becker takes his place at the podium for questions. Linda Barnett is the first to raise her hand as he recognizes her. "Captain Becker, where were you when the call was dispatched and did you respond directly to the scene?" He clears his throat, "I was in my office finishing some reports so I could take a leave on a personal matter. Lieutenant Ridge was assigned to the engine. I responded directly to the scene with the medic unit." He points to another reporter who asks, "What was your first reaction when you pulled up on the accident scene?"

Captain Becker gives to reporter a stunned look, clears his throat, and answers, "First I thought was I can't believe what I am seeing, and then I was preparing myself for fatalities with my crew. None of you can imagine seeing a fully functional fire engine leave the station and a few minutes later, it's a mangled piece of metal, rubber, and glass, I mean as shift officer, I feel that I am ultimately responsible." Linda Barnett raises her hand and asks another question with a follow up. "Chief, so how will the department operate being down an engine?" Chief Brewer cups his chin with his hand momentarily and then replies, "I have spoken with the chief of Middle Village. They will be loaning us an engine temporarily until the city replaces Engine One." The Chief recognizes another reporter, "Yes thank you Chief. Tim Tyler with Channel 8. How long will that take to get another engine?" The Chief replies, "The city father's are having an emergency meeting to address that. They are looking at the budget and costs involved. They tell me it may take a couple of months, but they are making it a priority."

Ms. Barnett raises her hand and directs her question to David, "Dr. Ridge, how is the family doing and how are you all holding up during this time?" Dr. Ridge clears his throat before speaking. "Right now, we are all waiting on the doctors and nurses as they fulfill their duty to keep our son alive. We are a family of believers in Our Lord and Savior Jesus Christ. Both the Ridge Family as the members of Gold City Community Church will be in prayer for Kelly and his partners. The power of prayer is very real and we believe strongly in that fact." He holds up his Bible as he finishes his statement. "God's Word is absolute in it's teachings and as long as we remain faithful to Him, He will remain faithful to us." As he finishes his statement, Bethany pops out and whispers something in her Daddy's ear. Dr. Ridge listens carefully and continues, "Excuse me! but me daughter Bethany just informed me that me wife has heard from our church secretary. A prayer vigil will be held tonight at 6 pm at the church." Ms. Barnett makes it a point to write that down.

During this conference, Rick has been watching in the wings. He thinks again of finding his best friend being pinned down by crunched, twisted and torn metal. Debris scattered both inside and out the engine. Then he realized, he forgot to make the most important call of any to make. He pulls out his phone and calls Annie. There is a brief pause as he waits for her to pick up. "Hey there honey, it's me Rick. I need you to call Sharon and give her a message." Annie replies, "Sure Love, I can do one better. She's with me here at the salon. As a matter of fact, she's under the dryer as we speak." Rick inquires, "Are they playing the news conference about the fire truck accident in Cherokee Hills?" Annie replies, "Yes they are and I have been watching. You and Kelly must really have your hands full right now."

Rick takes a deep breath, "Actually that's why I am calling. Kelly was on the engine when the accident happened. He's in critical condition here at GCH." All he can hear on the other end is Annie blurting out, "Oh! I will get Sharon and get over there right away, love you, bye bye." Annie hangs up and tries to collect her thoughts on how to break the news to Sharon. She only thinks for a few seconds and decides the direct approach is the best. She gets up from the manicurist table and walks over to Sharon. Sharon is just getting done with the hair dryer. "Sharon, we have to talk." exclaims Annie. Sharon excuses herself from the stylist. "Sure Annie, what's up?" Annie pauses briefly, "I just got off the phone with Rick. There's been an accident involving Kelly. He was on the engine and.." She is cut off by Sharon who is now becoming emotional. "But Kelly is on the ambulance today!" Annie tries to console her, "No sweetie, he was on the engine responding to a call and was in an accident."

All of a sudden, the look of curiousity on Sharon's face has turned to a terrified expression. All she can do is spit and sputter words as she tries to make sense of it all. "What? When? How?" Sharon begins to tremble and shake as though her whole world is collapsing in front of her. The very same man that she accepted a marriage proposal just a few hours earlier is now clinging to life by a mere thread. Annie quickly puts her arm around her and hold her tight as she begins to cry into her shoulder and states, "Come on now Sharon, Kelly is still alive, he's not dead. Let's get you to the hospital. I'll drive you." As they approach the salon exit, Bonnie, the owner states, "I couldn't help but overhear you. I know your credit is good Sharon, you can pay us later." Sharon nods and thanks Bonnie as they exit the salon. They quickly make their way to Annie's car. They get in and drive away from the curb.

At the hospital, the press conference has ended. The news media members are busy putting away their cameras and microphones. Just as Linda Barnett is getting into the van, she notices a small crowd starting to gather in the parking lot with signs of support for the firefighters, especially the Ridge Family. Although she has seen these types of gatherings before, these people are different. They are wearing dress slacks and polo shirts, and dresses and skirts. Several of them are kneeling on the grass and sidewalk and praying. She watches intently and thinks that she will monitor this activity to see what comes of it each day.

Back by the ER doors, Rick lights another cigerette and tries again to take this all in. The anguish builds up inside consuming his thoughts about his best friend and co-workers. With each puff of his cigarette, the emotions mount heavier and heavier. He paces the sidewalk, looking in multiple directions to see if he can locate Annie's car pull in to the ER parking lot. He takes two more puffs from the cigarette, looks up and sees Annie and Sharon pull in. The ladies get out of the car as Annie moves at a quick pace over to Rick and embraces him. He returns the embrace and focuses on Sharon, "I am sorry for you to get this news Sharon." She nods in agreement as best as she can as he extends a hug to her as well. The three of them do their best to compose themselves before entering the ER waiting room.

As they enter the waiting room, Bethany jumps up and darts over to Sharon, hugging her ever so tightly. Bethany exclaims, "Oh Sharon, I am so glad you made it here." Sharon returns the hug and states, "Me too! I am just so overwhelmed about all of this." Bethany gives an awkward smirk, "You should have seen how I found out about it. I pull in, see Rick, and he tells me Kelly IS the patient!" Bethany takes Sharon by the hand and leads her over to her parents. Bethany begins, "Sharon, these are our parents, Dr. David and Margaret Ridge." There is brief eye contact as Bethany continues, "Momma, Daddy, this is Sharon Renfro, Kelly's fiancee." Maggie has no problem extending her hands of love towards Sharon as she draws her near to her and exclaims, "There, there my dear. Please call me Maggie." Dr. Ridge on the other hand, has looked Sharon up and down and is already concerned about this woman who is in his son's life. He doesn't say much to her as his facial expressions are speaking louder than one of his sermons. Dr. Ridge's mind is filled with references to the "strange woman" mentioned several times in the Book of Proverbs. Chapter 23:26,27, sticks out in his mind as he mumbles to himself, *"For a whore is a deep ditch, and a strange woman is a narrow pit. She also lieth in wait as for a prey and increaseth the transgressors among men."*

Maggie overhears her husband's mumbled words, "What is that you're saying me husband?" David replies, "Oh I was just quoting Proverbs 23:26,27 to me self dear wife." Bethany immediately chides her Daddy as she remembers that verse reference he made in a sermon a few weeks ago. "Daddy! That's not the right thing to think right now. Please, leave your clerical collar at the church and focus on Kelly right now?" David looks a bit embarrassed by her chastisement and apologizes. "Forgive me child, sometimes the minister in me overrides me personal feelings." Maggie has noticed the exchange between her husband and daughter. She excuses herself from Sharon to investigate the family issue. Maggie asks, "What are you two discussing over here. Aren't we having other more important matters to deal with?" Bethany stands her ground with Momma, "Sure I can Momma. Soon as Daddy stops making references to the strange woman in Proverbs after meeting Sharon!" Maggie is quite shocked at what she heard. "Why David Seamus Ridge! I am dissapointed in what I am hearing. Surely you can put your opinions aside for now, please!" David looks at Maggie, "Aye, you're right me love. Forgive me Please!" Maggie just smiles at David with a look of mercy.

Maggie goes back over to Sharon and sits next to her. Sharon turns to look at Maggie, "Have you heard anything about Kelly's condition yet?" Maggie tries to be as gentle as she can be. "When we first got here, the Doctor told us that they thought he had what they called a Traumatic Brain Injury. They took him to surgery to relieve some fluid pressure on his brain. We've been waiting ever since." Maggie and Sharon just sit together in silence as David paces the floor. Bethany takes the initiative and taps Sharon on the arm to join her on a walk to the cafeteria.

As the two ladies make their way to the cafeteria, Sharon stops and turns to Bethany, "Beth, what happens to Kelly and me now?" Bethany looks puzzled, "What do you mean?" Sharon looks around the hallway distraught, "I mean what's going to happen to our relationship as a couple? Kelly and I had so much going for us. Now things have changed forever." Bethany looks straight in the eyes, "Look at me Sharon! Both of you are going to make it through this. Both of you!" Sharon pauses a moment and changes up the dialogue. "All my life I have been trying to figure things out. I had excellent grades in school, graduated with honors. My Dad was high up in government law enforcement so we had money." Bethany wants to say something, but is looking for an opportunity to witness to her brother's fiancee, so she let's Sharon continue to talk. "I first met Kelly when I worked at the nursing home where we met. I worked the Kitchen as a dietary aide and he tried to get my attention by stuffing the meal bell at the desk with a rubber glove. We chatted for a few minutes and he asked for my number, and I gave it to him. I had just broken up with an old boyfriend and thought he might be someone different. A few months later, I got into some trouble with the law and went to jail for like 6 months. Kelly was the only one who stayed in touch with me by visiting me at the jail or I would call him and we'd talk. I really think it was then where we started to develop a relationship."

Sharon pauses briefly as they enter the cafeteria. They both get a cup of coffee and sit down at a table. Bethany smiles and agrees with Sharon's last comment. "I remember that since it was the only thing Kelly would talk about for months." Sharon takes a big sighing breath, "Your brother became such a powerful force in my life, that I just knew right then and there that he was the man I wanted to spend my life with once I got out of jail. I did a complete 360 in my life and never had problems with the law again." Bethany places her hand on Sharon's forearm, "I just don't know why it is taking so long for him to propose to you." Sharon makes a depressed groaning sound, "That's the irony about today. He proposed to me this morning and now look what has happened. It's like some supernatural force is working against us and doesn't want us to have a happy life together."

Bethany is seeeing a mounting opportunity to witness, but she holds off just a bit more as Sharon continues. "I mean, I know there is some kind of God that controls everything. I was raised Catholic and had Catacism and was Confirmed. Kelly told me once that there was a Supreme God that ruled over all. But over the years, he even said that he began to question the existence of God." At this point, Bethany is on pins and needles almost ready to pounce like a wild animal, hoping for her chance to ask that one specific question to her friend. Sharon takes a sip of coffee, "Then one day he told me that he made a deal with God that if He would leave Kelly alone, then Kelly would leave God alone." Bethany can no longer hold back, "Sharon, can I ask you a question"? Sharon shrugs her shoulders, "Sure."

Bethany takes a deep breath and asks point blank, "If you were to die today, where would you go?" Sharon smiles really big and states, "That's easy, I would go to heaven like everyone else who is confirmed would." Bethany looks puzzledly at Sharon, "What makes you so sure of that?" Sharon emphatically states as she counts on her fingers, "Because I am a good person. I give to the needy on the streets, I help out at the food pantry each month and I run errands for the elderly with the Senior Cares Program. It's all about being a good person. God sees that and I know I am going to heaven." Bethany looks suprised by Sharon's answer. "Sweetie, you think doing works will get you into heaven?" Sharon replies, "Of course I do. My priest once told me God doesn't sweat the little stuff. If you have been kind to people, then you will be welcome into the gates of Heaven." Bethany pulls out her cell phone and brings up her King James Version Bible App on her phone. "Sharon, can I show you something from scripture that might make you see things a little differently?"

Suddenly Sharon becomes uncomfortable with the conversation and quickly changes the subject. "Can we talk about this another time? We need to keep our thoughts on Kelly right now." With this, Sharon finishes her coffee and asks, "Can we get back to the waiting area? I would like to know if they found out anything yet." Bethany nods in agreement and gets up as well. The two of them leave the cafeteria and return to waiting area after a short walk.

Bethany asks, "Have you heard anything yet on Kelly?" Maggie walks over to the two young ladies, "No one has come and given us an update on anything about your brother." Bethany turns and looks at her Dad, "How's Daddy holding up through all this?" Maggie looks Bethany directly in the eyes, "Your Father is like a Cedar of Lebanon in a hurricane. Right now nothing is showing emotionally on the outside, but I have been married to him far too long to not recognize the anguish he is experiencing on the inside."

Bethany goes over to her Daddy and asks, "Daddy, You're terribly quiet about all of this." To this Dr. Ridge replies, "Aye daughter and it's best that I should right now. Your mother and I have spoken while you were gone off with Sharon. We agreed that right now it is far better for me to be dad rather than a minister of The Gospel." Dr. Ridge glances over at Sharon and Maggie. He then turns to Bethany, "Come my child. This is a time for prayer and not for criticism." The four gather together as Rick has left to return to duty at the firehouse and Annie had to leave. Maggie added, "Sharon, Annie said she would take care of the hair salon bill." As David completes the circle of four he adds, "Join me now in a word of prayer for Kelly." Maggie and Bethany bow their heads. Sharon is noticeably uncomfortable with this, but joins them out of respect. She bows her head but does not close her eyes as David begins, *"Lord Jesus, we humbly bow in reverence before you now and ask that you will first and foremost forgive us of any sins in our lives and that you would reveal them to us. Please Father, watch over Kelly and protect him while he is in surgery. Please guide the hands of the surgeon and his team. Above all Father, whatever the outcome may be, grant us the wisdom and peace in this time of need. We ask this graciously in Your blessed name Jesus, Amen."* Maggie and Bethany unanimously reply, "Amen." Sharon remains silent as all four give a group hug and sit down on the couches.

Time seems to go on forever as they wait for some answer on Kelly's condition. Maggie quietly pulls out some yarn and knitting needles from he purse and begins to knit. She turns to Sharon and smiles saying, "Always carry a purse big enough to carry yarn and knitting needles. You never know when you will need them." Sharon just politely smiles back at Maggie and continues to read a fashion magazine. Bethany finds comfort in watching animal programs on the nature channel on television as David sits and reads the Bible and makes some notes for his Sunday Sermon.

One of the nurses comes out and says, "I'm Nurse Nelson, Lead Surgical Nurse, and you are the Ridge Family I hope?" David rises and moves toward the nurse, "Aye, I am his father David, This is me wife Maggie, our daughter Bethany and Kelly's fiancee Sharon." Nurse Nelson nods to acknowledge them all. "I came out to let you know that the surgeon will be out in a little while to let you know his condition. Unfortunately, I am not allowed to give you any information. Excuse me, I need to go back into the surgical unit." Nurse Nelson turns to walk away and David implores her, "Please, can't you even tell us if he came through the surgery?" Something about David's demeanor in asking her changes her mind as she does state, "I can tell you it's not bad news." She then turns and heads back into the surgery unit.

David and Maggie look at each other and embrace as Bethany and Sharon do likewise. David makes the decision to gather everyone around for more prayer. *"Father God, we are ready to accept whatever the final outcome from the surgeon will be. I just ask that you will give us strength as we receive this news from the surgeon. Thank you Father, Amen."*

CHAPTER 8

ANOTHER HOUR PASSES IN THE WAITING ROOM FOR THE RIDGE'S AND Sharon. David gets up out of the chair and starts pacing the floor. Maggie rises and addresses her husband, "David, what's wrong?" David looks up at her, "Aye Maggie, the nurse said the surgeon would be in shortly to tell us of Kelly's condition and it's been another hour since." Maggie tries to be reassuring to her husband. "I am sure there is a good reason for the delay." It is at this moment that the surgeon appears in the waiting room doorway.

"Good afternoon, I hope this is the Ridge Family." states Dr. Foreman. Bethany and Sharon both rise and join David and Maggie. David answers for the family, "Aye, we are the very same." The surgeon nods his head, "Good! I am Dr. Foreman, the surgeon for your son. I do apologize for the further delay, I got paged for something in ER and had to attend to that first before seeing you." Maggie looks at Dr. Foreman, "That's quite alright Doctor, Kelly isn't the only patient here to be seen." With this Bethany breaks in, "How's Kelly? When can we see him?" Dr. Foreman puts up both hands in a pausing gesture. "You will all get to see him in due time, however you all need to be brought up to speed on the situation." David gently touches Bethany's shoulder, "Thank you Doctor, please sit down and tell us."

The five all sit down as Dr. Foreman begins, "When Kelly came to us, he had some internal bleeding that we were able to stop. Kelly also had some pressure built up in the brain from a head injury sustained in the accident. We relieved that pressure and was able to stabilize him more." Maggie jumps into the conversation, "Can we see him now?" Dr. Foreman continues, "Soon, but please let me finish. He does have a few broken ribs and a concussion. His right arm has what we call a hairline fracture. What puzzles me is how ended up with the injuries he has for this type of accident." David looks very puzzled by the surgeon's comment. To this, Bethany chimes in, "What would make you say something like that?" Dr. Foreman looks her in the eyes and states, "Because in all reality, that type of accident he was in, should have killed him!" Maggie gasps as David quickly takes hold of her hugging her tightly. David's looks the doctor squarely in the eye and states, "Aye doctor, but it didn't. It is a miracle from God that he was spared."

Dr. Foreman gets up and prepares to leave. He turns to address the family one more time. "We are going to transfer him to the Intensive Care Critical Care Unit upstairs. We have placed him in a medically induced coma for the next 24-48 hours. He has been medicated pretty heavily to allow the body to heal while he sleeps." replies the surgeon. Sharon then asks, "When can we see him doctor?" Dr. Foreman takes an assertive stance, "After he's moved, we will let you see him through the glass doors of the unit. Dr. Foreman excuses himself and walk out of the waiting room.

The four of them embrace each other with reassurance as David takes the lead. "Maggie, Bethany, Sharon, let's all gather in a circle and give a prayer of thanksgiving to The Lord. The Ridge's take each others hands to form a circle. Bethany and Maggie reach their hands out to Sharon to include her. Sharon is a bit hesitant and feels on the uncomfortable side as Bethany gives her a nod of assurance. Sharon walks over and takes a hand each from Bethany and Maggie. Everyone bows their heads except for Sharon, who keeps her eyes open. David begins, *Father in Heaven, Master Physician, we humbly bow before you now and thank you for sparing Kelly's life. We now ask that you be with all of us at this moment and in the days ahead. Prepare us for the worst oh Lord, but may we rejoice in victory. We ask this of you in the Name of Jesus Christ, Amen.*"

They turn and gather all their belongings and walk to the elevator. Bethany pushes the call button and the doors open. They all board the elevator and go up to the second floor. The elevator doors open to the second floor right across from the entrance to the ICU/CCU Department. They are greeted by a charge nurse named Erin who greets them. "Hello,

I am Erin the charge nurse for this unit. Please follow me this way. He's right over here." She points over to Room 4.

They walk up to the glass doors and stare at the motionless body of Kelly. He is wearing an oxygen mask over his face and is surrounded by several different types of machinery that are connected to him in some way to monitor all of his body functions. The family just stares at him with mixed emotions of both joy and sorrow. They are all happy to see that he is alive, but it hurts them to see him that way. Maggie, Bethany and Sharon all huddle together in a group hug type of formation. David stands alone next to them just staring at his son. He says nothing and shows no emotions as he gazes at Kelly. Then all of a sudden David begins mumbling the 23rd Psalm. *"The Lord is my shepherd; I shall not want. He maketh me to lie down in green pastures: he leadeth me beside the still waters. He restoreth my soul: he leadeth me in the paths of righteousness for his name's sake. Yea, though I walk through the valley of the shadow of death, I will fear no evil: for thou art with me; thy rod and thy staff they comfort me."* He then finds himself not being able to finish the psalm as he can feel a rush of emotions he does not want to deal with at this time. He is afterall the Patriarch of the Ridge Family and must remain strong for his family members that are hurting.

Maggie takes out a hankerchief and wipes away her tears and then hands it off to Bethany who follows suit. Sharon just stands there in silence, reviewing the earlier part of the day in her mind as tears flow from her eyes. Bethany taps her on the shoulder and hands her the hankerchief as well. David turns to Maggie, "Me Love, why don't we see if you can spend the night with Kelly." Maggie turns to her husband, "I don't know if I can handle that right now." Bethany cuts in, "Yes Momma, why don't you stay the night." Sharon joins Bethany in agreement, "Yes Mrs. Ridge, that is a good idea." Maggie is almost convinced to stay the night until she recognizes a look in David's eyes and call him out on it. "No, no, I think you should stay with your son David. I am not strong enough right now to handle this." David replies in a calm but suprised tone, "What? But Maggie we haven't had anything to do with each other in years." Maggie snaps back, "Now David Ridge don't you dare use this as reason to not be with your son! Yes, you haven't spoken in years, but what difference does that make right now. For once in your life stop being Dr. David Ridge and be Kelly's father! Besides, we need to attend the prayer vigil at the church." David just stands there in silence as he takes the stern but loving chastisement from Maggie. Then, David looks ever so lovingly at Maggie and surrenders, "Once again me love, you have broken my stubbornness with the love of Christ." Maggie looks at her husband and smiles, "That's why I am your help meet me husband. You are the head of the house and I am the neck that turns the head." David Smiles in agreement, "Ah, Maggie, you are so right me love." In a teasing tone she replies, "An' don't you forget that now either!"

The ladies gather up their things and prepare to leave for the night. Sharon goes up to Dr. Ridge and prefers to shake his hand and walks out of the room to the hallway to wait for Bethany and Maggie. Bethany gives her Daddy a hug and whispers in his ear, "Be thankful that he's still alive and that it's for a purpose. Just like you remind me when I have difficulties." David nods and smiles at her as they separate. Maggie steps up to her husband and hugs him firmly, "Tonight will be good for both of you David." The couple kiss each other good bye for the night. Bethany looks back as she walks out of the unit, "See you in the morning Daddy, I love you."

The three ladies make their way out as Dr. Ridge finds himself alone with Kelly. He stares at him intensely as a tear starts to stream down his face. David gets permission from the nurse to enter the room and stay the night. There is some silence between the blips and beeps of the various equipment around Kelly as he enters the room. He takes in those few moments of silence to draw some peace in his mind. He walks over to Kelly and puts his hand on his shoulder, "Aye me boy, you sure paid a price today. I bet you would be thinking I would be the last one to have anyhing to do with you right now, but I am here." He takes his hand and wipes away another couple of tears running down his cheeks. "Just more proof that The Lord isn't done with you quite yet."

With every word he says and thought in his mind, he can't control his emotions. He breaks down finally and weeps long and hard for his son. He pauses for a moment and looks heavenward and prays, *Heavenly Father, I am hurting right now. Me Son, me oldest child lays helplessly before me like he was when he was a wee baby so long ago."* He pauses to wipe away more tears before continuing, *"Father I humbly ask, and maybe I am being a bit selfish here, but, please use this situation to make Kelly see YOU through all of what he faces down the road and bring him back to the fold. Father, I ask this in Your Holy Name, Amen."* Dr. Ridge lifts his head just as Kellys' attending nurse comes into the room. It just happens to be Charge Nurse Erin who greeted them when they came in to see Kelly. She introduces herself again and explains that she is Kelly's nurse for the evening. "Excuse me Mr. Ridge, it's Erin again. I will be Kelly's nurse. I need to check his vitals and do a physical assessment of him. It will only takes a few minutes."

Dr. Ridge smiles and steps aside, but not before giving her some correction. "Certainly me dear, but it's Doctor Ridge not Mister." Erin looks up at him and exclaims, "Oh? I'm sorry. What is your field of practice?" He smiles at her and quotes Matthew 9:37,38. *"Then saith he unto his disciples, The harvest truly is plentious, but the labourers are few; pray ye therefore the Lord of the harvest, that he will send forth labourers into his harvest."* Erin looks up and exclaims, "Oh, you're a preacher!" Dr. Ridge pumps up his ego a bit, "Yes child, I have me Doctorate in Ministry. I am the Senior Pastor at Gold City Community Church." Erin shows interest, "Oh, well I am a believer also. I just moved here from Montana and I am looking for a church to worship in." Dr. Ridge's ego increases dramatically, "Well then, might I offer ye an invitation of sorts to visit me church sometime?" Erin looks up from her assessment and smiles graciously, "Well thank you, I just might do that sometime. Maybe after things settle down for you and your family. I will however keep Kelly and all of you in my prayers." Dr. Ridge replies, "Your hesitance to me is irrelevant, however, a hesitance to Our Lord should never be." She finishes her work, "OK, everything looks good with Kelly from a medical standpoint right now. I will be in later to check up on him frequently throughout the night. Will you be spending the evening?" Dr, Ridge answers, "Yes me dear, I will be. I just need to take a walk around and maybe visit the chapel and pray a while. You know the power of prayer is our best weapon in a time like this." Erin nods in agreement and leaves the room. Just as David in leaving, she pops back in and hands him a visitor's pass to wear. "Dr. Ridge, you will need this on at all times while you are here." He accepts it with a smile and clips it to his shirt. "Thank you lass. I shall return in a bit." He then proceeds out of the unit and makes his way to the cafeteria downstairs first.

He enters the cafeteria and makes his way over to the coffee machine and makes himself a cup. Then he moves over a bit and takes a premade sandwich from the cooler. He goes over to the self check out, pays for everything and leaves. He makes his way to the chapel and starts to open the door, but is held up by someone calling his name. "Dr. Ridge! Excuse me, Dr. Ridge!" He turns and sees Tom Maxwell approaching in a wheelchair accompanied by an orderly. Dr. Ridge smiles and acknowledges him, "Hello Tom, nice to see you again." Tom Maxwell nods, "You too Dr. Ridge, but I was hoping to run into you." Dr. Ridge looks awkwardly at Tom, "Oh? How so?" Here now, we are both grown adults serving in the cloth. Please call me David." Tom continues after nodding in agreement, "I just heard about Kelly on the news earlier today and wanted to contact you and let you know that I am praying for all of you." David puts his head down briefly and raises it again, "Thank you Tom, I really appreciate that. Kelly needs prayer warriors. Lots of them! Those who are willing to stand up for their faith and use prayer as their best defense weapon against evil"

Tom tells Dr. Ridge of his experience with Kelly, "When I had the crash, Kelly was the paramedic on the scene that helped me, so I thought it was fitting to see you." Dr. Ridge shows interest, "Well now, isn't that a fine coincidence." Tom replies, "Honestly David, I have been starting to wonder if it was part of God's infinite plan for me to be here at this very moment in time." Dr. Ridge contemplates briefly what Tom Maxwell is saying and confides in him. "Say Tom, can I share some things about Kelly and me-self with you?" Tom Maxwell extends an open palm to Dr. Ridge, "Please continue."

Dr. Ridge takes a few moments to gather his thoughts. He finds that this is harder to do, since he has never really spoken about his relationship with his son to anyone. He has never even spoken to Maggie about it. Tom Maxwell tries to be reassuring as he notices Dr. Ridge's uncomfortable demeanor. "It's OK David! No, please take your time." Dr. Ridge takes a sip of his coffe and continues, "Well, you see Tom, Kelly and I were really close when he was a wee lad. I tried me best to be a good father to him. I played ball with him and took him to the Zoo. I taught him the Bible and he seemed to do very well with scripture memorization at one point in his life." Tom Maxwell seizes a moment and asks, "Then everything changed, right?" Dr. Ridge shrugs his shoulders, "Around his Junior year something changed in him. He was interested in cars more than God." Tom Maxwell looks awkwardly at Dr. Ridge, "OK, that sounds like a normal teenager to me." Dr. Ridge puts up his hands in a wait gesture, "No please, let me finish." Tom Maxwell surrenders as Dr. Ridge continues, "You see, he began to bring home both regular car magazines, and the kind of car magazines that had those scantily clad women on them and inside the pages. He kept going on and on about wanting this one car he saw in one of those magazines."

Tom Maxwell begins to show real interest and leans forward as Dr. Ridge notices, "I thought that might interest you, Tom." he says with a chuckle. Tom Maxwell becomes a bit embarrassed when he realizes the exact moment he became more attentive. "Ok, you got me there." He laughs at himself as Dr. Ridge continues, "He started working at food places like the Golden Rings and Burger World, working more and more hours." Tom Maxwell seems a bit puzzled and asks, "What's wrong with that? Most young people had no problems with burning the candle at both ends back then." Dr. Ridge puts his hand on Tom Maxwell's arm, "Yes, but you see Tom, He spent less and less time with God. Then, his obsession with cars, moved to girls much like the ones Solomon warns us of in Proverbs."

Tom Maxwell expresses enlightenment on his face as Dr. Ridge notices, "Yes Tom, exactly." To this Tom Maxwell asks, "Did you try to counsel him about his choices?" Dr. Ridge replies, "Aye, that I did, but it seemed to just go in one ear and out the other. I do know for fact that he did keep his virginity in tact for some reason or at least that's what he told me." Dr. Ridge finishes his coffee and continues, "This unfettered behavior carried on right up to his high school graduation." Tom Maxwell chimes in, "So did you decide to give up on him?" Dr. Ridge replies in a slightly irritated tone, "I most certainly did not!" Tom Maxwell sees Dr. Ridge's irritation and immediately apologizes, "I'm sorry Dr. Ridge, please continue." David takes a deep breath, "So on the day he graduated, I gave him a very special gift that held the treasures he had been seeking." Tom Maxwell asks, "And that was?"

Dr. Ridge replies, "That was the last thing he wanted from me. He opened it, saw what it was, threw it on the sofa in my den and stormed off. He moved out and sought after the worldly vices and turned from God." Tom Maxwell then asks, "Did you ever try to reconcile with him and try to heal those wounds?" Dr. Ridge replies, "I made several attempts over the years, but it did no good. One day he came out and told me that he wanted nothing to do with God anymore." Dr. Ridge sighs heavily then continues, "Every time our paths crossed, it was like we never knew each other. It happened again the other day when I came to see you. I ran into him here and the grief was intense for me. I never have stopped praying for him."

Tom Maxwell looks directly into the eyes of Dr. Ridge, "As hard as it may be to hear this but, your opportunity to make amends could be this moment in time right now." Dr. Ridge sighs heavily again, "Maybe Tom but, if he doesn't pull through, I will never be able to forgive me self and Kelly will be lost for eternity." Tom Maxwell tries to be reassuring, "David, your forgiveness is between you and The Lord. Kelly's relationship with The Lord is between the two of them. You cannot hold yourself responsible."

This time Dr. Ridge looks directly into Tom Maxwell's eyes, "I beg to differ with you Tom, but I was charged in Ephesians 6:4; *And ye fathers, provoke not your children to wrath: but bring them up in the nurture and admonition of the Lord*. You see Tom?" Tom Maxwell replies, "I think I do. You're blaming yourself for those decisions that Kelly made which you dissaprove of." Dr. Ridge looks aghast and fumbles through his words, "W-w-Well maybe, but I don't see where I failed."

Tom Maxwell pauses a moment before speaking, "David, you are obviously a man of integrity. You have done all you feel was required of you, but it's really up to the Lord now. I recommend you use this time in prayer and meditate on scripture." The two men share a moment of silence then Tom Maxwell asks, "David, may I pray with you?" Dr, Ridge nods in agreement as they bow their heads and Tom Maxwell begins, *"Father in Heaven, I want to thank you for giving me this chance to spend some time with Dr, Ridge and talk. Lord, I lift Kelly up before you and ask that you, The Great Physician intercede in Kelly's healing. I humbly ask that you would also be with Dr. Ridge and his family as they go through this time as well. I pray that Your will be done, no matter what the outcome. Father, use this time to repair Kelly's broken spirit and help him to find YOU again! If I can be that instrument Lord, then here am I. I realize now why you sent me to Gold City, and I am beginning to understand what my REAL mission is here, and I thank you Father. I pray this in the name of Your Son, Jesus, Amen."*

Both men raise their heads as Dr. Ridge speaks, "Thank you Tom, I needed that." Tom Maxwell shakes his head, "No David, thank you. If you will excuse me now. I need to get back to my room for the night. Good Night Sir." The two men shake hands as Tom Maxwell's orderly comes up and helps him exit the chapel. Dr. Ridge picks up his sandwich and slowly makes his way to the chapel door. He pulls out his cell phone and calls Maggie. "Hello Maggie me love. How was the vigil? He listens for her response and continues, You see me love, I was having a chat with Tom Maxwell a bit ago. Listen carefully, I need to be here with Kelly and fast and pray for the next few days. I need you and Bethany to minister to Sharon during this time as well. Please me Love, this is something I feel I must do for Kelly's sake." There is another pause as he listens again to Maggie's response. "Alright then, Good night me love."

He ends the call on his phone and gets ready to walk out. He turns briefly, looks up toward heaven, and exits. As he returns to Kelly's room, he stops at the Nurses Station and hands his sandwich to the nurse and states, "You can have me unopened sandwich me dear child. I won't be needing it right now." He enters room 4 and sits in the chair next to Kelly's bed. He opens his bible and will spend the next few days in prayer, meditation, and fasting.

CHAPTER 9

Maggie, Bethany and Sharon arrive at the church, where a crowd of believers is already gathering. As they get out of the car, the Channel 14 News van rolls up and Linda Barnett jumps out of the passenger seat. Her cameraman goes to work in the back by raising the transmitting antenna and linking up with the studio for a live broadcast. He hands the wireless microphone and an earpiece to Ms. Barnett and does a quick sound check. They will be going live at 6:30 and decide to try to get some pre-taped interviews from the participants.

Her associate picks up his camera pack and closes the doors to the van. First, they just walk through the crowd and simply observe the activity. Linda takes notes about potential interviewee's as she moves to the front of the gathering. There is a glass wall between two entrances where a single fire department helmet lays surrounded by flowers, and cards in support of the injured Firefighters. She turns to her cameraman and tells him, "Gary, let's get some more of this footage. I have some editing ideas for the story." Gary just nods in agreement and begins filming the makeshift tribute. Although all four men are alive, she is intrigued by the fact of only a single helmet.

As Gary records footage, Linda Barnett is doing a voice over to run later with her report. As she records, she is approached by the Youth Director who takes the liberty of introducing himself, "Good evening, I'm Associate Pastor Rob Preston. Thank you for covering this event." Ms. Barnett shakes his extended hand and asks, "This memorial area is very nice, but I noticed only one helmet is here and there were four of them injured. Can you explain that to me? He replies, "Sure. We offered this idea to all of the other families and they all agreed that it should be for Kelly mainly because this where his dad is Senior Pastor as well as he is the worst injured of the four of them."

The news reporter is quite impressed with what she is being told and asks, "That is great that even though they all share a common grievance that they are willing to do that. Would you be interested in repeating that on camera as part of the coverage?" Pastor Rob replies, "Sure I would whenever you are." She quickly goes over a few directions with Pastor Preston as Gary positions himself in a good spot. Linda Barnett takes her place in front of the camera with her interviewee just out of camera shot. Just before she gets the sign to start, she stops Gary and exclaims, "Wait a minute Gary! Let's save this part for when we go live." She looks at her watch and adds, "It's almost time to go live anyways."

In her earpiece she hears the lead in for the evening news. Gary starts a finger countdown while Linda hears the anchor lead announce "We go live now to Linda Barnett, who is live at Gold City Community Church. Linda?" She takes a quick breath and begins, "Good evening Christy, I am here at the church which is pastored by one of the injured firefighters from today's accident. Doctor David Ridge's son Kelly was one of them. He remains in critical condition at Gold City Hospital currently." The video switches to the tape of both the accident scene and the tribute area at the church entrance as she does a voice over the video. "Church goers and community members are gathering in tribute to paramedic Lieutenant Kelly Ridge who was injured earlier in a traffic accident while responding to a call with a neighboring department. As you can see from the video that a tribute area has been set up at the front of the church."

She pauses for a few seconds as the camera goes back to live where she continues, "Joining me now is Associate Pastor Rob Preston. He is the Youth Pastor here and he is going to tell us a bit more about the tribute area." Rob nods at her and begins, "Thank you. Originally we were getting this ready for all four of these brave men with that tribute area. However the families of the other injured firefighters have decided that this should be a stand alone tribute to paramedic Firefighter Kelly Ridge since he is the worst of the injured as well as it being the church where Kelly's Dad is the Senior Pastor." Linda pulls back her microphone and comments, "I look around and I will say that it's pretty impressive how you were able to put all this together in such a short period of time." Pastor Rob replies, "Well, honestly I wasn't alone. Our church secretary Lucy Doyle was really the mastermind behind most of what you are seeing. We are very blessed to have Lucy in our congregation. Her organizational skills are a true gift from The Lord." He points to Lucy who is to his right side about twenty feet away.

Just as he finishes his sentence, Maggie, Bethany and Sharon walk up on the interview. Pastor Rob notices them and immediately refers Ms. Barnett to them. "Matter of fact Ms. Barnett, here's Kelly's family members right here." Maggie looks rather cross at Pastor Rob for putting her on the spot, but Bethany steps in to ease her Momma's sudden displeasure. "Good evening Ms. Barnett, I will answer your questions about Kelly." Linda Barnett asks, "And you are?" Bethany assertively answers, "I am Bethany Ridge, Kelly's sister." She turns to Momma and Sharon and continues, "This is our momma, Margaret Ridge and Kelly's fiancée Sharon Renfro."

Linda Barnett acknowledges them as well and then asks, "How are you all holding up during all of this?" Bethany explains, "Our family believes strongly in the Power of our Great Physician Jesus Christ for our strength right now especially." Linda Barnett nods in the affirmative and continues to comment and ask another question. "I am sure of that with your father being the Senior Pastor here that your beliefs in God are strong, but how are you handling all of this really?"

Just as Bethany prepares to answer, Maggie surprisingly speaks up, "My dear lady, we also receive our strength through the power of prayer both as individuals as well as a congregation. The scriptures tell us in James 5:16, that we are to; *Confess your faults one to another, and pray for one another that ye may be healed. The effectual fervent prayer of a righteous man availeth much.* Our church believes very strongly in that prayer is the key to everything that tries us in life!"

Linda Barnett appears interested and then asks, "I don't see Dr. Ridge. Is he even here tonight?" Bethany answers, "No. We felt and agreed together as a family that he should stay with Kelly at least the first night and we will go from there. Momma will take the next watch and then I will stay with him for a night or two." The reporter then asks, "Can you tell us what the doctors are saying about his chances?" Again Maggie steps forward, "They tell us right now it's day to day effort. Right now a lot of is up to the healing power of God through prayer."

Ms. Barnett nods and then turns to Sharon, "I know you are his fiancée, but is there anything that you would like to add?" She smiles at Sharon and shakes her head no. Linda Barnett then turns herself to face the camera and finishes her report, "That's it from here for right now, unless you have any questions." There is a brief pause as she listens to her earpiece and closes the report, "In that case I am Linda Barnett, Channel 14 News. Back to you in the studio." She gets the signal from Gary that they are disconnected from the studio.

As they return to the news van to pack up, Linda Barnett is going over the interview with Maggie and Bethany in her head. Something that they said has caused a stir in her mind. Gary takes a brief pause from the editing console in the news van and notices his colleague's demeanor. He asks, "Linda? Is everything ok with you?" She stops what she is doing and looks up at Gary and replies, "Oh yeah, I'm good. I'll be right back in a few minutes. We can go over tonight's follow up broadcast later." Gary nods in agreement as she walks away from the van.

Linda wanders through the crowd looking for Maggie and Bethany. The things they said during the report has left Linda curious about many things. She looks towards the tribute area and sees the three ladies chatting with Pastor Preston and Lucy Doyle. She makes her way through the crowd of people moving closer to Maggie, Bethany, and Sharon. As she moves through the crowd, she can't help but take note to herself of all the smaller groups that are in prayer for Kelly and his brothers in Fire Service.

She approaches Maggie and exclaims, "Excuse me, Mrs. Ridge?" Maggie and Bethany both turn and notice Ms. Barnett. Maggie replies, "Yes my dear, how can I be of service to you again?" Linda looks around for a few mere seconds and answers. "Well, after we finished the interview and you walked away, something made me curious that I just had to follow up with you on. Maggie expresses a look of curiosity and asks, "Do you need more information for your news report or is this personal?"

Linda is quite impressed by Maggie's instant perception and responds,

"Nothing for my report. This is about a personal matter I wish to discuss with you if you have the time?" Maggie nods her head and replies, "Certainly child! Would you like to find a more private place to talk?" Linda Barnett nods and follows Maggie into the church foyer. They both sit at small bench inside the door next to the outreach ministry booth.

Maggie looks endearingly at Ms. Barnett and asks, "What can I help you with my dear?" Linda looks at her directly and responds, "There was something about what you said back there that made me think. You made reference to Gold City Community Church as being a praying church and that it a very powerful tool." Maggie nods, "Yes dear, that is correct." Linda asks, "Is that really it? I mean I grew up in a church, where they were more interested in your works than your faith." Maggie shows concern and replies, "It's quite a lot more than that. Please tell me more about how you were raised and how to believe."

Linda Barnett remains silent for a few moments as she puts together her past to tell Maggie about. She begins, "I was raised in a church that sort of sprung from a series of tent meetings in 1844." Maggie nods and agrees, "Oh yes, I remember me husband David telling me something about that when he was taking classes in seminary. I believe it had to do with something called The Great Disappointment. Please go on." Linda agrees, "Yes, something like that." There is a brief pause as Linda continues, "There was a married couple there that some time later, the wife claimed to have seen a vision from God like a modern day prophetess in her day. They started this church the believes that because God rested on and sanctified the seventh day of creation, that day is the day to worship on."

Maggie replies, "My goodness child! That's a strange sounding church." Linda continues, "Oh there's more. The church sat on a corner in the middle of a small village across the street from the local post office. It had the high pointed steeple above the front doors and looked kind of like one of those churches you see on a Christmas card. It was like it was the mission of the church to interpret scripture the way they wanted it to and not the way God meant for it. They even claimed that their so called prophetess even visited that church once." She pauses to clear her throat and continues, "Excuse me. The more I was raised, the more they emphasized how many souls that were witnessed to and saved. How many bible tracts I gave out, foods allowed to eat and foods forbidden to eat. It became more like a cult than a true Bible believing church." Maggie's again replies, My dear, that's not how a person comes to The Lord! The Bible clearly tells us that all we have to do is believe in The Lord Jesus Christ and be saved. It's what Paul and Silas told their jailer's in The Book of Acts Chapter 16:31 when they asked them what they had to do to be saved. Not only that, but several times in the four gospels, Christ told us that all we had to do was to accept Him as your own personal Savior, repent of your sins and never go back to them."

Linda Barnett's interest is increasing with what Maggie has told her. She comments and asks, "I remember that about the jailer's belief, but I thought that you had to do more than just believe." Maggie is reminded of another verse that might help, "Let me read in Roman's Chapter 10 and Verse 9; *"That if thou shalt confess with thy mouth the Lord Jesus, and shalt believe in thine heart that God hath raised him from the dead, thou shalt be saved."* She puts her Bible down and states, "That's all there really is to it to begin your walk with The Lord."

Linda looks at Maggie and very stoically and asks, "That's it? That's all I have to do?" Maggie looks very tenderly at her and replies, "Yes dear, that's just about it." Linda inquiries, "Don't I have to recite some phrase to do this if I want to accept what you are offering?" Maggie is quick to correct her by saying, "Oh, it's not what I am offering, it's Jesus Christ that is doing the offering. I am just the vessel He chose to make available to you. Some believe they have to say a certain phrase or speech, but it's really between you and The Lord how you approach Him. Just say what's on your heart and He will do the rest."

Linda replies, "I don't know, I guess I can give it a try. I really am moved by what you shared with me and I want the same thing you have. So much has been missing in my life and I want to make it right. There's something new welling up inside me that is feeling good right now. I want to know who your Jesus is and not the one that I was raised in believing." Maggie replies, "That's the main problem with most people today. They want Jesus to be what they want Him to be and not who He really is." Maggie asks, "Is there anything else that I can help you with? He's waiting for you right inside that door." Maggie points to the sanctuary doors as she finishes her sentence. Linda Barnett nods and walks to the sanctuary door and enters it. She kneels down in a pew and pours her heart out to The Lord. *"Um Jesus? Hi! I'm not very good at this since I haven't prayed in a long long time. So I will just lay it out for you, Ok? Please forgive me for all these years of not trusting in You. Something is happening in me that I have never felt before. I like how it feels and I want more of it. Please come into my life and save me! Mrs. Ridge told me that was all I had to do, was believe in you and trust in you and I would be saved, and so I say, yes and please! Well, Jesus I guess that's it, so I will say thank you and um Amen."*

Linda Barnett gets up from the pew and returns to the church lobby, but Maggie is no longer there at the bench. As a matter of fact, she is nowhere to be found. She wonders for a moment if she was actually chatting with Maggie or if she encountered an angel, but shakes it off as ridiculous thinking. As she leaves the church entrance, she sees Maggie, on her cell phone, getting into their car and driving away. She smiles brightly as she returns to the news van.

Gary has been waiting patiently for her to return and asks, "Where have you been? You said you'd be back in a few minutes and it's been a half hour." Linda just smiles and replies, "I'm sorry for that Gary. I was talking to Kelly's Mom off camera and the time just got away from me. She is quite a compelling woman to chat with." Gary just chuckles smugly and replies, "Yeah, those preacher's wives can appear to be that way." Linda Barnett looks directly at Gary and replies, "You know, I think she's more real than that. I give her lots of credit for maintaining her feelings the way she is dealing with all of this." Gary replies, "Yeah ok! You believe what you want to. Me personally, I'm not really into this God stuff. I can't relate to the idea that there's one supreme being who rules the galaxy. I mean, it's like a force surrounding us that we make it or break it in life."

Linda Barnett shakes her head slowly and replies "Ok Gary, that makes you the first person for me to be in prayer for." Gary smugly responds, "Why? Did she proselytize you to her church? Linda replies, "As a matter of fact she led me to find what was missing in my life. Gary, I received Christ as my Savior tonight and I want to live my life for Him! Gary replies in a very hostile and angry way, "Really? How about if you keep your new found church stuff to yourself, ok? Somebody pretending to talk to someone or something out there cosmically is not my thing. Besides, we need to get done and get back to the studios."

Linda puts her hands up and answers, "Ok, ok. You're the boss here." She smiles at him in a sarcastic manner and helps to finish up. Gary closes the sliding door and makes his way to the driver's seat and gets in. Linda follows suit on the passenger side. Gary starts the van and drives away commenting, "Man, I am glad to get away from all that religious junk. These kind of stories really curdle my skin." Linda can't resists and asks, "Sure it's not guilt your feeling?" Gary just glances at his colleague in disgust. After a short trip, they arrive back at the news station. Gary hands Linda a videotape and stares, "Here you go. I noticed the van needs gas so I am going to fill it up and then come back in a little while to help you finish editing."

Linda nods in agreement and exits the van. Gary gestures an open handed wave and drives off. Linda Barnett goes into the station and stops at her desk for a moment, checking her messages and then continues on to the editing room. She enters and sits in front of a large console and slides the video tape into the player and begins the editing process. She stops several times at her interview spot with Maggie and replays the part about the power of prayer over and over. Then she finds herself thinking about their conversation afterwards. She smiles and continues with her work.

Another hour passes and Gary still has not returned from refueling. She begins to worry about her colleague until she hears a knock on the door. It is not Gary coming in, but news director Steve Hirsch. She pauses the playback and acknowledges her boss. "Hey Steve! You haven't seen Gary, have you? He was supposed to come help me finish up in here when he got back." Steve looks directly at Linda and states, "That's why I came in. Linda, Gary will not be back." She looks surprised by this and asks, "Why, did another big story break so he took another reporter?"

Steve carefully explains, "Linda, how do I put this gently?" He sits in the chair next to her and continues, "He was on his way back to the studio and a drunk driver crossed lanes and took the news van head on. Gary was killed instantly. Police said he wasn't wearing his seatbelt." He gets back up to leave and turns back saying, "I thought you should be the first to know." Linda looks at Steve with a stunned look and replies, "Well, thanks for telling me."

Steve exits the room and Linda sits in the chair motionless for a few minutes. Tears begin to stream down her face as she realizes what she has just been told. She begins to cry in the privacy of the editing room for Gary. Not for his physical death as much, but for the eternal torture his soul is facing for refusing to accepting Christ as his personal Savior.

CHAPTER 10

Two days have now passed since Kelly's accident. Dr. Ridge sits in the same chair next to Kelly's bed. He has not slept or eaten at all during this time. It is early morning and the sun is up. The sun rays make their way to the window in the ICU room. Dr. Ridge pulls back the curtain and greets the day. "Good Morning Lord! My, this is a fine day you have given me and I thank you for it." As he looks out the window, he notices a small crowd has gathered on the sidewalk below the window. He sees that they are carrying signs of support for both Kelly and for the Ridge Family as a whole. His heart is warmed even more as he reads things like; *We Love You Ridge Family* and *We Are Praying For You.* He is filled with a great admiration for those people. He turns and looks at Kelly. All he still sees is the sleeping form of his son amongst the beeping machines and wires. He looks up to the heavens, *"Well Lord, what do you have in store for us today? I see You sent some special people to remind us of Your goodness to us and Your love for Your people."*

There is a knock on the door and Nurse Erin enters and addresses her patient first and then acknowledges Dr. Ridge. "Good Morning Kelly. It's time for your morning assessment. Also, good morning to you Dr. Ridge. Will you be having something to eat today or are you still fasting? Dr. Ridge tries to straighten his hair with his hand and states, "Ah, that me child, is up to the Lord and if He has heard me prayers. Until then, I will continue with me fasting." As Nurse Erin makes her way around the bed, examining Kelly and writing down notes for her report, there is another knock on the door.

A tall thin handsome man in a white lab coat enters and introduces himself. "Good morning, I'm Dr. Stevens. I have been monitoring Kelly's progress and have been his attending Doctor for the last 48 hours. I presume that you are Mr. Ridge, his dad?" As he prepares to answer the doctor, Nurse Erin excuses herself from the room. Dr. Ridge pulls his stomach in and puffs his chest, "Aye, that I am, but I am Dr. Ridge, Minister of the Gospel." Dr. Stevens lets that response just roll freely off and continues, "Well that's nice!"

Dr. Stevens begins to look at machines and write down several notes as he moves around Kelly's bed. As he moves around, he makes a series of positive sounds, "Uh-huh!" and then he continues to write down more notes. He then turns to Dr. Ridge and comments "In all my years of practice I have hever seen anything like this. Kelly has somehow achieved record levels of recovery that I have never seen before." Dr. Ridge just stands there smiling politely and nodding periodically knowing all too well what has been happening.

Dr. Stevens then makes a final statement to Dr. Ridge, "If there are any other family members that need to be here, I suggest you contact them and have them get here so we can discuss your son's prognosis and treatment plan." Dr. Ridge looks a bit puzzled and asks, "Excuse me Doctor but, is there some bad news laced in all that medical mumbo jumbo you just blurted out?" Dr. Stevens just smiles at him and states, " Please, just get your family here. I will be back in one hour to fill you all in at the same time." He then turns and leaves the room. There is an overwhelming rush that moves through Dr. Ridge. Although, he still seems a bit bewildered about what Dr. Stevens has said. He reaches for his phone and calls Maggie and let's her know what's going on.

Back at the Ridge home, Maggie is moving about the kitchen making breakfast for her daughter and her guest. Bethany and Sharon come down together and help Maggie with the breakfast preparations. Maggie looks up, "Good morning ladies. How did you sleep?" Bethany looks at her mother and says, "Honestly Momma, the last two nights have been miserable. Since Daddy called and insisted we stay home for a couple of days, both of us have gotten very little sleep." Maggie looks lovingly at her daughter, "Yes me child, I can relate. However, he is your father and he felt he did what he thought was best for all of us." Bethany shrugs her shoulders, "Maybe so, but it would be nice to hear some news about Kelly."

About this time there is a ringing of the phone. Maggie gets up from her chair and goes to answer the phone. Sharon and Bethany talk amongst each other. "Sharon, how do you really feel right now?" Sharon replies, "All I want right now is to walk into Kelly's room, find him awake, and give him the biggest hug in the world." Bethany smirks, "You know Sharon, I was just thinking the same thing. He is my brother, and I do love him so much, despite our differences." Sharon agrees and comments, "I don't know Bethany. There have been so many times in the last couple of days, I've wondered what will I ever do without him."

About this time, Maggie comes bursting into the dining room, "Girls, girls, that was Daddy. He said that the doctor had some news on Kelly's condition, and we were all supposed to be there in one hour to meet with the doctor." Bethany and Sharon immediately jump out of their chairs and bring their dishes to the kitchen sink, with Maggie right behind them. Quickly, they all work together to wash, dry, and put dishes away. They all get their purses and leave the house, get into the car, and are off to the hospital.

After a short drive, they arrive at the hospital and move as quickly as possible for the elevator inside to head up to the Intensive Care Unit. As the three ladies approach the ICU doors, they slow to a paced and graceful walk. They are buzzed in and met by Nurse Erin at the door. "Good Morning ladies. I believe you all know your way to his room." Maggie makes her way to room four and knocks on the door. She enters before Dr. Ridge has a chance to acknowledge her. Bethany and Sharon, follow in right behind her. "David, we're here. Where is the doctor you spoke of?" David puts up his hands, "Patience me Love, patience. The nurse was to contact him once you all got here."

After a few minutes, there is a brief knock at the room door. Dr. Stevens enters and greets everyone. "Good Morning all. I am Dr. Stevens and I am Kelly's primary physician. I am glad you all made it here so quickly." David introduces everyone, "Good Morning again. This is me wife Maggie, me daughter Bethany, and Kelly's fiancee Sharon Renfro." Doctor Steven's nod at each of them as they are introduced. As he shakes

Sharon's hand, he notices the engagement ring on her finger. "Well I see your son has very good taste in women." Sharon blushes a bit and Dr. Stevens regains his composure. "I called you all together to discuss what is happening with your son, brother and fiancee." He turns and looks at Kelly before continuing, "I looked at his CAT Scan this morning and there is no evidence of any brain swelling whatsoever. He still does have a hairline fracture to his arm, as well as various cuts and bruises on his face and hands." He looks down briefly at his notes and continues, "The Electro Encephalogram or EEG as it is commonly referred to is showing increased brain activity. His labs are slightly elevated in his white cell count. That is normal as the white cells are busy fighting off infection."

Sharon suddenly interrupts him, "That's great, but what does it all mean?" Dr. Stevens ignores what he sees as her rudeness for interrupting him, "With all these sudden improvements, and if all continues to go well, then we will reverse the coma tomorrow and bring him back to consciousness." All four of them gasp at the same time as David begins to puff out his chest and exclaims, "It's a true miracle from God in Heaven. That's what it is!" Maggie cuts him off, "Now me husband, if The Lord wants us to experience a miracle, I don't wish to miss it." Bethany adds, "Now Daddy, you told us growing up, that if we are to experience a miracle then we are not to rush it and let it happen on it's own. Besides you taught me that a miracle is an unexpected supernatural intervention of God." David is a bit taken back by her comment, "Did I now? When did I tell you that me child?" Bethany smiles brightly, "At my sixteenth birthday party!"

David responds rather snidely, "Well I guess I did at that! At least one of my children heeds my teachings." Maggie immediately chides her husband, "Now David Ridge this is not the time to be critical!" Their conversation is becoming more heated when Sharon breaks in to the exchange, "Please, both of you, with all due respect, we are losing our focus on Kelly right now." Bethany pipes up in support of Sharon's comment, "Momma, Daddy, she's right! We need to keep our feelings in check for Kelly's sake. After all, he's my brother too!" David and Maggie look at each other in an agreeing glance as David replies, "Quite right me daughter. Your Momma and I apologize for our words in front of you both." To this Sharon responds, "Thank you Dr. Ridge."

During all this, Dr. Stevens has remained in the room witnessing all the tension. The other three regain their composure as David turns to the doctor, "I apologize to you sir on witnessing our frustration with all of this. However, I must admit this is a true showing of healing from God." Dr. Stevens shows some ire towards him, "Really! Modern medicine is what is responsible for your son's improvements, and you want to give credit to some universal entity that you believe exists?" Dr. Ridge asserts himself by standing his Biblical grounds, "I most certainly do! God is the Master Physician that makes all things possible. The power of prayer is a force of its own. That's the trouble with this world today. It has decided to worship the creature and not the Creator! That's in the book of Romans Chapter 1 and Verse 25."

Dr. Steven's increases his ire, "Dr. Ridge, I do respect your title, however your belief in some space entity you feel exists is something that I strongly disagree with you on. To put it more bluntly sir, I am an atheist. I do not share your beliefs. I can not believe my abilities and training coupled with all those years of medical school was the result of a so called god, and not my own doing!" To this David replies, "I see, and where did you think your talents and abilities came from? The scriptures say in Romans 1:28, *"And even as they did not like to retain God in their knowledge, God gave them over to a reprobate mind, to do those things which are not convenient."* Dr. Stevens replies, "What does that have to do with anything? My degrees came from a lot of hard work and studies in my field by grasping the concepts and doing the applications."

David returns Dr. Stevens words back to him, "And of course, all that just happened. Then again scripture also tells us in Romans 8:5-8, *"For they that are after the flesh do mind the things of the flesh; but they that are after the Spirit the things of the Spirit. For to be carnally minded is death; but to be spiritually minded is life and peace. Because the carnal mind is enmity against God: for it is not subject to the law of God, neither indeed can be. So then they that are in the flesh cannot please God."* Doctor Stevens has heard all he wants to hear of Dr. Ridge's mini sermon and takes that comment as a final insult to his profession and quickly and abruptly exits adding, "The Anesthesiologist will be here in the morning to bring him out of the coma. Please keep your religion to yourself and your family. Good Day Mr. Ridge!"

As he walks out, David blurts out, "It's not a religion, it's a relationship." He then turns to the others as though the heated exchange with Dr. Stevens never happened and exclaims, "Do you all know what this means dear ones? It means that it sounds like God is hearing our petitions for Kelly and has begun the healing process to his body." Sharon walks over to Dr. Ridge, "Dr. Ridge sir, I want you to know that I am having difficulty understanding a lot of this whole situation, but I promise you that when this is all over, I know that Kelly will be the best thing that ever happened to me, and I know he will be very happy that he married me." Dr. Ridge looks directly into Sharon's eyes, "I believe you me dear, but you have such a long way to come before you are ready. So much to learn about the sanctity of marriage." She nods her head at him, "I know that, and I am willing to take those steps if this all goes the right way." Bethany is puzzled and asks, "What do you mean Sharon? Of course everything will go the right way. Just learn to trust in God and it will all work out." Bethany walks up and puts her hands on her shoulders, giving a type of squeeze hug and adds, "Besides, I am going to be here for you to help you along the way." Sharon however, can't see through her own selfishness, "I know in my heart Kelly was meant to be the one to take care of me forever, so he better pull through." Both Bethany and Dr. Ridge are taken back by Sharon's reply. They both roll their eyes, look at each other and just leave it at that.

Meanwhile, Maggie has made her way over to Kelly's bed. She reaches for her son's hand and holds it tightly. She leans forward toward his ear, and whispers, "I know you may not be able to hear me or know I am here but, I love you very much Kelly. So does your father except he's too stubborn to admit it sometimes. I can't wait to hear your voice again really soon. Let the Lord take control of your body and bring you back to us." She then pulls her face back a bit and kisses Kelly on the cheek. Her hand moves across his arm and she touches his cheek with her hand.

She moves away from the bed and makes her way over to the corner of the room and sits in one of the chairs. Bethany steps up to the bedside and just stares at her brother. She closes her eyes for a few seconds and prays for him. She moves away and goes over by her Momma and places her hands on her shoulders. Finally, Sharon walks up next to the bed and just starts crying. Suprisingly to her, Dr. Ridge steps up and places his arm around her and pulls her into his embrace. He whispers in her ear, *"Oh taste and see that the Lord is good: blessed is the man that trusteth in him."* "That's from the book of Psalms, Chapter 34 verse 8." Sharon musters a smile at Dr. Ridge and wipes away her tears from her eyes as best she can.

There is a sudden lull of slience in the room as everyone pauses their speaking at the same time. This awkward moment quickly subsides as David turns to the ladies and speaks, "My dear family, Sharon included, I think we can all see what is happening to Kelly. I believe it to be appropriate at this time to seek the Lord in prayer for what He has given us and what lies ahead." Maggie and Bethany raise their heads and nod in agreement. Bethany even adds, "Not only that Daddy, but our church has been in constant prayer all this time since the accident. Sharon, although impressed that Dr. Ridge has included her in the family circle, is suprised, and simply raises her head and smiles. She is having a difficult time trying to grasp on to something with all these changes happening around her. All she can think about is focused around her feelings and what life without Kelly would be for her.

Maggie and Bethany bow their heads while Sharon just stares at Kelly and remains silent. Dr. Ridge begins, *"Father in Heaven, so much is happening right now that quite frankly is overwhelming in many ways. Father, I ask for clarity through all this calamity. I ask for grace and wisdom yet again oh Lord. Please continue to do your miraculous work in Kelly's life and make him completely whole. Lord, in the name of Jesus, make it so! Amen."* The three Ridge family members open their eyes to see Sharon still staring at Kelly. Bethany puts her hand on Sharon's shoulder, "Sharon? Are you alright?" She turns to Bethany and replies, "I don't know. This is way too much for me to take in right now." Bethany asks, "Is there anything that I can do?"

Just before Sharon answers her, there is a knock at the room door. Another man in a white lab coat with a slightly portly build enters the room and introduces himself. "Good Day everyone, I am Doctor Mazak. I am Kelly's Anesthesiologist. They told me I could find you all here. I wanted to let you know what has been happening and what will be happening with our patient." David speaks for the family, "You are here today? Dr. Stevens told us it would be morning before you would come to see us about Kelly." Doctor Mazak replies, "Well I thought you might want to hear some good news a lot sooner than tomorrow." He smiles at them and continues, "When Kelly came to the Surgical Department he appeared to be in a critical situation. As the surgeon probably told you already that some pressure that had built up on his brain had been relieved. His fracture on his arm was treated and reset. Because of the type of accident it was and considering his injuries, the surgeon wanted Kelly placed into what we call a medically induced coma." Dr. Ridge asks, "What is that exactly?" Dr. Mazak continues, We administer a combination of three drugs called Propofol, Pentobarbital, and Thiopental which puts him into a very deep sleep to increase the repair process his body needs right now."

Maggie inquires, "So, how much longer are we talking here before he wakes up?" Doctor Mazak turns to her, "Well I am working with Respiratory Therapy and they are monitoring his breathing. They tell me that he is showing good signs of trying to breathe on his own." Bethany pipes up, "So that's a good thing right?" Doctor Mazak is suprised by her question, "It most certainly is young lady!" He turns back to address them all again, "We are looking at starting the process this afternoon, but I need you all to know that it will take several hours after that before he begins to wake up." He pauses briefly before continuing, "We will wean him off the drugs and we will stop the ventilator once he shows signs of primary breathing on his own." He pauses again to be ready for more questions. However he needed to add, "Please be aware that because of his injuries and being in a medically induced coma, he will not remember very much of what happened or may have memory loss all together." Bethany asks, "How long will it be before he gets his full memory back?" Dr. Mazak looks at Bethany and states, "Right now it's hard to say. Besides, with the memory loss he may also experience fits of anger, mood swings, and need some motor skills retraining. It's really going to be up to him."

There is a feeling of contentment from everyone in the room except Sharon who asks, "But there is still a chance that he could die also, right? I don't know if I could spend my life without his caring for me!" Doctor Mazak tries to be as reassuring as possible, "No matter the outcome, we are doing the best we can for him." With this, Doctor Mazak acknowledges everyone again before leaving, "If you will all please excuse me, I have other patients to see." David speaks for the family, "Certainly Doctor, and thank you for the information."

Bethany steps up and tries to console Sharon, "Well I think everything will work itself out. Don't you worry about it." Sharon rejects what Bethany says and decides to leave the room." She blurts out, "I can't do this right now. I need to get something from the cafeteria." "Would you like some company Sharon?" Bethant asks. She is visibly uptight and rejects Bethany's offer, "No thanks, I just need some coffee and try to clear my head." Bethany nods and answers, "Okay." With that, Sharon exits the room. David can no longer contain himself with courtesy, "I do not know how Kelly could get himself involved with the likes of her?" Maggie chides, "Now David, is that a proper christian attitude to take right now?" David looks at his wife, "Maybe not Maggie, but I am having my own difficulties accepting her into our family. I am not exactly sure she would be good for the Ridge reputation." Bethany feels she needs to expresss her viewpoint and steps between them, "Please, both of you! We can try and work those details out later. Let's just worry about Kelly. I am sure Sharon will come around in time."

Sharon has made her way to the cafeteria. She gets herself a cup of coffee and goes to a table and sits down. Before she takes a sip, she looks around and reaches into her purse. She pulls out a single serving size bottle of whiskey and adds it to her coffee. She proceeds to drink her coffee when she is approached by a man in a wheelchair. "Excuse me Miss, I can see you are upset about something. Do you need an ear to listen to your troubles?" She looks up to see Tom Maxwell in front of her. Quickly she tries to shun him away, "Please leave me alone. I am not looking for company right now!" She bounds from the chair, grabs her coffee cup and almost runs from the cafeteria. She makes her way to her car, gets in, drives cautiously out of the lot. Once she is on the main road, she accelerates rather quickly from the hospital.

CHAPTER 11

THREE HOURS HAVE PAST AND SHARON HAS STILL NOT RETURNED TO THE room. Bethany is getting concerned. "Momma, I am getting worried about Sharon. She's been gone to the cafeteria a long time." Maggie looks at her daughter, "Maybe you should go looking for her." Before Bethany has a chance to respond, David interrupts, "No, both of you stay here with Kelly. As head of this house, I will go and try to find her. Afterall, if she is going to be part of our flock, then it is the shepherds job to find the lost lamb." David then leaves the room and heads for the cafeteria.

As he enters the cafeteria, he is stopped by a familiar face. "Hey, Dr. Ridge. How is everything with Kelly going?" Dr. Ridge recognizes Tom Maxwell and smiles, "Aye, we just got the news they will be in to take him out of the coma very soon sometime this afternoon." Tom Maxwell replies, "That's great news to hear. I have been in constant prayer for his recovery." Dr. Ridge is very grateful, "Aye Tom, thank you so much for that. Say, I am looking for someone and I thought you may have seen her." Tom inquires further, "I have seen several people today. Can you please give me a description?" Dr. Ridge goes on to describe Sharon to him, "A young lady with blonde hair, very pretty thing. Came in about three hours ago?" Tom Maxwell thinks for a minute, "I think that description does ring a bell. A lady matching that description came in, had a cup of coffee and sat down right over there. I approached her and asked her if she needed to talk about her troubles." Dr. Ridge interrupts, "And?" Tom Maxwell continues, "She basically wanted to be left alone. As a matter of fact, after telling me that, she got up and bolted from here. That's the last I saw of her." Dr. Ridge rubs his chin with his hand, "Thank you Tom. Thank you so much." Dr. Ridge turns and leaves to return to the room.

As Dr. Ridge enters Kelly's room, Bethany immediately pounces on him. "Were you able to find her?" Dr. Ridge looks directly at his daughter, "No Lassie. she wasn't in the cafeteria, however, I ran into Tom Maxwell, the evangelist from the plane crash. He told me she was there, but had run out when he tried to talk to her." Bethany puts her head down and walks away mumbling, "I hope nothing bad has happened to her." Maggie walks up next to her and puts her arm around her daughter, "I am sure The Lord has everything under control." Maggie states. Bethany looks up and nods to her Momma, but then decides to try to call her on her cell phone. She dials Sharon's number and there is no answer. This intensifies her worrying and blurts out, "Oh! She's not answering her phone!" Her Daddy reinforces his wife's comment, "As your Mother said, The Lord has it all under control."

Bethany gets up from her chair and looks out the window. She is still hopeful that she will see Sharon in the parking lot returning to the hospital. She looks at the screen on her cell phone to see if she may have missed Sharon's return call. Her wandering mind is broken by Dr. Mazak entering the room. He tries to emulate a positive tone in his greeting, "Good Afternoon again everyone. We are ready to begin the wake up process. David and Maggie embrace as Maggie comments, "Alright doctor, the Ridge Family is ready." Dr. Mazak reiterates a previous comment, "As I had said earlier, the waking up process could take a while. I wanted to do it later so he could possibly be awake by tomorrow morning. That will be up to Kelly though and how his body responds." With this Dr. Mazak turns and administers the waking medications into Kelly's I.V. line. He turns back to Dr. and Mrs. Ridge, "Alright, that's it. Now comes the waiting period before he wakes up. Please remember what I said about his memory." Both parents nod in agreement as David adds, "Thank you Doctor, for everything." Doctor Mazak acknowledges their thanks by a nod and leaves the room.

David consoles Maggie quietly for a few moments and then looks over at Bethany and smiles. Bethany returns her Daddy's smile and quickly returns to worrying about Sharon, despite what her parents had told her earlier. Maggie sits down in her chair and begins to knit. David takes his seat in another chair, opens his bible and begins to read it.

Several more hour pass and there is still no sign of Sharon returning to the hospital. The quiet of the room is broken by Charge Nurse Erin entering and speaking, "Good Evening everyone. I will be going home for the night shortly, But there is a Rick and Annie Smith outside the unit waiting to speak to all of you." Bethany expresses a stunned look as Dr. Ridge steps over to her, "Thank you Child. Bethany and I will come out to speak with them." He turns to Maggie and explains, "You remember Rick. Kelly's partner on the ambulance?" Maggie nods her head yes as David continues, "He probably wants to know how Kelly is doing. I will fill him in and send him on his way." Maggie agrees again with a head nod as David adds, "You stay here with Kelly and we'll be back in a few minutes." Bethany and David leave the room.

As they come out, Rick turns and extends his hand to shake Dr. Ridge's as Annie steps over to Bethany and hugs her. Rick begins using a quiet tone of voice, "Hello Dr. Ridge, Bethany. How is Kelly doing?" Dr. Ridge answers cautiously, "He's getting better. The Anesthesiologist just reversed the coma earlier tonight. Now it's a waiting game for him to wake up." Bethany adds, "Thank you for giving us some privacy before you came by." Annie replies, "Oh you're very welcome."

Rick looks down at the floor briefly then makes eye contact. He is hesitant with his words at first, but explains why he is there. "There is another reason why we came by. Actually, I am on duty and I asked Annie to join me here at the hospital to speak with you." Bethany asks, "Ok then, what's going on?" Rick tries to choose his words carefully, "I just finished a call to Taylor's Ravine for a car that crashed the guardrail and went into the ravine." Rick sighs heavily before continuing, "When we got there, we found the car slammed into a big oak tree at the bottom of the ravine." Bethany begins to panic, "Please, no!" Dr. Ridge places his hands on Bethany's shoulders as Rick continues, "The car had a strong smell of alcohol when we approached. As we got closer to the patient, the sheriff's deputy showed me the I.D., and it was Sharon's." With this news, Bethany just loses it and buries her head in her Daddy's chest. Rick adds, "They called us out because of the damaged guardrail." He takes a deep breath while Annie runs her hand across Bethany's back in a supportive way as Rick finishes his news, "As Lead Medic today, I had to check the patient, and it was indeed Sharon slumped over the steering wheel." Bethany, who is now sobbing looks up and asks, "B-But, you were able to save her weren't you?" Rick looks Bethany straight in the eyes, "I'm sorry Bethany, but we were too late. Apparently, she died on impact with the tree."

Bethany quickly turns to her Daddy and continues her crying. She is sobbing so hard that she is making a large wet spot on the front of her Daddy's Shirt. She is obviously visibly distraught about the loss of her future Sister-in-law. Dr. Ridge does his best to console his grieving daughter, "There there me child. We have to remember even though she's gone, we must realize that she made her own decision." Bethany pushes herself back away from her Daddy and replies, "I know you are right Daddy, but its just that--" She sobs even harder and runs off as Annie follows behind her calling out to her quietly, "Bethany, wait." She turns to Rick, "See you later!" Rick waves and smiles to his wife in response.

As Rick turns back to Dr. Ridge, he is met with an extended hand. "I thank you Rick for letting us know Sharon's fate." Rick smiles and accepts his hand in return as Rick ends his part of the conversation. "You're welcome Sir. Please let me know when Kelly wakes up, no matter what time it is. I need to get back to work now." Dr. Ridge replies, "Very good me boy. Good night." Before Rick leaves he comments and asks, "You know Dr. Ridge, I am very impressed by your foremost trust in God through all this. If Kelly does come out of this, can I meet with you and talk about it sometime?" Dr. Ridge nods in approval and Rick turns and walks away. Dr. Ridge enters the ward and returns to Kelly's room smiling about Rick's inquiry."

Upon entering the room, David notices Maggie leaning over the bed and stroking Kelly's head and cheeks She has been humming some Irish Lullabies to him as though he could hear each one of them. Maggie looks up at her husband and asks, "Isn't it good to know who Kelly's friends are?" To this David repiles, "Aye me wife, it's a sure thing." David puts his hand on his forehead and sighs in frustration. Maggie notices this and inquires, "David? What's wrong?" David mumbles a bit to himself before speaking, "Aye Maggie, it's far worse than you may want to hear." Maggie looks at her husband, "Now David, you know that I am a stronger woman than that." David nods his head in agreement and replies, "Aye, you're right as usual me love so here it is." He pauses briefly and then begins, "Kelly's partner Rick just told us that Sharon was in a terrible accident and did not survive." Maggie clenches her chest and exclaims, "Mercy Dear Lord, Mercy!" She is not taking the Lord's name in vain when she says this, but more as a prayerful response much like David in the Book of Psalms.

Maggie looks lovingly at her husband, "But David, what are we going to tell Kelly when he wakes up? She was his girlfriend for so many years." David replies with a sarcastic remark, "Aye, what are the chances of his memory being lost about that?" Maggie immediately calls him on the carpet for that remark. "David Seamus Ridge! That is NOT funny at all. You keep stepping up on that soapbox of yours and it's gettting very old." David looks at his wife and states, "Yes me love. It's a terrible habit I need to put off right now."

Maggie maintains a very calm demeanor as she speaks properly to her husband, "You need to be Daddy, and not Dr. Ridge the Pastor. Especially right now!" David mutters to himself for a few seconds and responds as lovingly as he can, "Alright me love, I'll do it for you." To this Maggie snaps back, "If you are doing it for me, then it's for the wrong reason. You've been letting this angst consume you for too long." David quietly ponders what Maggie has said. Rather than admit defeat, he quickly changes the subject. "I think it's my turn to go home and get a good night's sleep in me own house and in our bed. This way, you can have some time with your son." Maggie agrees with him wholeheartedly, "Now I think that's the best thing you've said all day!" David gathers his things and kisses Maggie on the cheek adding, "G'night me love. See you tomorrow." Maggie just smiles and says nothing more as her husband leaves for the night.

Maggie moves around the room straightening up some things on a nearby counter. She looks around the room to see if there is anything else she can clean. She can't help herself, since this is something that has been instilled in her. She turns and goes back over by Kelly. She looks tenderly and compassionately at him and is compelled to sing a Lullaby to her son in Gaelic. She begins to sing it a second time, but this time in english. As she finishes, Bethany returns to the room. She is still visibly shaken a bit about Sharon. However, her time with Annie has helped to calm her down. She walks over to her Momma and comments, "You were singing Fairy Lullaby to Kelly." Maggie smiles and says, "Yes I was! I used to sing it to Kelly when he was a baby. I even sang it to you my child." Bethany smiles at her and replies, "I may not remember the Gaelic, but I do remember the tune."

Momma looks appreciative at Bethany and asks, "Are you doing better me child?" Bethany looks aroung the room and says, "Yes Momma, I am doing better. It's just the shock of it all accompanied by some guilt." Maggie moves closer to her daughter and inquires, "Bethany? What do you mean by some guilt?" Bethany looks down at her lap and then raises her head. She rolls her eyes a bit before she states, "Sharon didn't have to die. I mean, I was supposed to be her maid of honor at their wedding." Maggie wraps her arms around her duaghter and tells her, "There there my precious one. I am so sorry for you." Bethany pulls back from her hug and continues, "But the worst part about it was that I had the opportunity to witness to her and share Christ the night of Kelly's accident. I waited too long and blew my chance with her. For all I know it was my fault that she did not accept salvation."

Momma sees the genuine concern in her daughter's eyes and reassures her, "You still planted a seed didn't you dear one?" Bethany hesitantly states, "I think so." Maggie continues, "Well now, it's in The Lord's hands if she was able to cry out for salvation or not." As Bethany continues to look up at Momma, she adds, "But Momma, Kelly's partner Rick said that there was alcohol involved and that she died on impact according to her injuries." Momma tells her, "Maybe there was a moment between hitting the tree and death, that she had time to surrender to God." To this Bethany perks up and blurts out, "That's right Momma, but I guess we will never know until we are taken to our eternal home in Heaven." Momma agrees, "That's right me little love. We will have to wait and see." In the back of her mind, Maggie knows the truth but for now, this is the best way to answer Bethany.

Maggie sits a while and just holds her hurting daughter close. As a silence falls across the room, Bethany looks up at her Momma and asks, "How has all of this affected you Momma? I mean, you always know the right thing to say when someone is hurting. Maggie looks her daughter in the eyes and tells her, "Oh me precious child! This whole trial that The Lord is allowing us to have is more than I can handle." Bethany looks awkwardly at Momma and declares, "But Momma, you always seem to have things under control. From what I have witnessed in the last few days, you have been incredible."

Maggie politely accepts the compliment and replies, "Thank you Bethany, but my strength is drawn from our Lord's mercy and grace. Without Jesus Christ in my life, I would have fallen apart by now." Bethany smiles fondly at Momma and says, "I hope I can remain strong like you when I am faced with these kinds of trials when Jon and I are married." Momma smiles in return and quips, "Not to mention all the grand babies from you both also!" Both women chuckle to each other after Momma's comment.

With another brief pause, Bethany changes the subject. "Momma, tell me about Daddy. I mean, about how you two met and how you've remained married for so long." Maggie brings her index finger up to her lips as though she is pondering where to begin. She exclaims, "Let's see, where do I start?" She pauses again briefly and then starts, Well, your Daddy was fresh out of seminary when we first met. I was invited to a church service one Sunday where a new young minister was coming as a guest speaker." Bethany sits up and gives her attention to Momma as she continues, "He did a sermon on the Book of Ruth and her trials and her rewards. I was so captivated by his message that I felt that I had to be sure to meet and greet him afterwards." Bethany slips in a sarcastic comment, "Back when Daddy had hair, right?" Momma is amused by the question and giggles before answering, "Yes dear, a long time ago."

Maggie continues, "After dismissal, I went back to meet this new young man who spoke so eloquently of the scriptures." There is another pause. "When we shook hands, he introduced himself as Pastor David Ridge, Minister of The Gospel of Jesus Christ." Bethany again chimes in, "That sounds like Daddy alright!" Momma agrees and continues, "As we spoke to each other, he noticed my Irish accent and began speaking to me in Gaelic. We hit it off from the get go in that conversation. Then out of nowhere, he asks me out to dinner the next evening in Gaelic, so no one else could understand him but me." Bethany jumps in and asks, "You know, you never really taught Kelly and me any Gaelic while growing up." Maggie nods and replies, "We wanted to raise you kids up as Americans, since you both were born here. Daddy and I still speak it to each other privately in our home or when you kids were not around us." Bethany nods with an understanding expression on her face as Momma continues, "We were married just after he got his Master's Degree a year later. He went on to receive his Doctorate while we were establishing our first home and here we are today." Bethany adds, "And we all lived happily ever after!"

At that moment Maggie stops herself as she faced the reality of the situation facing her now. Her strength has indeed come from The Lord, however Bethany's last comment hit her emotions unepectedly. She starts to fall apart a bit, but pulls herself back together. Bethany notices the momentary pause and asks, "Momma? Are you Okay?" Maggie looks at Bethany and replies, "Yes dear one, I am fine. The Lord just had to remind me of what Paul told us in Second Corinthians 12 verse 10, *Therefore I take pleasure in infirmities, in reproaches, in necessities, in persecutions, in distresses for Christ's sake: for when I am weak, then I am strong.*" Bethany smiles brightly and nods in agreement.

Bethany looks at her watch a moment and notices the time. "Momma, it's getting late so I am going to go home and get some sleep. Besides, Daddy may need me also." Maggie agrees and turns back to Kelly. As Bethany gather her things, her cell phone rings. She answers it and is suprised by the voice on the other end. "Hello, Bethany Ridge speaking." Her sadness and her demeanor changes drastically to the positive. She hears, "Hello Bethany, this is Jon. I have some good news for you. The school has to shut down for some emergency repairs on a water main break." Bethany smiles even brighter and asks, "So what are your plans?" Jon replies, "Well, I thought I would come down and visit for a few days with my sister Dawn. I would love to be able to see my girl." Bethany excitedly says, "Yes! But we have some tragic news we are dealing with here involving Kelly." She pauses to hear his comments and continues, "Kelly was in a very bad accident and is here at the hospital. I am here with Momma. I was just getting ready to leave when you called." There is another pause as Jon tells her, "In that case I will leave right away and see you in the morning. I love you Bethany." Bethany replies, "Love you too, bye bye." She hangs up her phone and gives Momma the good news. She all of a sudden is behaving like the last several hours never happened. "Momma, Jon is coming home for a few days to visit unexpectedly. I need to definitely go home now. You stay the night with Kelly and we will all be back tomorrow. Good night Momma."

Maggie acknowledges her daughter's departure with a wave and a smile. As Bethany walks out, she turns back to look at Kelly and looks to the Heavens asking, *"Alright me Lord I trust you fully, but I only wanted to ask, how much longer."* She sits in the chair next to Kelly's bed, says a small prayer and falls asleep, secure in her Lord's Will.

CHAPTER 12

THE NIGHT HAS PASSED, AND IT IS A NEW DAY IN GOLD CITY. CHARGE Nurse Erin knocks softly on the door to Kelly's room, and enters to do her morning assessment. She tries her best to be as quiet as possible as Maggie is still sleeping in the chair at bedside. As she puts her clipboard down, she accidentally bumps the empty water cup off the bedside table. It hits the floor and causes Maggie to wake up. Erin notices her waking and immediately apologizes, "Oh Mrs. Ridge. I am so sorry for waking you. You looked so peaceful as you slept." Maggie, although a bit sluggish, graciously accepts her apology. "That's alright dear, I need to be up and start me day." As she says this, she looks at the wall clock and suddenly increases her speed some. "Oh, I am late getting up. Do you mind if I use the bathroom and freshen up some?" Erin gives her a nod and tells her, "Sure you can do that. It's that door right there." Erin point to the closed door just to the left of the entry door.

Maggie thanks her and proceeds to the bathroom as Erin begins her assessment of Kelly. First she writes down the date and time, then flips the chart back a few pages to review previous assessments. After a few minutes, she starts with pulse, breathing, and blood pressure. As she reaches for his wrist, she notices Kelly raise his left index finger and then puts it down. Erin is surprised by this and calls out to Maggie. "Mrs. Ridge? Kelly moved his left index finger!" Maggie comes hurriedly out of the bathroom and moves up next to Kelly at his bedside. She looks down at her son and grabs her chest when she sees him curl the fingers of his left hand and relax them.

Maggie is elated by seeing this, that she quickly grabs her phone from her purse and calls her husband. The phone rings a few times before David answers, "Hello? This is Doctor Ridge spea..." He is cut off by Maggie, "David, it's Maggie! Kelly moved his left hand. Did you hear me David? He moved his left hand!" David puts his hand up in a stopping gesture as he replies, "Slow down me love! I can hear your excitement. He moved his hand you say?" Maggie confirms her words again, "Yes David, I've seen it me self." As she speaks, David moves his hand to his forehead and replies, "Praise the Lord! He has heard our pleas." He pauses briefly and continues, "Alright me love, I am on my way." Maggie ends the call and moves back over to her son. Back at the house, David quickly gathers his suitcoat, Bible and keys. He rushes out of his study and exits the house, slamming the door behind him. As he makes his way to the car, he fumbles with is tie and tightens it around his collar. He opens the door and tosses his suitcoat on the passenger seat and carefully puts down his Bible as he gets in. He starts the car, pulls out of the driveway and heads to the hospital post haste. Bethany has already left for work.

At the hospital, Maggie is bouncing around the room in sheer excitement because The Lord is doing His work as the Master Physician. Erin does her best to finish with the assessment amidst Maggie's joy. As Erin picks up her things, she looks at Maggie and smiles brightly. She adds, "Mrs. Ridge, maybe if you start talking to Kelly, it might accelerate the waking process. Maggie nods her head in agreement and dashes back over to Kelly's bedside. She places her left hand on his shoulder and her right on his hand. Then she leans over to his right ear and says, "Kelly? Kelly? Can you hear me son?" Kelly remains still and does not move. Maggie tries again, "Kelly? It's Momma, please wake up." There is still no response. As Erin starts to exit the room and asks, "Would you like me to see if Bethany is a available to come up?" Maggie turns to Erin and says, "Yes, please, by all means." Erin nods and exits the room. She returns to the Nurses Station and calls Bethany. She finds that Bethany is not answering her extention so she hangs up. She rolls her chair back to get up just as Bethany enters the ICU and heads right to Kelly's room. As she enters she calls out, "Momma, it's Bethany, I'm coming in." She gives Momma a big hug and greets her. "Good morning Momma Did you sl......" She is immediately cut off by Momma, "Bethany, Kelly moved his hand!" Bethany replies, "Oh Momma that's wonderful news. Have you called Daddy yet?" Momma subdues her emotions a lot more and answers, "Yes of course I did. He should be here any moment." Just as she finishes her sentence, there is a slight knock on the door and David enters. "Good Morning family, I see everyone is present. Has the boy moved anymore yet?" Maggie looks directly at David and tells him, "No husband, YOUR son hasn't moved since I called you. David is stunned by the sound of Maggie's reply and exclaims, "Aye woman? What brought that on?" Maggie becomes a bit more harsh and answers, " If he moved again, would I have kept it from you?" Once again, hearing his wife's tone, he surrenders, "Aye, maybe so me wife." He quickly changes the subject as Bethany just watches the banter between her parents. He then reaches his hand out to Bethany in a gesture of love. Bethany then extends her hand and arm in a likewise gesture, and smiles. David turns back to Maggie and suggests, "Maggie me Darlin', why don't we go to the cafeteria and get some breakfast together?" Bethany jumps in quickly, "That's a great idea Momma. I can stay with Kelly while you and Daddy go." Momma reluctantly agrees and goes with her husband while Bethany stays in the room.

Dr. and Mrs. Ridge make their way through the hallways and down to the cafeteria. They enter the cafeteria together as Maggie goes to a table and sits. Dr. Ridge goes to the coffee dispenser and prepares two cups. He brings them to the table and hands Maggie a cup while he sits down. There is a few moments of silence as they each take a sip from their cups. David begins, "Might I get you something to eat from the food bar, me love?" Maggie ponders for a moment then replies, "Just a bagel with cream cheese and a fruit cup please." David smiles at her and states, "Certainly me love, If you don't mind me having a full breakfast of bacon and eggs? I need to finish me sermon for Sunday and I'll need the extra protein." Maggie smiles at him in approval and nods. David gets up and makes his way to the food bar and orders his food. He goes to the cooler and gets the fruit cup while he waits for his order. He makes sure to grab the bagel and cream cheese for Maggie. After a short time, he returns with the order and separates it between the two of them. David asks the blessing on the food and they enjoy breakfast together.

Meanwhile back in Kelly's room, Bethany has done her best to tidy things up while Daddy and Momma are having a much deserved break. She sits down and turns on the television. As she flips through the channels, her phone rings and she answers it. "Hello?" She quickly becomes giddy as it's Jon's voice on the other end. "Hello Bethany! How am I supposed to find you? I thought that I would stop by when I got into town and see you right away." Bethany's mood quickly changes to a somber one as she explains things, 'Oh Jon, I am up in the Intensive Care Unit. remember I told you that Kelly was in a very serious accident and has been here for the last several days." Jon is very supportive, "Oh Bethany, yes I remember. I will get there as soon as I can. Sounds like I am needed more than I thought!" Bethany tries to calm him some, "Now Jon, I don't need you as an ICU patient too!" Jon chuckles a bit, "I think I am safe. Dawn is doing the driving. I will get there soon like within the next few hours." Bethany perks up a bit and replies, "Okay Jon that sounds great. I can't wait to see you." As she finishes her sentence, she turns her head back toward Kelly who is now awake and staring right at her. This startles Bethany, as she yells out. "AAH!!"

She has just alerted the nursing staff and they start rushing in to see what's wrong and ask, "What's wrong!" Bethany points at Kelly and exclaims, "L-L-look! Kelly's eyes are opened." Sure enough the nurses look and see that his eyes were indeed open. Kelly just lays there in silence, expressing a bewildered look, trying to figure out his surroundings and situation. Bethany asks out of curiosity, Why isn't he saying anything?" Nurse Erin looks at Bethany, holds up her index finger and says, "Just a minute Bethany. " Erin turns back to Kelly, "Kelly? My name is Erin. Can you hear me?" There is a moment of silence and then Kelly responds somewhat groggy, "Uhm!" Erin then turns to Bethany and suggests, "Why don't you use the phone at the Nurses Station and call your parents at the cafeteria." Bethany agrees and calls the switchboard to have her parents paged to the line. "Good morning Amy, I need you to page Dr. David and Maggie Ridge to the phone please?" She waits patiently for them to answer as she hears the page overhead. "Doctor David or Maggie Ridge, please call the hospital switchboard on the white courtesy phone. Dr. David or Maggie Ridge please call the hospital switchboard on the white courtesy phone."

After a few minutes, Bethany hears her Daddy's voice on the phone and speaks excitedly, "Daddy, it's Bethany. You and Momma need to come back here right away! Kelly has woken up." She hangs up and waits for them at the ICU desk. Dr. Ridge and Maggie enter the unit and meet Bethany at the desk. Maggie inquires "What are you doing out here dear? Why aren't you in the room with Kelly?" Bethany simply replies, "Because I came out to call you and just waited so we could all go back in together." Maggie smiles and they move forward towards the room. Dr. Ridge hesitates, "Tell you what Maggie, you and Bethany go in. I'll wait out here and then come in when it's comfortable to." Maggie once again has to chide her husband. "David Seamus Ridge, you will do no such thing! Do I need to rehash a previous conversation?" David decides not to push any further and replies, "No me love, that won't be necessary." Maggie, Bethany enter the room as David follows behind them.

As they approach the bed, Nurse Erin is finishing her In room assessment. Erin comments, "He was awake briefly and then went back to sleep. This is common with coming out of a coma. He will regain full consciousness, but it will take some time." Doctor Ridge smiles at Erin and replies, "Thank you lass! We will stay with him now." Erin nods, smiles and exits the room. Maggie comments, "I hope it won't be too much longer." Bethany agrees, "Me too Momma. I miss talking to my brother." David feels he needs to step in and be husband and father. "Patience me loved ones, patience. When The Lord decides it is time for him to wake up fully, he will."

Maggie just can't contain herself. She looks at David, then turns to Bethany, "See, your Daddy just has to be Mister Obvious again!" David becomes quite insulted by her comment and asks, "And just what do do you be meaning by that?" Maggie looks directly at David and tells him, "Don't be playing coy with me David Ridge, you know exactly what it is I mean!" Their argument is getting more and more heated until Maggie calmly states, "Sometimes David your absurdity to the obvious is tiresome. Please, I will ask you like I did a few days ago, just be Daddy and leave the clerical collar at home." David again realizes his error and quickly apologizes to her, "Aye Maggie, once again you slay me heart with love. I will do my best from here on out to leave me collar at the door." Maggie smiles and accepts his apology, "Thank you me husband, and yes I forgive you." Bethany quickly jumps in, "I think you both needed to do that. I am glad to see the tension has broken between the two of you." Maggie and David share a hug and then invite Bethany in for a group hug. They all chuckle with each other briefly before they hear a familiar voice they haven't heard in a while, "Somebody want to fill me in on this loving moment?" Immediately, they turn towards Kelly's bed to find their son and brother awake with eyes open sluggishly.

Bethany calls out as she moves to the bed, "Oh Kelly, I have missed you so much." She pauses briefly and then adds, "Well, actually we all have." Maggie and Bethany begin to show love and gratitude to Kelly while David slips out the door hoping to avoid any unnecessary confrontation with his son. Maggie continues, "Kelly, your Dad and I have been so worried about you." Kelly rolls his eyes and states, "I believe you about your worry, but Dad? Yeah right!" Maggie tries to reassure her son, "Now Kelly, your not being fair to him." Kelly changes the subject to avoid any more lectures from Momma. He rolls his head back and forth on the pillow and asks, "What happened? Why am I in a hospital bed? Things are really sketchy to me right now." Bethany asks, "Can you remember anything Kelly?" Kelly looks around and slowly moves his hand up to his forehead, "Last thing I remember is boarding the engine for a call." Maggie moves closer to him, "Is there anything else you can remember besides that?" Kelly answers, "N-No I can't. Everything is so foggy to me. Please tell me what happened."

Bethany looks her brother in the eyes and explains,"Wednesday morning you were responding to a call on the engine as duty officer. Engine One made a left turn at Table and Mountain, and was struck on the passenger side by a driver in a big rig that was being pursued by the police. Kelly is still puzzled and asks, "Wait! Wednesday? What day is this?" Maggie cuts in, "Kelly, son, it's Saturday morning. You've been in a coma since then." Kelly is visibly overwhelmed with everything that he is being told. "Wait, hold on, this is just too much to take in." With his last few words, he fades off back to sleep as Maggie is reassuring to him. "Alright Kelly, you get some more rest. We can talk more later today when you are more awake." Bethany looks at Momma, "Oh Momma, what if he asks about Sharon? Who's going to be the one to tell him?" Maggie looks at her with a schemed expression and tells her, "We will leave your Daddy to tell him that one." Although a bit shocked by Momma's comment, Bethany giggles under her breath and agrees, "Ok Momma, that will be his privilege." Momma adds, "Yes and let's pray for both of them when it happens." There is a pause in their conversation, then Maggie asks, "Bethany, why don't you see if your father is still outside the unit." Bethany agrees, "Sure Momma! Be right back." She turns and gleefully exits the room to find her Daddy. Meanwhile, Maggie turns back to Kelly and watches him as he sleeps.

After a short period, Bethany returns with her Daddy right behind her. She exclaims, "I found him in the family waiting room going over his sermon notes for Sunday." David adds, "Aye, that she did. Can you believe it? Right when I was getting to the best part too." He pauses a moment and continues, "Has the lad said very much?" "Actually Daddy, he is a bit confused about things. I have to get back to work and Momma has shopping to do. We both thought you could bring him up to speed the next time he wakes." David expresses a lost worried look and blurts out, "W-What am I supposed to tell him?" Maggie pauses, looks her husband in the eyes, "You, me husband, can tell him about Sharon." Again David asks, "Now how do you suppose I do that?" Maggie reassures him, "Now David, how do you give bad news as a minister of The Gospel?" She says nothing more and exits the room as David mumbles to himself, "Bah! First she wants me to take off the collar and be Dad, then she wants me to put it back on just the same." All he can do right now is pace the floor and wait for him to wake up again. In his mind, he mulls over and over to himself just how to break the news to his son. They haven't spoken to each other for years now, and he has to be the one to tell him the sad news of Sharon's passing. As the next few hours pass, David finds himself mulling over how to explain this tragedy. Unlike most occurrences, this one brings heavier consequences.

A couple of hours have passed since Maggie and Bethany left. There is a knock at the room door as Maggie returns from her errands. She enters the room and asks, "Hello again me husband! How did it go with Kelly? How did he take the news?" David looks at Maggie with an awkward look and replies, "Aye, he didn't take it at all! The lads been sleeping ever since you left. However, I will still tell him, unless you want to." Maggie cuts him off right away, "No you're not mister! You're not going to make that excuse. You will tell him as his Dad."

David finds himself again at a point if surrender, throws up his hands and replies, "I will tell him, I will tell him!" He turns back to Kelly's bed to find him wide awake. Kelly asks, "OK old man, what is it that's so important to tell me? Mom is pretty adamant about it so what is so urgent?"

David looks firmly at his son and begins to explain, "You see son…" Kelly cuts him off abruptly, "Before you continue, where's Sharon? I was hoping she would be here." David takes a deep breath before continuing, "That's what I need to tell you. I know we haven't spoken to each other in years, and whether you choose to believe me or not is up to you." He takes another deep breath, "Kelly, Sharon will no longer be with us." Kelly asks, "What? Have you chased her away too?" "No no no, it's nothing like that. Matter of fact we were ready to welcome her to the family, until." Kelly interrupts, "Until what then?" David hesitates no longer and comes right out with it. "Kelly, Sharon passed away a couple of days ago. She's dead son!" Kelly becomes somewhat confused, "What? Come on old man, not funny."

Maggie senses a need to step in and does so, "It's true son. She couldn't handle the situation of your accident and left the hospital the day they gave you the medication to wake you up." Kelly asks, "So didn't you try to stop her from leaving?" Maggie replies, "She said she needed some time, so we respected that." Kelly then asks, "So how did you find out about her death?" Bethany has entered the room quietly as Momma and Daddy were explainung things to Kelly. At this point she steps into the conversation, "Later that night, Rick came by with Annie and told us." Kelly becomes more distraught as Maggie consoles him, "I know Kelly, but it will all work out in time. Just be thankful for the time you had together." Kelly reconciles himself to accept this news, since Momma has explained it in her loving and nurturing way." David begins to see the irony in all his efforts to communicate with his son as pointless and declares, "Well, I did my part. I am going home to finish me sermon notes for Sunday. Good Night me love!"

Maggie decides the best recourse is to just submit to her husband, "Alright David, I will see you at home." She turns back to Kelly, "You know son, he's really trying hard to let by gones be by gones and be a father to you. I wish you could see that and go easier on him." Kelly looks up and smirks sarcastically at Momma and states, "I could, but sometimes it's more fun for me to see him get frustrated." Maggie continues to chastise her son, "Now come on, you were raised better than that! You need to respect your Daddy. He does love you and cares for you deep down." She pauses and leans over her son and kisses him on the forehead and continues, "Now Bethany and I are going to leave you for the night. Get some rest and we will see you after Sunday Service. We love you Kelly! Good night Son."

As they leave, Kelly lays there and ponders all that was told to him earlier. Tears run down his cheeks as he remembers Sharon and all the good times they had. He knows that he has a long road ahead of him. He thinks, "What about the other firemen on the engine? Why did this have to happen to him?' These questions continue to mull through his mind as he drifts off to sleep for the night.

CHAPTER 13

A NEW DAY UNFOLDS IN GOLD CITY. TO MANY OF ITS RESIDENTS, IT IS Lord's Day. The day for them to worship in church. As for Kelly, it has become nothing more than another day. Just as well, there's not much to do when you're lying in a hospital bed staring up at the ceiling or scanning the room for something to find interesting. He moves his hand a bit to activate the nurse call button. A friendly voice comes over the room speaker, "Yes, may I help you?" Kelly clears his throat before speaking, "Can someone please come in and help me reposition? I am so uncomfortable right now." A very brief pause is immediately followed by a cheerful response, "You sure can. Someone will be right in."

The nurse resets the call light and enters the room a few seconds later. She assists Kelly with his request and quickly has him repositioned and comfortable in no time. Before leaving, she turns and asks, "Is there anything else I can do for you before I go?" Kelly just smiles and shakes his head no. The nurse leaves the room as Kelly returns to his time of deep thought. He remains like this, drifting in and out of consciousness for the next couple of hours.

The next thing Kelly knows, there is a knocking on his room door. Bethany's voice calls into the room, "Kelly? It's Bethany! I have a couple of special people with me to see you." She proceeds to enter the room followed by Bethany's fiancée Jon and his sister Dawn. Bethany cheerfully acknowledges her brother, "Hey big brother, look who came back to visit me for a bit." Jon leans over the bed and smiles at him saying, "Hey there Bud, I heard about your situation and wanted to see you." Kelly looks up and replies, "Come on, you're here to see Bethany and came with her to see me because you were obligated to." Jon, who is taken back by that comment quips, "Well I see you still have your sense of sarcasm." Bethany quickly steps in, "All right you two, be civil to each other." Jon, replies, Hey, this is how future brother's in law treat each other." He smiles at her as he finishes the reply.

Kelly's attention is suddenly drawn to a very attractive woman standing in the room. She stands about five feet nine inches with white pumps dressed in a powder blue dress with a white flower print. She is blond haired and blue eyed. She is definitely a "looker" by Kelly's standard. He boldly asks for an introduction, "Would someone please introduce the lovely young lady behind you?" Jon quickly apologizes and proceeds to introduce his sister. "Kelly Ridge, this is my sister Dawn. She brought me down to see Beth. She stayed for church, then brought us here to see you." Dawn steps forward to the bed as Jon speaks. Kelly smiles at the sound of a sweet voice speaking. "Hello Kelly, it's very nice to meet you. I have heard quite a lot about you in the last couple of days." His smile widens more as he replies, "The pleasure is very much mine. Dawn, was it? She smiles and replies, "Yes." Kelly adds, "That's such a lovely name for such a lovely looking girl." To this Dawn replies, "Thank you very much for the compliment Kelly."

Bethany sees something happening between the two of them and interrupts, "So, big brother, did you have a good night's sleep?" Kelly looks at Bethany, "Not really. All night I was fighting this emotional battle inside. Like my whole world has been turned upside-down." Bethany looks straight into Kelly's eyes, "Everyone's world has been turned upside-down with all this. Momma, Daddy, me, we ALL have been affected." Dawn feels compelled to come into the conversation, "Kelly, did you ever stop and think that this might be God working in your life?" Bethany waves her hands in a no motion at Dawn. Kelly surprises everyone in the room when he replies, "As much as I feel about God right now, I will let that comment go for the time being." Bethany steps up and adds, "Dawn, his relationship with The Lord is a delicate subject." Dawn replies, "In that case, I will just excuse myself and wait for you two in the family waiting room." She turns and gets ready to exit when she hears, "Wait, don't go. Please stay a bit longer." from Kelly's lips.

Bethany and Jon look at each other and express a curious smirk. Dawn replies, "OK, if you really want me to." She steps forward closer to the bed as she says this. Kelly asks, "Dawn, how did you get to be so bold in approaching someone who is a stranger to you?" She replies, "Because The Lord tells me in the scriptures that I am to have a bold and loving spirit to whomever I make contact to with." Kelly is very impressed with her answer and responds with, "I sure do wish I felt that same approach with people."

At that moment, Dawn is compelled to reach for Kelly's hand and assures him, "Maybe this is too bold, but I don't care right now. You can have that same feeling, if you I just surrender yourself to The Lord." Kelly looks very directly into Dawn's eyes and tells her, "You know, If you were anyone else, I would tell you to get out, but.." He tightens his hand with her before continuing, "There is something curious about you Dawn that I can't place right now. What is it you do for a living? Have I met you somewhere before?" Dawn replies, "I work as a Flight Attendant for one of the major airlines, so I spend a lot of time in Capital City." Kelly smiles and asks, Will you please stay a while longer? I think you are a very attractive lady." Dawn is a bit embarrassed by his comment to her. Her face does reflect a pink hue as she gently lets go of his hand. If you really like I can stay as long as you would like me to. But for right now you get yourself better and we will see what happens." Dawn steps back away from his bed and gestures to Bethany towards her. Dawn tells Bethany, "I need to step out now. I will wait in the family waiting room." She is compelled by something unexplainable that has come over her. Rather than show any further embarrassment, she turns and exits the room.

Bethany turns to Kelly and inquires about Dawn, "Well I see you made some points with Jon's sister." Kelly cautiously answers Bethany, "Yeah, well, maybe. She's a bit too much God, church and Bible for me." Jon adds, "I don't know Kelly, you seemed to enjoy having her in the room." Kelly defends his actions, "Yeah, that or I'm just attracted to a good looking blonde!" Jon quickly defends her, "Watch it buddy! That's my sister you're talking about." Kelly changes his tone and replies, Hey, Whoa! I wasn't meaning to offend anybody." Bethany jumps in and reassures him, "It's okay big brother, no offense taken." Kelly looks around a bit and then states, "Ya know what? I am getting really tired right now. This visit has really worn me down." In his mind, Kelly figures this may be a good excuse to avoid anything more about Dawn. He did enjoy the new visitor and keeps her in mind.

Just as he completes his comment, Momma enters the room. "Blessed Lord's Day everyone!" Momma exclaims. Bethany and Jon both reply, "Blessed Lord's Day to you Momma/Mrs. Ridge." Momma makes her way to the bed. She leans over and kisses Kelly on the forehead and asks, "So, how is me son doing today?" Kelly looks up at Momma and replies, "I was just telling these two that I could use a nap about now." Momma shows concern, "Me poor boy! Well Momma's here now and I will take over so you can rest a while." Bethany turns to Momma and asks, "Didn't Daddy come with you?" Momma turns to address her daughter, "He's parking the car and will be up shortly."

Momma pauses for a moment and acknowledges Jon, "Well Jon, what did you think of the morning message?" Jon smiles and replies, "As far as I can say, Dr. Ridge hit another one out of the park." Kelly has fallen asleep during this conversation. Bethany agrees, "Daddy definitely delivered another om target, to the point sermon." She then changes directions with her conversation, "Momma, we brought Dawn with us and she and Kelly hit it off really well." To this Bethany is immediately chastised by Momma. "Now child, that's not something good for Kelly right now. He's not even over Sharon's death and you are busy playing matchmaker." Bethany defends her actions by saying, "Oh Momma, nothing was intended to happen. We just thought it would be a nice distraction for him. Only thing is, it might have worked." Bethany giggles as she says this.

As she finishes her sentence, Daddy enters the room and announces, "Here I am, that nice distraction you all seem to be looking for." Everyone in the room laughs as Jon replies, "Hello Dr. Ridge, and you are not the distraction we were referring to." Dr. Ridge smiles at Jon and gets "puffed up" with his next comment. "You know, I just met this lovely girl in the Family Waiting Room. She was at church this morning, and she told me that my sermon was "top-notch" in her words. Bethany rolls her eyes at him and replies, "Now Daddy, you know perfectly well that that was Jon's sister Dawn. Daddy quickly deflates himself, chuckling jovially. "Oh I know, me young lass, but I got the response that I was figuring I would."

Momma, Bethany and Jon all smile at each other sharing visual cues regarding Daddy's sense of humor. David turns to his wife, "How are things going with Kelly?" Maggie turns to her husband, points at Kelly, and states, "See for yourself. He's sleeping right now. Tell you what, you stay with him while the rest of us go to the cafeteria and get some lunch." David replies, "Why don't we all go and get something to eat and come back later so he can get his rest?" Bethany chimes in, "I'll get Dawn from the waiting room." She turns to leave as Jon adds, "I will let the nurse's know." They both walk out of the room as Maggie turns to David and asks, "Are you sure he will be okay with us going to eat?" David reassures her, "Why Maggie, it's no different then when we go home for the night."

Maggie continues her persistence, "I know David so, why don't you stay with him and be there for him if he wakes up again?" David shrugs off the comment by adding, "Besides, he hasn't wanted me to be there for him in years. What makes you think that he would want that now?" Maggie defends her comment, "Do I have to remind you David that you are still his father?" David quickly submits, "No me love, you don't need to remind me of that! I will stay here with our lad. Please just bring me back a sandwich." Maggie nods in agreement and leaves the room. Doctor Ridge turns back to Kelly, leans over him and says, "Now I don't know whether you can hear me or not, but I hope this accident has awoken you up to The Lord's mercy and grace. He could have taken you from us, but He chose not to." Tears begin to roll down his face as he continues, "Oh me son! I am pleading for you to come back to Him. Walk away from all this worldly lust and seek Our Heavenly Father again."

Again he wipes the tears from his cheeks and steps back from the bed. In his mind, he still wonders if Kelly heard his heartfelt plea. He resolves himself to the fact that The Lord heard him and that's all that really matters. He moves over to the chair in the corner, just out of Kelly's view. As he sits down, one of the nurses enter the room to speak with the family. She sees Dr. Ridge and engages in conversation with him, "Oh Dr. Ridge I'm glad I caught you. Dr. Stevens is going to be here in about an hour to see Kelly. He wants to speak to family members as well." Dr. Ridge nods and replies, "Ah thank you lass! Can I contact me family in the cafeteria and have them come back up?" The nurse nods in agreement and tells him,

"Of course! Just use the room phone and dial 0 for the switchboard, and they will connect you to your family members. " Dr. Ridge thanks her again and she leaves the room.

Dr. Ridge does as he was directed and calls the switchboard. He is greeted by a friendly voice, "Gold City Hospital, how may I direct your call?" He proceeds, "This is Dr. David Ridge. Me son Kelly is a patient in the ICU. The rest of the family is in the cafeteria and I need to be connected to them." The operator replies, "Anyone in particular you need to speak to?" Dr. Ridge responds, "Yes! Me wife, Maggie Ridge please?" She asks for a moment, "Hold the line please. I will have you connected in a couple of minutes." Dr. Ridge thanks her and patiently waits.

In the cafeteria, Maggie has been eating and enjoying the company of Bethany, Jon and Dawn. They are approached by one of the cafeteria employees who walks over and politely interrupts the conversation, "Excuse me, but are you the Ridge family." Maggie looks up and replies, "Yes dear, I am Mrs. Ridge. What can I help you with?" The employee replies, "There's a Dr. Ridge on the white courtesy phone and he would like to speak with you." Maggie stands up and thanks her as the employee points her in the direction of the phone.

She makes her way over to the phone and picks up the receiver, "Hello, this is Maggie Ridge speaking." David begins immediately, "Maggie, it's David. Kelly's Doctor will be here within the hour, and he wants to talk with us about Kelly." Maggie expresses an immediate concern, "What's wrong David? Is there a problem with our son?" David calmly reassures her, "No me Dear, everything is fine. He just wants to give us an update on his care." Maggie's anxiety is quickly dispelled, "Oh, well then I will let everyone know and we will be right back up. See you soon David, bye bye." She hangs the phone up and goes back to the table. "That was Daddy. The doctor wants to meet with us within the hour about Kelly's care. We need to return to his room and await his arrival."

Everyone gets up at the same time and resets their chairs. Bethany grabs the sandwich her Daddy asked for from the table as they all make their way out of the cafeteria and head for the elevator. When they get back to the room, they find Daddy pacing the floor at the foot end of the bed. Bethany hands Daddy his sandwich, "Here's your sandwich Daddy!"

Daddy nods and smiles in thanks. Bethany sits in the chair in the corner as Momma sits in the one at Kelly's bedside. David, Jon and Dawn remain standing as they wait for Dr. Stevens to arrive.

The hour passes, and there is a slight knock on the room door. Dr. Stevens announces himself and enters the room greeting everyone. "Good afternoon all, I am glad you could all be here. I wanted to take some time with you and update you on Kelly's progress." Everyone waits with eager anticipation as he begins, "I've been through Kelly's vital signs record, labs, x-rays, scans and overall care. I really must say that I am amazed at the improvement that has happened. Somehow, he has made more progress than any other patient in my medical career." As they hear the doctor speak, they can't help but not contain their smiles. The Doctor notices this immediately comments, "I can see this is sounding very good to you. As a member of the medical community, the science here is phenomenal. Dr. Ridge begins to chuckle out loud and replies, "Science you say! Good man, have you no consideration for Our Great and Heavenly Physician who makes all healing possible?"

Dr. Stevens becomes visibly angry and bursts out at Dr. Ridge, "Wait! You still expect me to believe that some universal cosmic life form is responsible for this progress? That's just a bunch of hogwash! Science and Medicine do serve a purpose here also." David replies rather smugly, "Hogwash you say?" David turns to Maggie and states out loud, "Do you believe that me wife? The man still thinks it's all of this is because of him!" Dr. Stevens continues his work and deliberately ignores the clamor between Dr. Ridge and Maggie. He looks at the monitors and flips through Kelly's medical chart and enters notes into the record. Maggie then decides to confront Dr. Stevens. She looks directly at him and asks, "It doesn't sound like you are a believer in The Lord Jesus Christ! He is performing a miracle right before your very eyes and you deny him."

The Doctor decides to put Maggie in her place and end the conversation. "Mrs. Ridge, with all due respect, as I told your husband. Your son's progress can not be assigned to some universal diety performing some kind of miracle as you call it is preposterous. I am an athiest and I DO NOT prescribe to your thinking! Assigning all this progress again to your way of thinking is medically and scientifically impossible." He makes a few more notes and then addresses the family one last time before leaving. "Regardless of who or what is increasing his healing, if he continues to improve, we will move him to a regular unit in the next few days. Good day!" He picks up Kelly's chart and exits the room.

David and Maggie just stare at each other silently. Bethany breaks the silence, "Wow! That was both informative and rude all at the same time." Dawn has remained silent through all the briefing. Jon, on the other hand comments, "Beth, you have to remember that we live in an unsaved world." David and Maggie agree with Jon in unison, "Aye!" Dr. Ridge looks at his watch and informs the family of the time. "Well, it's almost time to get ready for evening service. Let's leave Kelly to get his rest for the night." They all agree as Maggie leans down to Kelly's ear, "Kelly me boy, we are all going to leave for the night, ok?" Kelly awakens and replies, " Alright Momma. Can you ask the nurse for my sleep meds for the night?" Maggie nods as the other four exit the room.

She turns to leave and then turns back to Kelly and asks, "Just how much of that conversation with the doctor did you hear?" Kelly just smiles at his Momma and tells her, "Momma, you always taught me to tell the truth and I will tell you that I just woke up as you said you were leaving for the night." She smiles and nods again, gently rubbing his shoulder. She turns and exits the room just as the nurse enters the room and fulfills his request.

As the nurse turns to leave, Kelly asks, "Say, can I ask you a question before you leave?" The nurse looks at him and repiles, "Sure. What else can I do for you?" Kelly answers, "It's nothing related to my care. It's more of a query. You know, to get your opinion on something." The nurse nods her head and replies, "Sure, whats your question?"

Kelly begins, "Did you ever in your life, lie about something to your mom or dad?" She pauses in thought for a few moments and then answers his question, "Well, when I was a little girl, my mom asked me if I took a brownie before supper. I lied and said I didn't but she caught me in the lie." Kelly asks, how did she find out you lied?" The nurse chucked a bit and said, "It really wasn't that hard. I had brownie smears all over my face."

Kelly smiles widely as the nurse returns the question, "How about you?" Kelly answers, "Well, I just lied to her for the first time in like 20 years. She and my father just had it out with the doctor about whether or not he believed in God. It was beginning to get really hostile. Before she left she asked me if I heard any yf it. I told her I slept through the whole thing, but I heard every word." The nurse rolls her eyes a bit then asks, "So she caught you lying?" Kelly vehemently answers, "No, amazingly enough, she believed me." The nurse compliments him sarcastically, "Well, congratulations on being successful this time. Just remember, she is mom and she might have seen right through it and let it go for now. I do know this whole delimma has been very difficult for her especially." As she leaves the room, she turns down the room lights. Kelly ponders her words for a moment and then settles himself into the mattress and drifts off to sleep.

CHAPTER 14

It is now Monday and a new day has begun in Gold City. Kelly is sleeping peacefully in his room, when he is awoken by a loud bang from the outside. For a moment he is puzzled by the noise and just credits it to thunder. This is not the case, considering there's not a rain cloud in the sky. The weather is clear and sunny as the morning hours continue.

A few minutes later, one of the nurses comes into the room and rouses Kelly awake. She touches his shoulder and speaks, "Mr. Ridge, please wake up. My name is Amy, and there's a breaking story on the news you might want to see." She reaches for the television control as she finishes her sentence.

She turns it on just as a news update is starting. "*Good Morning everyone, I'm GCTV Reporter Linda Barnett coming to you live. We are standing down the block from Gold City Chemical Company, where an early morning explosion has occurred leveling a section of the building and injuring more than 20 people. Right now, it is believed the injured are from an outside contractor. We are being told that they were digging a trench next to the building and struck a gas line, which set off the explosion. Gold City Fire Department is on scene and have called in units from Middle Village and Cherokee Hills to assist. We are also being told that Battalion Chief Brewer will be having a press conference shortly with a update. Back to you guys at the station.*"

The nurse turns to Kelly and asks, "Are you OK with this or would you like me to change channels," Kelly replies, "Leave it on! I want to hear what Chief Brewer has to say." The nurse assures him, "Sure thing Mr. Ridge."

Kelly smiles at her and corrects her, "Thank you and by the way, it's Kelly." The television returns to Linda Barnett at the news conference. *"Hello again, this is Linda Barnett reporting live. We are awaiting Chief Brewer with an update on the explosion at Gold City Chemical this morning." Just as she finishes her sentence, Chief Brewer steps up to the microphone. "Good Morning, my name is Battalion Chief Michael Brewer. I wanted to give you an update on this morning's explosion. At approximately 7:05 this morning, a private contractor working for Gold City Chemical was digging a trench next to the South side of the building when they struck a gas line running from outside the building in and under he south wing of the plant. There was a chain reaction explosion that blew out a portion of the South wall that injured 20 people. These are both contractor and plant employees. Of the 20 injured, 2 were fatalities from the chemical company. Their names are being withheld pending notification of family members. Gold City Hospital has been put on high alert and are making arrangements to accept patients. There will be no questions at this time."* Kelly turns to the nurse and asks her to turn off the television.

As she turns it off, Charge Nurse Erin enters the room and addresses Kelly, "I see you heard the news." She pauses briefly then continues, "Dr. Stevens planned on moving you in a day or two, however with the explosion ICU beds are needed, so he ordered you to be moved today. As a matter of fact within the next hour as soon as we have a room for you." She turns to walk out and Kelly asks, "Erin, will it be a private room?" She tries to be reassuring, "I'll do my best with the Hospital Nursing Supervisor, but I can't make any promises." She smiles at him as he returns a nod, and both nurses leave the room.

About thirty minutes later Erin enters the room with the new room information. "Well Kelly, I have good news and bad news." Kelly turns his head toward her and replies, "OK, let's have it in that order." Erin makes a sighing breath and begins, "Well, the good news is that we have a room for you. It was the only available bed right now. The bad news is that it's a double room and you have a roommate. The bed is also on the window side of the room." Kelly inquires, "How long before this happens?" Erin replies, "Any time now."

Then Nurse Amy comes in, followed by the hospital transport aide. She gathers his personal belongings and helps the aide move Kelly onto the transport gurney. His belongings are put on the gurney by his legs. They move him out of the ICU and take him to his new room on the medical unit.

The nurse stops at the Nurses Station on the medical unit for few minutes as the transport aide continues to the room. The aide turns the gurney to go in head first and enters the room. Kelly has been lying quietly in the bed the whole time. He notices that the room is empty and silently reacts to it. Just then, Nurse Amy enters to help transfer him to the bed. She comments, "OK, I just found out your roommate is in therapy and will be back in a while." Kelly justs nods and asks, "Ok, can you please draw the curtain between us before you go?" Amy smiles and nods, doing what he requested and leaves with the transport aide. Kelly closes his eyes and goes to sleep.

About an hour passes when Kelly is awoken by movement and clattering on the other side of the curtain. His roommate has returned and is looking forward to finally having someone else in the room to talk to. The aide assists him into his bed on the curtain side at his request. He motions to the aide to draw back the curtain so he can meet his roommate. The aide looks around the curtain and asks, "Excuse me sir, but the gentleman in the bed over here wishes to meet you. Would that be alright with you sir?"

Kelly seems a bit apprehensive at first, but nods his head in approval. The curtain is pulled back to reveal, none other than Kelly staring into the face of Tom Maxwell. Kelly exclaims, "You have got to be kidding me!" Tom Maxwell is equally surprised and replies, "Well, paramedic Lieutenant Kelly Ridge. I never imagined that my roommate would be you." Kelly answers back sarcastically, "Lucky for you, and I wouldn't have never imagined it, so let's just leave it at that!"

Tom Maxwell tries to divert the conversation another direction. "Look, I may not be your most favorite person right now. I am supposed to be leaving tomorrow, so I won't be in your life much longer. Please call me Tom." Kelly agrees with a nod as Tom Maxwell continues, "So since we have the next 24 hours together, let me ask you, Do you still want to live the kind of life you are living?" Kelly looks Tom in the eyes and asserts, "As long as it doesn't include you, my life will return to normal as it's meant to be!"

Tom thinks to himself for a moment, and then asks, "Why are you showing me such hostility? I mean, what did I ever do to offend you?" Kelly sighs and then replies, "Because I am tired of Christians like you that think your so perfect!" Tom chuckles to himself and then replies, "Oh yeah right! This coming from the most decorated firefighter in the fire department's history. I've heard all about you since I have been here." Kelly's ego starts to inflate with Tom's comment. He can't help but reply with a big grin, "Hey, when you're good at something, don't be afraid to let it be known." Tom stares at Kelly in astonishment and replies, "I get it! You're one of those guys that thinks he's all that and a bag of chips." Tom pauses briefly and corrects his last statement. "On second thought, you think you're the whole potato chip factory."

As they continue to banter back and forth, their conversation is starting to become more heated. Kelly suddenly blurts out, "You have no idea how hard my life was, growing up the son of a preacher!" Immediately Tom changes his course on talking to Kelly. He calms his voice and tries a different tactic. "So you think you were the only one with a rough life? Now I am going to tell you my story and then we can decide who's had it worse, ok?" Kelly justs looks at him and replies, "Whatever."

Tom whispers a silent prayer to himself and then begins. "I grew up in a loving home with a younger brother and a younger sister and two of the best parents anyone could ever ask for. We didn't go to church much, except for when Mom helped out at one of the local Baptist Churches." Quickly Kelly interrupts, "See, you weren't raised to go to church every Sunday and Wednesday night." Tom replies, "True, but I did attend. Please let me finish." Kelly nods in both yes and no headbob as Tom continues, "In my teen years, I had a friend who invited me to another Baptist Church where they had a boys program called the Brigades." Kelly shows some interest, "We had something like that when I was younger, except the church called it Trailblazers. We earned badges and went camping and stuff."

Tom is surprised that he said something that rang a bell to Kelly, "That's right! We did all kinds of outdoor activities camping, sports, etc., and we earned badges just like in the boy scouts." Kelly looks up and replies, "OK, So we have a little bit in common. What else?" Tom's emotions are filling him with joy as he continues his story. "Well, a big part of that also was doing scripture memorization to earn badges as well." Kelly agrees, "Yup! My dad was big on that one with having to be a preachers kid, but we didn't earn badges for that."

Tom replies, "Well, ok. Each group is different I guess." He continues, "I distinctly remember my teacher as an older teen that had long hair. He kind of looked like the Jesus that was portrayed in all of the Catholic pictures." Kelly sarcastically asks, "Did he have that glow over his head too?"

Tom does his best to ignore his comment and continues, "One night as he told us about Jesus, it really hit home with me. That night I went home and knelt by my bed and asked Jesus to come into my heart. I continued in church for a couple of years after that up to the time I got into high School." Kelly verbally jumps on Tom, "See, you became Mister Perfect from that point on."

Tom makes a stopping motion with his hands, "Hold on, I'm not done! I got mixed up in the wrong crowd and fell away from church. I experimented with alcohol and drugs at first, like pot and hash. Before I knew it my grades started to suffer and I failed Algebra 3 with Trig my junior year and I was not able to play football my senior year." Again Kelly interrupts, "Wow, all that from doing a little pot and hash. I tried some pot at a party one time. Didn't really affect me though. At least I don't remember it affecting me."

Tom chuckles to himself. He pauses to get a drink of water from his cup. He moves his hips to reposition himself on the side of the bed. Kelly is beginning to show more interest in the testimony. Tom continues, "We had a policy at our school that you had to pass all of your curriculum in order to play sports the next semester. I was devastated because I had three major colleges scouting me for full scholarships and I had dreams of a career in football. All of those dreams were washed away, and I had no one to blame but myself."

Kelly has really become intrigued by Tom's experience. He replies, "Wow, I didn't realize how much that cost you, I mean I was involved in sports, but.." Tom interrupts Kelly this time, "But hang on, it gets worse. I spiraled down into a drunken and drugged out state for several years after that. I left home after high school spending 5 years wasting my life away.

All I did was work and party and went to heavy metal rock concerts. I was getting so drunk and wasted on just about every drug other than heroin. It was only by the grace of God that I didn't overdose. When I got addicted to crystal meth in San Diego, I hit rock bottom. I couldn't get enough of it. After an injury at work and over a year on workman's comp, I turned into a crystal meth addict."

Just as he finishes his sentence, his room phone rings, "Excuse me while I take this. My wife is supposed to call and let me know when she is coming to pick me up." He turns and picks up the receiver. Kelly justs wanders the room with his eyes, looking out the window and back to the clock on the wall. His pain level has risen, so he calls for his nurse. After a few minutes, the nurse enters and gives him some pain meds through his I.V.. Before she leaves, she turns to Kelly and informs him, "Dr. Stevens has ordered some follow up X Ray's tomorrow morning." She turns and exits the room just as Tom finishes his call and hangs up.

He takes another drink of water then starts, "Where was I? Oh yes." He pauses slightly, "One night as I was overdosing on crystal meth. As I laid on my bed it felt like my heart was going to explode. It was beating so fast, I got really scared. I got up from my bed and grabbed a Bible off my bookshelf and literally had to dust it off. I laid down on the bed and held it across my chest and poured my heart out to God. I asked him not to take me home, because I knew he still had something for me. I prayed that whatever he wanted me to do, wherever he wanted me to go I would do it if he would just spare my life at that moment." Once again Kelly's sarcasm surfaces again, "Ah, the bargain for your life stage!" Tom recognizes Kelly's sarcasm and refers to a Bible text, "But, you see my life at that point was exactly how it was described in Isaiah." He picks up his Bible and reads Isaiah 64:6 to Kelly, "In Isaiah it says, *But we are all as an unclean thing, and all our righteousnesses are as filthy rags; and we all do fade as a leaf; and our iniquities, like the wind, have taken us away. That was me at that time."*

Something different is happening to Kelly as he speaks with Tom. Rather than shrugging him off or pulling away, Kelly is slowly being drawn in. Tom continues, "Suddenly my heart stopped racing and I stopped having the cold sweats. There was a great peace that came over me like angels were attending to my body. I was a feeling that was hard to explain.

I opened the Bible and just started reading where it said that Jesus would come from the North and the East. He would be crowned King of Kings and Lord of Lords. I knew what the Lord was telling me to do at that point in time." Tom looks at the clock on the wall and notices the time, then turns back to Kelly, "Wow, I didn't realize we have been talking for so long. It's almost Noon." Kelly replies, "At first, I thought I didn't want to listen to you, but I can relate to some of what you're tell me."

Tom suggests, "Then let's have our lunch respectively and I will finish my story afterwards." Kelly nods in agreement and they eat lunch. An hour passes and Kelly looks over at Tom and asks, "Are you ready to finish? I am ready for a nap in a little while, but I am willing to hear you out."

Tom nods, sits up at the side of his bed, and continues, " I was to go home, and get away from the drug scene in San Diego. So I went back to where I grew up. The very next day I called my brother and he flew out to help me drive my car back. I left everything and went home 3 days later. I weaned myself off the crystal meth, but I still continued to drink and smoke pot with my friends there." Kelly quickly goes on a verbal attack, "So, I was right! You just did one of those bargain for your life prayers! That sounds like you really didn't mean it!" Tom replies, "Yeah well, I was still pretty young and immature then. But anyhow, About a year after I left California, a good friend invited me to church and I decided to go back.

I immediately broke down at the altar and I gave myself to Christ that day. I stopped drinking, drugs, swearing, pornography, everything that Labor Day weekend and I never looked back. As I prayed, I was reminded of what David requested of The Lord in Psalms 51:7." Tom reaches for his Bible and opens to Psalms 51 and reads, *"Purge me with hyssop, and I shall be clean: wash me, and I shall be whiter than snow."*

"From there, I got involved in the ministries of the church like the bus ministry and Sunday School and even became one of the leading bus captains in the church. My pastor started encouraging me to go to Bible college and get a degree to become an evangelist or pastor."

Tom covers his mouth with his fist to clear his throat. He takes another drink of water and is impressed by Kelly's curiosity. He continues, "An evangelist who I just so happen to know from playing football in high school encouraged me to go on the road with him. I wasn't ready to surrender to full-time ministry yet. I ran from the calling of God for several years after that, knowing that God was trying to get me to give up all the things of this world for him and go to school to become an evangelist." Kelly asks, "You mean you were given all these opportunities and you still resisted?" Tom agrees and replies, That's right! But, it took a nasty motorcycle accident, as well as a friend and my church pastor for me to finally see where the path was that God was leading me down."

"They both reminded me that there may not be another chance for me to answer God's calling." Kelly sarcastically replies, "Ya Think!" as Tom finishes, "I sold everything I could and had thrown the rest away. All I took was a few books and some clothes and traveled back to California to attend Bible College for an evangelist degree."

Kelly tries to throw an old lifestyle at Tom and states point blank, "And you went back to smoking pot and drinking again, right? Tom replies rather firmly, "Wrong! It was not easy go to school full time and work full time to pay my tuition, but The Lord gave me the strength to get through it. I graduated with a degree in Evangelism in 4 years, and that's my story."

Tom is still amazed with Kelly's attentiveness during this whole time. He looks at the time and excuses himself. "Look at the time. I need to get to the chapel and meet with The Lord." Tom hobbles to his wheelchair and starts to leave. He stops and turns back to Kelly, "See you later." Kelly just nods and turns towards the window and falls asleep. Tom exits the room and heads for the chapel.

All this is broken as he is nudged awake by the X-ray Technician. "Mr. Ridge? Excuse me, Mr.Ridge?" Kelly slowly opens his eyes and replies in a groggy manner, "Yes?" What is it?" He looks up and notices a pretty brunette standing over him. She identifies herself, "Good Morning! My name is Cassie and I'm from X-ray. I'm here to take you to your tests. She carefully helps him into the wheelchair and roll him to the door, Kelly asks. "Where's Mr. Maxwell?" Cassie looks at Kelly and replies, "I don't know, maybe he's in the chapel. Just as they roll out the door, the nurse meets them, "Oh! Mr.Ridge, I'm glad I caught you before you went down."

She holds up a folded piece of paper and continues, "Mr. Maxwell was discharged earlier this morning. He wanted me to give this to you." She brings the paper down to his hand. Kelly opens it and begins to read Tom's note:

"Dear Kelly,

I wanted to thank you so much for your care when my plane went down over a week ago. I also wanted to thank you for our talk yesterday and letting me share my testimony with you. I also want to wish you well on your recovery, and hope you can return to work as soon as you're able. The day of the accident you told me in that you made a deal with God, and that if he left you alone, you would leave him alone. As I told you on the ambulance, you may have given up on God, but he has not given up on you.

Sincerely,
Tom Maxwell"

He folds the paper back in half and puts it in his lap as the technician rolls him out. The road to recovery has begun.

CHAPTER 15

IT'S BEEN EIGHT MONTHS SINCE KELLY'S ACCIDENT AND HE IS PREPARING for his first day back at the fire station. The road to recovery has been a difficult one for Kelly. As he drives down the road, he is reminded of what happened before, during, and after the accident. There wasn't just physical therapy to recover, but mental and emotional issues to talk through. He found Bethany to be a very good listener. Especially when it came to Sharon. He found out how and why she died as well as how her parents handled her burial. He tried making contact with them during the last eight months and was refused.

While discussing Sharon with Bethany, he was told that she had found out Sharon's parents had her cremated and buried in the indigent cemetery out by the county courthouse. Kelly learned shortly there after that her parents ended up in a divorce over her death. Later on, her Dad lost his job with the county and her mom ended up committing suicide.

He pulls his car into the employee parking area behind the firehouse. He enters through the back door into the Apparatus Bay and stands still. Medic One is in its usual spot and Engine One's spot is filled by a brand new engine. Well, new by Kelly's standards and six months old by others. He puts his duffel bag down and walks around the truck and stops at the pump panel step behind the cab. As he takes in the view, a familiar face walks up behind him and asks, "Can you find the hose stretcher for me?" He immediately recognizes the voice of his partner, Rick Schmidt. Without turning around he counters by asking in a true sarcastic response, "Only if you can go to the medic unit and find the Fallopian Tubes!"

He turns to find Rick Schmidt walking over to him. Both men share a handshake and a "guy hug" together as Rick asks, "How ya been partner?" Kelly rubs the back of his neck with his hand and replies, "I've been doing good. The phone calls and visits off and on from Annie and you really helped me through many rough spots." Rick puts his hands on his hips, shrugs it off. He looks at Kelly and replies, "Hey! Your not just my partner, you're my best friend. Not only that but Annie really liked Sharon and now you." There is a brief pause as Rick changes subjects, "So what do you think of our newest edition?" He touches the crew compartment while he is asking. Kelly is in awe of the new engine and replies, "Wow, it's pretty awesome looking." Rick adds, "Yeah, it's only six months old. Took a couple of months to get with city approval and finances and all. In the interim, Middle Village loaned us one of their reserves to use."

Just then they both hear a commanding voice call out behind them, "Lieutenant Ridge, paramedic Schmidt! Fall in!" Both men turn and find Captain Becker standing behind them with a serious look on his face. It quickly fades to a smile as he approaches with his right hand out to shake Kelly's hand, "Welcome back to the job. Why don't you go and get ready for shift roll call in about 15 minutes." Kelly nods and heads for the crew lockers as the captain turns to Rick and tells him, "Don't go to far, I will need to go over something in roll call that might interest you." Rick nods and heads for the medic unit to start inspecting it for supplies.

Fifteen minutes pass and Captain Becker enters the Apparatus Bay and calls out, "A Shift, fall in!" Rick stops what he is doing and moves to the front of Medic One as Kelly joins him at attention. The engine crew of Hawks, Wilson, and Stillman stand in front of Engine One also at attention as Captain Becker begins, "At ease men!" Everyone changes to the military at ease position as the Captain continues, "First off, I want to officially welcome Lieutenant Ridge back to the shift." They crew all cheer and clap as the Captain calls for order, "Alright men let's continue. Second, Firefighter Ropino has tendered his resignation officially, citing the accident with the old Engine One has seriously affected him mentally and emotionally. Firefighter Wilson will be joining us from C shift to take his place, as that shift will be taking on a couple new recruits from the academy." Everyone turns and acknowledges Wilson and return to the at ease position.

Again Captain Becker continues with his meeting notes, "At 1500 hours today, we are all to meet at City Hall, both engine crew and medic unit for a recognition ceremony in the council chambers. Dress Uniform will be in order and Middle Village will be covering calls during that time. Just a heads up, I will announce right now that we will have two paramedic Lieutenants on our shift. You will hear more about that later, but for now, we will as a shift, congratulate paramedic Schmidt on his promotion." Everyone claps again as the Captain finishes, "Finally, just remember you are all representatives of Gold City when you put on that uniform. That's all men, finish your equipment checks and let's stay safe out there. Dismissed!"

Everyone goes back to their tasks as Captain Becker returns to his office. Kelly turns and grabs Rick's shoulder and congratulates him, " Hey congratulations partner, although it is a little unusual to have two lieutenants on the same shift." Rick replies, "Yeah I know but, that's apparently what it is for now." Kelly adds, "I guess we'll find out what this is all about at three o'clock." Both men finish their equipment checks and close everything up on the rig. They turn together and head towards the day room when tones drop followed by the dispatcher's voice, *"Gold City Medic One, respond to the city ballfield for a groundskeeper with chest pains. Repeating, Gold City Medic One, respond to the city ballfield for a groundskeeper with chest pains at 07:30."*

Immediately both men turn and head for the ambulance. Rick calls out his position to Kelly, "Shotgun!" Kelly replies, "Sounds good, but I get the next call! Remember, I still out rank you." As they jump in respectively, Rick grabs the radio microphone, Dispatch, Medic One is en route." As he waits for the reply, he turns to Kelly and says, "Deal!" Rick hears dispatch copy him and replaces the microphone back on its clip. They roll out as Rick activates the lights and sirens.

A few minutes later, they arrive at the city ballfield. They notice the groundskeepers surrounding their co worker that needs help. One of them has met the ambulance as they arrive and walks them over to their patient. One of the other groundskeepers had brought a chair over to the patient to sit in. Rick kneels down next to him and begins his assessment. Kelly pulls the notepad from the trauma bag, grabs his pen, and stands ready to write down the vitals as Rick dictates them. As Rick assesses the patient, the patient exclaims, "You know I really am feeling a whole lot better." Rick looks at his patient and asks, "Are you sure about that? Your blood pressure and your breathing is telling me something else." The patient looks around at his coworkers an asks, "What do you think fellas?" Bill, the grounds supervisor, looks at the patient and says, "I think you should let them take you Fred." Fred shrugs his shoulders and agrees. Rick asks, "Can you walk to the ambulance on your own?" Fred nods yes and is walked to the ambulance. Kelly has gone back and opened the back doors. As they help Fred get in, Kelly is distracted by something about the tree line. He can't quite place his finger on it and returns to the moment at hand. He closes the back doors of the ambulance and walks around to the driver's side. He gets in and begins to pull off the field. As he rolls for the main road, he can't help but stare at the side mirror reflecting the tree line. Then he just shakes it off and continues to drive to the hospital.

Upon arrival at the hospital, Kelly follows protocol and pulls into the ambulance bay. He parks and opens the back of the rig and helps Rick take the patient into ER to be seen. After they hand off the patient, Kelly is stopped Nurse Ashley, "Hey Kelly, nice to see you up and running." Kelly Replies, Thanks Ashley, it's good to be back." Rick looks at Kelly and suggests, "Ya know what partner, I think Nurse Ashley likes you. I've seen how she's always been around you."

He turns and joins Rick as they head out the door to the ambulance. Kelly remains as driver as Rick takes passenger side. As they drive away, Kelly turns to Rick, "Hey, I wanted to congratulate you personally for being promoted to Lieutenant now." Rick turns to him and replies, "Thanks partner, that really means a lot." To this Kelly responds, "You're welcome! You deserve it Rick. You have come a long way here in just putting up with me as your partner." Rick chuckles a bit then replies, "Shouldn't it be the other way around?" They both share a laugh and arrive back at the firehouse. Rick heads for the report room as Kelly makes his way to the crew quarters. He makes his way over to his bunk and lays on top of the bedding. He puts his hands behind his head and mulls over things in his mind. You would think that eight months later, everything would come back to memory. Finally, the light bulb comes on in his head as he realizes six words and then it all makes sense to him, "Tree line, Plane crash, Tom Maxwell." He begins to think back to the plane crash, the ambulance ride, sharing the room, the talk, and the letter. He remembers most of it and wishes he could forget about the rest.

He sits up on the side of the bed, puts his head in his hands and tells himself, "Come on Kelly, keep it together! That was eight months ago and this is now." He decides to go to the day room and see if there is a magazine to read or something. He finds the updated continuing education board containing pamphlets and journals and decides to sit down and read up on the latest medical protocols. As he reads the latest on stroke care, once again, tones drop and he hears, *"Medic One respond to Andrew's Market for a 45 year old female having a syncopal episode, repeating Medic One respond to Andrew's Market. Forty-five year old female, syncopal episode at 09:40."*

Kelly makes his way to the driver's seat and gets in, followed by Rick in the passenger seat again. Rick calls in their response over the radio and they roll out. Upon arrival at Andrew's Market, they quickly get out their equipment and go inside to find their patient. An employee directs them to the business office at the front left side from the entrance. Rick begins his assessment and finds everything to be in order. He asks his patient, "How often do you have these fainting spells?" She looks up and replies, "No, never! This is the first time it's happened. I was doing fine and then got dizzy. I must have passed out, but I am fine now." Rick tells her, "Do you still want us to take you in and get checked?" She shakes her head slowly and replies, "No, I will take myself in." Rick nods in agreement and turns to Kelly, "You got the Medical Refusal form handy?" Kelly opens the clipboard, pulls the form out and hands it to Rick, "Here you go!" Rick exchanges paperwork with the patient and packs up the trauma bag. As they exit and head for the ambulance, Rick suspects possible pregnancy but says nothing.

Not much is said between the two of them this time as they return to the firehouse. Rick once again heads for the report room to file the run on the computer program. Kelly straightens things up inside the ambulance and goes to the kitchen to see what's planned for lunch. Hawks and Wilson are already starting to prepare things. Kelly exclaims, "Hey guys, what's for lunch?" Hawks looks up and replies, "We're having cold cut sandwiches for lunch. We figured something quick and easy with the plans for this afternoon." Wilson adds, "Not to mention fresh cut tomatoes and onions to go with it." Kelly, in his usual sarcastic tone replies, "I'm glad I'm on the medic unit and not the Engine." He smirks at Wilson as he finished his comment.

Rick enters the kitchen and notices the onions being cut, "Oh Wilson, I see Hawks has you doing the hard work while he does the easy stuff." Wilson stops cutting and looks up at Rick and replies, "I see you've spent too much time around Ridge. You can be just as sarcastic as he is." Rick leans against the counter, crosses his arms, smiles and replies, "No, that's just one advantage to being a paramedic instead of a hose jockey." Hawks jumps in to defend his firefighter, "Just keep in mind, you both had to start as a Basic." Kelly puts up his hands in surrender, "Okay, we're leaving!" Both paramedics turn and exit the kitchen. As they exit, Hawks yells out, "You guys have supper tonight!"

Rick turns to Kelly and asks, "So how do you like your first day back so far?" Kelly shrugs his shoulders, "It's fine I guess. Kind of a slow day so far." Rick nods in agreement, "I know. Things have been that way lately. It's like Gold City has taken a vacation from any type of emergency." Kelly replies, "Well just remember partner, it's always the calm before the storm." Rick shakes his head, "Man, now you're beginning to sound like that preacher guy you cared for 8 months ago." Kelly stops what he is doing, puts out his index finger and replies, "Look partner, that preacher guy is in my past and I intend for it to stay there. Seems like my life has been really miserable since I met him." Rick looks at Kelly and asks, "Maybe there's more to God than I thought." Kelly ignores Rick's comment and begins straightening up his gear locker.

Tones drop, followed by the voice of the dispatcher, *"Gold City Medic One, respond to Gold City High School. Student with possible nose fracture. Repeating, Gold City Medic One respond to Gold City High School for a student with possible nose fracture at 11:00."* This time Rick gets to the driver's door first and proclaims "My turn to drive! I had the last two so you get the next two." Kelly agrees as he pushes the garage door button and gets in the passenger side. Rick starts the rig and pulls out while Kelly activates the lights and sirens.

As they roll away, Rick turns to Kelly and asks, "So, what do you think? Bathroom brawl? Hallway confrontation?" Kelly replies, "I don't know. Maybe one of those, but I guess we won't know for sure until we get there." Upon arriving at the school, they are met by an attractive brunette in a dress suit who identifies herself as the Assistant Principal. She walks them into the office where a young girl is being interviewed by the school resource officer. She continues into the nurses office where they find a 17 year old boy moaning and groaning in pain holding his nose.

Kelly squats down next to the patient and identifies himself, "Hello, I'm Lieutenant Ridge with the Fire Department. Can you tell me who you are and what happened?" "I'm Donny and I think my nose got broken!" He states emphatically as he holds the gauze to his nose. He continues, "Ya gotta give me something. This pain is intense." He continues to moan in pain. Kelly asks, "Can you tell me how it happened?" He reaches up to Donny's face to examine the nose. One of Donny's buddies is with him and answers for him. "Yeah, he got walloped by that blond girl out there." Kelly replies, "Rick, why don't you go and talk to her." Rick nods and goes out to the waiting area. He see a young girl in a pink blouse, blue jean skirt sitting next to the school resource officer.

He walks over and introduces himself, "Hello Miss, I'm Rick from the fire department. Can you tell me what happened to your hand?" She is sobbing and is not able to answer clearly, so a friend answers for her. "Her name is Julie and she just moved here a few weeks ago. Her parents are missionaries to South America. Anyways, Donny in there has been making passes at her a lot. This morning he made another pass at her and got a little too personal by touching her shoulder, so she punched him squarely in the nose."

Rick looks shocked by the explanation as her friend continues, "Well, Donny drops like a rock to the floor screaming in pain. Assistant Principal Jones comes around the corner right after it happens and breaks it up." Julie nods in agreement with everything her friend says. Rick looks at Julie and replies, "Wow, looks like you got a pretty good right cross for such a petite build." He pauses before continuing, "Did you need to ice that hand?" Julie shakes her head no and replies, "It's a little sore, but I'll be ok." This reply really stuns Rick and leaves him speechless for a few seconds.

He then stands up and returns to Kelly, who is ready to walk the patient out to the ambulance. They are escorted back to the ambulance by Assistant Principal Jones and the school resource officer. As they put him on the gurney and get him comfortable the resource officer pulls out a pair of handcuffs and puts one loop on Donny's wrist and the other on the gurney side rail and explains, "Sorry Donny but her parent's are pressing charges for assault. I have to detain you and place you under arrest." Just then Sylvio and Minster pull up behind the ambulance in a squad car. The resource officer exchanges some information with Sylvio before he gets into the back of the ambulance and Kelly closes the door behind him.

They take Donny to the hospital and turn him over to the ER staff with Sylvio following close behind. Kelly and Rick retrieve their medical supplies and leave in the ambulance. On the way back to the station Rick strikes up a conversation about the call. "So Kelly what do you think really happened with that kid?" Kelly turns to Rick and replies, "I think it was exactly as it was reported to us." Rick looks puzzled by this and asks, "How did you come to that type of conclusion?" Kelly chuckles to himself and begins, "Back when I was in high school, there was a similar incident I remembered." He pauses briefly and continues, "One day, the school bully, a senior, picked a fight with a sophomore. The senior was becoming more aggressive and pulled a knife on the sophomore kid. He lunged at the kid with the knife. The kid grabbed the guys arm mid lunge, broke his wrist, and swept his legs. The bully dropped to the floor like a rock and the sophomore walked away." Rick blurts out, "Wow! You think this was the same type of thing?" Kelly replies, "Minus the broken wrist and the leg sweep, it had a familiar ring." Rick asserts, "So it was self defense plain and simple! Kelly finishes the story to Rick, "Turns out, a few weeks later that the sophomore had self defense training. After that, nobody tried anything confrontational with that student. Matter of fact, a lot of the girls that drove cars to school asked him for an escort to their cars when they went home."

They arrive back at the firehouse, and this time Kelly heads for the report room to file the run. After about five minutes, he joins Rick in the kitchen and comments, "You know, filing is becoming easier and easier to do. Longest five minutes of my day." Rick chuckles a bit and goes to the refrigerator to pull out the cold cuts and vegetables for lunch for Kelly and himself. Kelly stops the refrigerator door from closing and grabs the mayonnaise and a can of cola for each of them and places it on the dining room table. Rick has made himself a sandwich and sits down. Kelly does the same and joins Rick as well. Both men are silent as they start in on their sandwiches. Kelly gets up and goes to the cupboard to look for some chips as a side. He finds an empty shelf and turns to Rick, "Add a couple of bags of chips to our shopping trip later." Rick holds up his index finger and replies, "Noted, and entered into the log." Kelly returns to the table and they continue eating while talking with each other. Rick swallows a bite and asks, "So, what are we doing between now and the ceremony? We have some time to kill." Kelly looks at his watch, then replies, "Well, I don't know about you, but I am going to lie down for a bit. I'm unusually tired for a first day back." He gets up, cleans up after himself, and adds, "After all, I may need the rest pending on what happens with the ceremony."

Kelly walks out of the kitchen and heads for the sleeping quarters. He sits on the bed and unzips has duty boots and removes them. He places them at his bedside and raises his legs up to the supine position. He stares up at the ceiling as memories again flood his mind. The mention of the school bully in high school has conjured up memories of the argument he had with his dad about his graduation gift. He relives that moment over and over again in his mind. The yelling and screaming at each other that occurred. He looks himself over and thinks, "What is wrong with me? Ever since the accident, I am feeling tortured from my past!" He finally decides for himself that he will do whatever it takes to regain his sanity. He swings his legs over the side of the bed and gets up. He goes to his locker to get his hygiene kit and walks to the bathroom to get washed up for the ceremony.

After a few minutes, he returns to his locker to put away his kit. He changes his undershirt to a fresh one and pulls out his dress uniform to change into. He sits down at the bedside chair and reaches for his boots, when the inevitable happens.

CHAPTER 16

ONCE AGAIN, TONES DROP AND THE VOICE OF THE DISPATCHER IS HEARD over the radio. *"Gold City Fire Department and Battalion One, respond to a traffic accident with possible ejection. Olive Grove Highway between Crescent Road and Billy Drive. Repeating, Gold City Fire Department and Battalion One, respond to a traffic accident with possible ejection. Olive Grove Highway between Crescent and Billy. Time out at 13:05."*

Kelly quickly puts his duty boots on, zips them up and heads for the apparatus bay. He pushes the garage door open buttons for both rigs and dons his turnout coat and grabs his helmet. Rick joins him and dons his turnout coat and gets his helmet as well. As they do this, the engine crew of Hawks, Wilson and Stillman join them and board the engine. Captain Becker comes out of his office with his turnout coat and red helmet in hand. He tosses the helmet on the Officer's Seat and puts his coat on. He boards the engine and closes his door just as Hawks releases the air brakes and rolls out of the bay. Lights activated and sirens blaring, Engine One announces its intentions to the oncoming traffic followed by Medic One. They bring both vehicles up to response speed and head for the call. This call will take a few minutes longer to get to since it is up in the hill and ravine areas outside of the city.

They arrive on scene to find two vehicles collided head on. One on them is a convertible and the other is a medium size sedan. Kelly and Rick notice the driver of the sedan is shaken up, standing next to his car, and talking to the Deputy Sheriff on scene. The occupants of the convertible are no where to be found. Captain Becker approaches both of them and explains, "Both the driver and passenger in the convertible were ejected up and over a nearby stonewall at the road side." Kelly measures it up quickly with the eyes to about a six foot high embankment. Rick tosses Kelly the trauma bag while he gathers other equipment to assist. Kelly makes his way to a nearby driveway and proceeds around behind the embankment wall.

As he comes to a flattened part of the driveway, he sees the body of an elderly female laying face up in the center. He quickly makes his way over to her and kneels down next to her. He quickly begins his assessment of his patient. Not as slowly as most medical calls, however, just as meticulous. This female patient has suffered major trauma and needs serious medical attention. He quickly discovers that she has arm and leg injuries mainly, besides the probable head and neck injuries. He treats her injuries, checks her vital signs, and prepares her for transport. As he is doing this, she cry's out, "Have you seen my husband? Where's my husband?"

Apparently it was her husband who was the other victim ejected from the convertible. All Kelly could do was remain focused on his job at that time. He looks at her and replies, "Ma'am, right now you're my patient. I am working on you. We'll get a couple of others to look for him. But as for now, you are my priority." As Kelly is caring for his patient, Stillman and Wilson approach him from behind. Wilson taps Kelly on the shoulder and asks, "Everything ok here Kelly?" Kelly nods and replies, "Yeah, I'm good for now. She says she can't find her husband. Why don't you two go up farther and see if you can find him." Both men nod in agreement and continue up the driveway which turns to the left and rises behind Kelly.

As they continued on, Rick and Captain Becker arrive with the gurney and backboard. Kelly applies a cervical collar around her neck to prevent any further neck and spinal injuries prior to placing her on the backboard. Then Kelly, Rick and the Captain position her on the backboard and secure her to it. While moving the backboard to the gurney, the woman again cries out, "My husband, my husband! Why can't you find my husband?" Kelly looks her directly in the eyes and replies, "Ma'am, Ma'am! There is another team taking care of him. Again, I need you to stay calm and remain my priority, Ok?" She reluctantly nods in agreement as they roll her down to the ambulance.

While she is being loaded in, Battalion Chief Brewer approaches Rick and pulls him aside and tells him, "Go ahead and get her to the hospital. We have a second unit coming for her husband." Rick replies, "Yes Sir!" and finishes closing the back doors before getting into the driver's seat. Rick calls back to Kelly through the passage way, "Kelly! The Chief wants us to go ahead to the hospital. Another unit is on the way for the other patient." Kelly signals ok with a hand gesture and a nod to proceed. He calls the ER and gives them a patient report and their E.T.A. to the hospital. He continues to give care while talking to ER over the radio. As the ambulance makes its way down the curving hillside of Olive Grove Highway, Kelly looks at his patient and reads her face clearly as she continues to worry about her husband. Kelly can do nothing more to assist the woman in her anguish. All he can do is resign himself to his duties.

After several more minutes pass, Rick pulls Medic One into the ER ambulance bay. He brings it to a stop and shuts off the engine. Kelly finishes with his care and makes ready to move the patient. Rick opens the rear doors and signals Kelly for the ok to unlock the gurney and pull the patient out. Kelly nods and she is taken into the ER. They transfer care to the hospital staff and separate, one to supply and the other to report finishing.

About ten minutes pass and they meet up back at the ambulance. The front door to the bay is opened and the two paramedics begin to exit the bay. Over the radio they hear Chief Brewer calling, *"Medic One from Battalion One, stand by at GCH. I need to talk to you!"* Kelly picks up the radio microphone and replies, " Medic One copies, standing by at GCH."

In a matter of a short time Chief Brewer pulls up in front of the ambulance. Kelly and Rick have gotten out and are standing in front of Medic One as the Chief joins them. "Hi fellas, how are you doing?" Both paramedics answer with a smile and a thumbs up gesture. Chief Brewer smiles back and replies, "That's the spirit guys." He pauses briefly and continues, "By the way, there was a reason why I had you two take the wife right away." Rick looks at the Chief and replies, "Yeah, you told us a second unit was coming for the husband." The Chief looks directly at both of them and states, "Truth is, the husband died at the accident scene. So in reality the second unit was the Coroner."

Both men drop their jaws momentarily at this news. But as usual, in his normal form of sarcasm, Kelly reasons, "I had a feeling about that." Chief Brewer chuckles back in the same sarcastic manner, "I had a feeling you would Ridge. Anyways, I thought I should let you know that." He heads back to his vehicle and opens his door. He turns back to Kelly and Rick and adds, "Oh, so you both know and this is especially for you Ridge. Incident stress debriefing is available if you need it. I mean with this being your first day back and all." Kelly just smiles in agreement as the Chief finishes, "And because of the call and how late it is, the ceremony will be rescheduled to a later date."

Chief Brewer returns to his car and drives off. Kelly just stands there for a few minutes not moving at all. His mind is trying to grasp the outcome of the call. Was all the effort he just made all for nothing? How horrifying for her husband to be ejected so far up into the air on a hilly driveway and to land on a hard surface and die." Rick looks at Kelly to get his attention, "Hey partner! Could things have been any worse?." Kelly comes back to reality as they get in the ambulance and head out. He looks at Rick and replies, "Reminds me of an incident back to my training when I first wanted to be an EMT. The paramedic I was with told me about one of his first calls. He responded to a call where two big rigs collided head on and caught fire, welding the two tractors together. Rick asks, "I take it both drivers were killed? Kelly replies, I believe so, but the worst part was when they managed to pry the two apart, they found a Volkswagen Bug crushed in the middle. People in that car would never have known what had happened to them." All Rick could do was look at Kelly and blurt out, "Ouch!" Kelly changes subjects, "While we're out, we might as well stop at the market and pick up supper fixings." Rick looks over and asks, "You have something in mind?" Kelly replies, "I'm thinking of a good old fashioned spaghetti and meatballs tonight. What do you think?" Rick gives a sideways nod and answers, "Sounds good to me."

Rick pulls Medic One into the supermarket parking lot and parks in an empty area away from the entrance in case they have to roll again. They enter the store with Kelly grabbing a hand basket, and head for the pasta aisle. Just before Kelly enters the aisle, Rick tells him, "I'm going to see about some garlic bread or breadsticks a few aisle's down." Kelly replies, "Ok. Meet you at checkout in say ten minutes?" Rick replies, "Sounds good to me." They split off and Kelly begins shopping for sauce and spaghetti noodles. He meanders slowly down the aisle checking out all the different brands and varieties. He decides on six large jars of name brand sauce and starts looking at the pasta choices. Rick stops in the aisle and passes Kelly a shopping cart instead adding "You can fit more in here than that little basket."

Rick goes back to the bread aisle as Kelly continues his quest for the right spaghetti noodles. At the end of the aisle he finds the bulk sizes of noodles on the lower shelf and squats down to investigate the prices. As he is squatting, a woman in a very nice skirt and heels enters the aisle and begins shopping right next to Kelly. It becomes harder for Kelly to concentrate on his shopping when the same very attractive woman is right next to him. After a couple of curious glances, Kelly rises up to a stand position with several large boxes of noodles and places them in the cart. He smiles politely at the woman and turns to move down the aisle. The woman glances at Kelly and smiles. Kelly's sinful pride starts to well up inside him as he musters up the courage to make a pass at this beauty next to him.

He is taken totally off guard when the young woman, glances momentarily at his name plate and then asks, "Kelly? Kelly Ridge? Is it really you?" Kelly is taken back by her question of recognition of him. He can only stutter in response, "Uh, uh, um! I'm sorry but have we met before? I can't for the life of me place who you are." The woman replies in her confidence, "You don't remember me, do you? We met eight months ago while you were in the hospital." Kelly reacts more positively to her by replying, "Oh yes, I remember. You were one of my nurses! So nice to see you again." She starts giggling and replies, "No silly, it's me Dawn! I'm your sister Bethany's future Sister-in-law. Her fiancée Jon is my brother. I came with them to visit you one Sunday after church."

After hearing this, Kelly is embarrassed by his own comment. He appears flustered then becomes apologetic, "Uh! Uh! Um! Oh boy, I am so sorry. It's been a long time you know?" She smiles at him and replies, "It's ok! It's just nice to see you again and in an upright position compared to the last time I saw you." Kelly thinks he hears something sarcastic in that comment but shrugs it off immediately. As he continues to visit with Dawn, memories of her in the hospital room begin to flood his mind. He remembers the dress she wore as well how her hair was styled. Like him, she looks very different now in a upright position. Kelly is compelled to ask her, " So you've come back to town for another visit?" She smiles wider and replies, "Jon wanted to come and visit Bethany, and I had a few days off from my job so, I thought I'd come down with Jon and spend some time looking around."

Kelly is puzzled by her comment and inquires, "Some time looking around for what? There's nothing really that great about Gold City." Her eyes dance a bit as she replies, "Oh I don't know. Gold City seems like a nice place to me. In fact, I'm looking at getting a place here because I do see one thing great about living here." She smiles deliberately at Kelly and finishes with, "You know, get married, settle down and raise a family." Kelly just expresses a puzzled look more for show, instead of letting on that he knows exactly what she is implying. He tries to defer the idea on the merits of living so far away from the more Metropolitan areas, "You know, Gold City is such a smaller place to really make something for yourself. I have worked and lived here for a long time and I think you could do a whole lot better elsewhere."

Dawn emboldens herself and replies, "I think I have a very good reason to move here. Let me tell you something, I don't back down that easy Kelly! After we met, I was so compelled by meeting you." He is blown away by her response that he scrambles in his mind for a comeback to her. He is immediately relieved of that by three attention beeps over his radio. *"Gold City Medic One respond to the front of Jensen's Pharmacy for a sixty-nine year old male who tripped on the curb and fell. Repeating, Golds City Medic One respond to Jensen's Pharmacy for a sixty- nine year old male who tripped and fell at 1605."*

Kelly looks up at Dawn and ends the conversation, "Well, duty calls! Excuse me please? Kelly turns and makes his way to the front of the market. He puts his groceries on the counter and asks the clerk if they could come back for them later. The clerk agrees with him as Rick joins him by the doors. The call is just three businesses down from the market. They see the man from where they are as Rick starts heading that way. Kelly heads for the ambulance to bring it closer to the patient.

The elderly man has been helped to a nearby bench in the interim. Rick comes upon him and begins his assessment. "Hello sir. I'm Rick from the Fire Department. How are you today?" The man looks up at Rick and gives a snotty reply, "How do you think I feel young man? I tripped on that confounded curb there." Rick continues his assessment as the elderly man continues rambling. "Pretty silly if you ask me putting a curb where a man's supposed to walk! I've got the right mind to complain to my city council about that."

Rick is already suspecting a concussion and asks, "Did you hit your head at all sir?" The man looks rather annoyed at Rick and replies, "Confounded young man, I did no such thing!" As Rick feels the man's head he takes note of a bump on the side of it. He responds by asking, "Then how do you explain this bump right here?" The elderly man becomes a bit embarrassed and makes a nonsensical comment, "Because the chicken couldn't cross the road."

Kelly has pulled up with the ambulance and joins Rick. He overhears the man's comment and asks Rick, "Possible Concussion?" Rick nods in the affirmative and asks the man, "Sir, I think you need to come with us in the ambulance to be checked at the emergency room." The man declines the offer, "No thank you boys, I'll be fine right here. My nephew will be out with my prescription shortly. He can take me in." Kelly and Rick look at each other and then Kelly goes inside the Pharmacy to check the man's story. He returns shortly and looks at Rick and slowly shakes his head in the negative. Rick looks back at the man and suggests, "Tell you what! There's a crowd gathering around so why don't we continue this in the back of the ambulance."

Kelly goes to the back of Medic One and takes out the gurney. He moves it over to the bench and lowers it for the patient. The man looks at the gurney and exclaims, "Well look at that! It's a bed on wheels!" Rick agrees, "That's right and it's all for you right now." The old man smiles and let's Rick and Kelly help him onto the gurney. They load him into the back of the ambulance and Kelly closes the doors after Rick. He gets into the driver's side and pulls away for the hospital.

As Kelly drives down the road, he can't help but overhear Rick's conversation with his patient. Rick asks the patient, "Has this ever happened to you before sir?" The man replies, "Nope! first time I had to ride in one of these fancy campers." Kelly snickers under his breath as Rick continues, "No sir, I mean tripping or falling down before?" The man looks puzzled a bit and replies, "Well, I've taken a trip to Europe many years ago." Rick is definitely convinced that the man is suffering a concussion from indeed hitting his head. He calls into the ER on the radio med channel as Kelly goes back to concentrating on his driving.

After a short period of time, he pulls the ambulance into the ER receiving bay, he ponders the encounter he had with Dawn earlier at the market. He can't help but think of the possibilities of her being his new girlfriend. Her hair was perfect and her makeup was so much different than Sharon's. He thinks to himself how refreshing it would be to be with someone who doesn't look like the poster child for a make up manufacturer. He still loved her when she was alive, although there were times he felt like she wore it a bit heavy.

He is brought back to reality when he feels Rick tap his shoulder from the back and ask, "So are you going to let us out or just sit there all day?" Kelly refocuses himself and replies, "Yeah, sorry! Give me a second." He exits the driver's seat and goes to the back doors and opens them. They take the patient into ER and pass him off to the ER team as usual. Kelly gets a couple of items from supply while Rick reports off to the doctor.

As they get back into the ambulance, Rick asks, "Ready to go back to the firehouse?" Kelly nods in the affirmative and they roll away. The silence in Kelly is deafening to Rick as they continue down the street. Rick turns and asks, "Hey partner, if it was any quieter over there, I'd think you were dead. is everything ok?" Kelly looks over to Rick and replies, "Oh sorry. I just got a lot on my mind you know with the first day back and all." Rick responds in a suspicious tone, "Uh-huh! Well just remember that you were the one that used the word slow earlier." Kelly quickly retorts, "Yeah and you just said the Q word!" They return to the firehouse and back Medic One into its spot in the apparatus bay, totally forgetting the food from the grocery store with all the activity from the afternoon. Just as Kelly stops the rig and places it in park, Captain Becker walks up to the driver's side window. Kelly acknowledges him properly as he gets out. "Hey Cap!"

Captain Becker replies in a stern voice, "Did you forget something Ridge?" Kelly looks in an awkward manner first and then realizes what the Captain was asking and answers, "Oh no!" He calls out to Rick as he opens the door of the ambulance, "Hey partner, we got to go back to the market and get the supper fixings." He is stopped immediately by the Captain, "Wait a minute! Before you go flying out of here I should tell you that you don't have to go back. There was a very pretty blonde that came here and dropped it all off for you. She left this note that I was supposed to give you." He hands Kelly the hand written note. Kelly takes the note and closes the door to the ambulance.

Rick makes his way to the report room as Kelly heads for the kitchen. As he enters, he sees the grocery bags on the dining table along with five boxes of garlic breadsticks. He looks in the first bag and finds five industrial sized cans of tomato sauce and seven two pound boxes of spaghetti noodles. In the other bag is twenty-five pounds of ground beef and six bags of potato chips in various flavors. He takes the note and opens it and begins to read;

> *"Dear Kelly,*
>
> *I hope you don't mind me helping you out with the groceries and bringing them to the station for you. I thought you might appreciate the gesture of kindness. I am going to be in town for a few days and I was hoping we could get together and chat. Meeting you eight months ago at the hospital really meant a lot to me. More than I even realized myself. If this would be ok for you, please call me at the number enclosed and we can make arrangements to meet. By the way, in case you doubt this, the phone number is really mine. It up to you to find out for yourself. Also, just so you know, I AM NOT SORRY for being so forward with you.*
>
> *Till your call,*
> *Dawn"*

As he read the note, he was so taken off guard by it. He didn't know if he would be ready for another relationship yet. He folded the note and put it in his chest pocket. Rick joins him in the kitchen and they prepare the supper meal for the station. Gold City would remain quiet for the rest of this night.

CHAPTER 17

AFTER 48 HOURS THE SHIFT ROTATION HAS PASSED AND IT IS KELLY'S TIME off from the fire station. This shift has been filled with a myriad of calls from traffic accidents to seizures and strokes to welfare checks. Finally a chance to catch his breath and have some time to himself. As he gathers his things from his bedside table, he finds the note that Dawn wrote him on his first day back. He opens the note and reads it again to himself. He ponders for a moment, then picks up his cell phone and dials the number on the note. It rings a couple of times and then he hears, "Hi this is Dawn." In his mind he figures it's an answering machine and waits for the beep. Then he hears, "Hello? Is someone there? He feels somewhat embarrassed and hangs up. He puts his phone in his left pants pocket and finishes with gathering his things.

He makes his way over to the locker room and begins sorting his clean uniforms from his dirty. His cell phone rings and he answers, "Hello?" There is a female voice at the other end who replies, "Hi Kelly, it's Dawn. I see you called me." Kelly tries to deny this but is caught off guard, "What? Huh? What makes you think it was me that called…". Dawn cuts him off right away, "Because I got your number from Bethany and programmed you into my contacts. When you just tried calling, it came up as you!"

Kelly cringes to himself under his breath, "I need to talk to her about that." To which Dawn responds, "What do you want to discuss with Bethany?" Realizing he might have been a bit louder than he thought, he quickly shrugs it off. "Oh nothing. Nothing important." All he hears is a "Uh-huh!" from the other end. Kelly tries to recenter things in order to be in charge of the conversation. "So I called you and you called me back. What did you need of me?" he asks. She once again makes a bold remark to Kelly, "What I need and what you can do for me are related in more ways than one." Kelly's mind is just exploding with pure shock of how bold Dawn is with him. Although he is seeing it as having a viable opponent, he is awestruck over her straightforwardness. So he deflects it as best he can and replies, "Again, what do you need?" To which Dawn replies, "I wanted to tell you that if you want to take me out, there is something big happening tonight that I would really like for you to take me to." Once again Kelly's mind pops with the directness of her that he trips over his words, "Yeah, um, sure, ok. Where and when?" She answers him with, "First, wait to hear from Bethany and we will go from there." He feels that he has no choice but to surrender and replies, "Ok, that sounds good. I will wait for her call." Dawn answers, "Great! Can't wait to hear back from you, bye bye."

Kelly is just astounded in one way, yet strongly attracted in the other. He puts his cell phone in his pocket and finishes with his locker and closes it up. He looks at his watch and leaves the building for his car. Rick is already at his car and is getting ready to leave. Kelly stops him briefly, "Hey I have been meaning to ask you Rick. You haven't had a cigarette all shift. What gives?" To this Rick replies, "When you had your accident, It was a pretty hard pill to swallow. It upset me so much that I was smoking up to five packs a week, compared to my normal two packs per week." Kelly replies, "Oh wow!" Rick continues, "Annie was starting to worry about my health and asked if we could look into smoking cessation classes through the hospital. Eight months later I am smoke free and either chewing gum or having a lollipop ." Kelly responds simply, "Well of that helps you then so be it I guess." Rick agrees and closes the discussion, "Yeah thanks. I'll see you later partner." Kelly replies, "Sounds good. I'll give you a call tomorrow. Too bad our days off go by so fast." Rick waves in agreement and adds, "Wasn't sure how to tell you this but Annie and I have been attending Bible studies at your dad's church." With this he gets in his car and drive off.

Kelly is about to do the same when his cell phone rings again with Bethany's name on the screen. He answers, "Morning little sister! What can I do for you?" Only Bethany asks, "Say, if it's your day off, do you have any plans for tonight?" Kelly replies, "I am on my days off and no big plans really for now. Why?" Bethany hesitates a bit, "WelL, I was wondering if you would swallow your pride with Daddy and come to the house for dinner tonight around 4:30? Momma is good with the idea and she thought it might be an opportunity for Daddy and you to make amends!" Kelly thinks about for a bit and replies, "I don't think that would be a good idea. You know Dad and I haven't spoken to each other in years." Bethany thinks for a moment and then asks, "Isn't there any way that I can convince you to change your mind?" Kelly is silent for a few moments then replies, "Naw, I better not. It's..." Bethany cuts him off by adding, "Jon and his sister Dawn will be here too."

Kelly immediately rethinks the idea and agrees with one stipulation, "Oh? Um? Well in that case I will as long as Dad stays civil, otherwise I am out of there." Bethany replies, I will talk to Momma and see if she can keep him in his corner so we can all enjoy our time together, ok?" Kelly is still a bit hesitant but agrees, "Ok, but remember if he starts anything about me leaving or church, I'm gone!" He can hear Bethany's excitement on the other hand and finishes the call. "See you at 4:30 little sister, bye." He ends the call and puts his phone in the cup holder in the armrest. He pulls out of the fire station and heads for his house.

He arrives at his home on the North end of Gold City. It is a small two bedroom ranch style house. He enters through the front door and puts his duffel bag down on the couch to the left. He makes his way to the kitchen to the right to see what's not spoiled in the refrigerator while he was away. Nothing really appeals to him so he just grabs a soda and closes the door. He picks up his duffel bag and drops it in his bedroom to the right and goes to his man cave to the left. He turns on the television and sits down in his recliner. He just flips through the channels, not finding anything good to watch. Of course this time of morning, there is nothing more than talk shows and movie channels. He settles on a movie and relaxes himself into a nap.

But this turns out to be no ordinary nap. His mind goes to work on him again, re-living the last eight months. He envisions the front of the big rig tractor just before impact, Tom Maxwell, remembering Sharon, and meeting Dawn at the hospital. He tosses and turns in the recliner as he relives these different parts of his life over and over. He recalls the last 8 months of rehabilitation of learning to reuse some parts of his body again. All of these visions are shattered as he is startled awake by his cell phone ringing. He picks it up and sees that it is Rick calling him. He pushes the accept button and answers, "Hey Rick, how ya doing?" Rick replies, "What took you so long buddy? I have been calling for the last two hours. I was about to call Sylvio and see if he could do a welfare check on you" Kelly looks around the room and asks, "What time is it? I must have nodded off." He pulls his phone away quickly and glances at the time and then returns it to his ear. Rick is suprised that Kelly is speaking to him, "Hey I'm glad you are still speaking to me after what I told you before I left earlier this morning. You know, about taking Bible studies from your dad's church." Kelly replies, "That's ok my friend. I can't fault you for falling into that trap." Rick asks, "What trap? Annie and I have had our eyes really opened up to what was missing in our lives for so long." Kelly avoids the subject by changing it, "So why did you really call?" Noting that he has slept away half of the morning already.

Rick asks, "So, do you want to come over tonight and just kick back with Annie and I?" Kelly replies, "No, I just got invited to my folks house for dinner by Bethany tonight." Rick responds with some astonishment, "Wow! You're going to enter the lion's den? From our chats about you and your Dad, I'm surprised you would dare enter that realm." Kelly answers him by saying, "I know but, Bethany is trying to guarantee civility and.." Rick's curiosity is peaking, "And?" Kelly takes a deep breath and replies, "And Bethany's fiancée's sister is going to be there and I think she likes me." Rick replies, "Whoa! Are you ready for that? I mean it hasn't been that long since Sharon's been gone." Kelly denies any interest in Dawn, "I don't know, I'll just go to humor my sister. I am not planning on anything happening right now in reference to dating." Rick closes the call, "Alright partner, Annie needs me so I need to go. Talk to you later." Kelly responds, "Okay, bye bye."

Kelly decides to get up from the recliner and take a shower figuring maybe he needs something else to focus on rather than always re-live his past. He finishes the shower and puts on deodorant and fresh clothes.

He's not very hungry at this point and decides he may have a light lunch after a bit. He wants to save his appetite for dinner at Momma's house. He hasn't been there in a while, but he can still remember the feasts she seem to always have with what looked like no effort to prepare in his eyes. He thinks back to the day is when he was a younger child. It seems he can always still remember the smell of fresh baked rolls and some kind of roast for dinner.

He remembers the enjoyment of gathering around the table the way a family was supposed to. He thought about the many enjoyable talks they would have as they ate and shared some memories. He started to fondly remember the times when his Daddy was exactly that, and not Dr. Ridge, Master of Divinity. Seemed like as Kelly went into his teen years, that Daddy was beginning to meld the two together.

Kelly assures himself that that was probably the time when they began to grow apart as a father and son. In retrospect, as Kelly began to rebel in his teen years, the strain on their relationship was creating a giant rift in the home. Arguments between Kelly and his Dad were becoming more and more frequent. There were many times, either Momma or Bethany would have to referee them. He quickly shakes off these memories and returns to the present day. He makes himself a peanut butter and jelly sandwich and heads back to the recliner. He turns his television on and spends the rest of the afternoon watching prepaid movies.

Time quickly passes and he realizes that it is time for him to get ready to leave for his parent's house. Although he feels somewhat apprehensive, he remembers who else will be there and refocuses on that. He puts on his best dress shirt and slacks, and leaves for his parents. He really doesn't feel like he needs to completely dress up since all it is is Momma and Daddy's place. It's not like he's going to see the President of the United States or a Hollywood Celebrity. He gets in his car and takes the short drive to their house. As he arrives, he notices the different cars in the driveway. His parent's car is in the garage. He recognizes Bethany's car next to another car with rental markings on the rear bumper that he figures is for Dawn and Jon. Their driveway is two car lengths deep so he pulls in behind the rental and parks.

He makes his way to the front door and moves his index finger to the doorbell. Just as he gets ready to push the button, the door comes flying open and Bethany blurts out, "Well well well, look who decided to finally show up!" This action takes Kelly off guard and surprises him completely. He calls out, "Hey, whoa! What are you trying to do to me? Age me another 30 years?" Bethany just smiles deviously at her big brother and replies, "Now wouldn't that be fun to see. Anyways, come on in and welcome home." Kelly deflects her comment and replies, "First, this is not my home. Second I am here as your guest." Just as he finishes his sentence, Dawn walks into the entryway and states in a playfully disappointing voice, "Awe, and I was hoping there was nothing that could change your mind about coming." Kelly's attitude changes immediately as he smiles at Dawn, and quickly notices her outfit. His mind is going off like the Fourth of July in his head. "Well, I could stay for a little while I guess. After all, I wouldn't want you to have wasted your money on such a great looking outfit." he replies. Dawn returns the smile and replies, "Thank you handsome!" The three of them make their way to the front room.

Maggie enters from the kitchen and goes over to embrace Kelly before he can sit down. As they separate from the hug, Maggie cups his cheeks with her hands and says, "Oh Kelly, it's so good to see you and that you have come back to the house." Kelly replies, "Thank you Momma." He pauses for a moment and continues, "So where's Dad hiding himself? Did he have to get the fattened calf brought in?" Maggie jumps in and chastises him, "You will show him some respect me son. Please do not make a mockery of the scriptures in this house. Besides, it took a lot of work and reasoning to get him to agree to this."

Kelly respects her request, "Of course Momma. I see your haven't lost your touch in giving me what for." Maggie nods in agreement as David enters the room. "Sorry for the delay. I had some church matters to attend to." He looks over at Kelly and declares, "Well, the Prodigal Son returns to his family and home!" Maggie immediately chides her husband, "David! I am not allowing Kelly to be disrespectful and I am holding you to the same account." David quickly backs down, "Yes me love. Whatever you say, I will do." David moves over to the fireplace and leans against the mantle. Bethany feels the need to cut the tension in the room and begins, "Well, I don't know about the rest of you, but I am so glad that we are all together as an immediate family as well as our future extended family." She smiles at Jon as she says this while Dawn turns and smiles at Kelly. In his slight embarrassment, he awkwardly smiles back at her hoping that her glance was not implying anything. But he knows in reality what she is meaning. Kelly tries to change the subject, "So, how long before supper is ready?" Momma replies, "It shouldn't be much longer. Just waiting on the biscuits to finish up." Kelly smiles and replies, "Good, I have been looking forward to some home cooking again." To this Momma responds, "Well then I know the biscuits will be put to good use in your belly."

David stands quietly next to the fireplace mantle and just stares at his son. Kelly is certain of this as well, because every time he looks over at his Dad, he looks the other way. Again the tension in the room is building. He gets up and declares, "I need some air! I'm going out on the back patio for a bit." Dawn immediately asks, "Would you care for some company?" Kelly just shrugs his shoulders and replies in a nervous way, "Yeah, um, Sure I guess if you want to." Dawn steps over to Kelly and they both make their way out to the patio. David looks at Maggie and just shakes his head in bewilderment.

Out on the patio, Kelly very loudly and obnoxiously takes a deep breath followed by several short deep ones. As Dawn follows him out, she asks, "Is it really that hard for you to be here this evening?" Kelly replies, "You have no idea how difficult this is." Dawn looks at him and asks, "Care to talk about it?" Kelly turns to her and replies, "Not really, I mean not right now. I don't know, my mind is so full of a lot So much confusion, so much anger." Dawn replies, "So how are you going to deal with all of it?" Kelly sits down in a patio chair, looks up at Dawn and replies, "I wish I knew how." Dawn sits down next to him and asks, "Have you ever thought of taking it to The Lord?" Kelly quickly becomes defensive, "You know, that's the LAST thing I need right now! " He sees the look of disappointment on Dawn's face and he tries to pull back his reply, "Look! I know you mean well and I am sorry for snapping at you. I made a deal with God several years ago that if he stayed out of my life, I would stay out of his. All was working out really good until this past year."

Dawn thinks quietly for several seconds and expresses an Ah-ha look and replies, "I think I figured out what your problem is." Kelly looks back at her in astonishment and asks, "Ok, I'll bite! What are you thinking?" Dawn is very careful about answering, "Well, first off, I have noticed that when someone else approaches you about God, you become very defensive about what you feel is an acceptable type of relationship with Him." This time, Kelly shows a very open interest in what she is saying. She continues, "With me, you don't do that. That says something to me and it should say something to you. Kelly Ridge, YOU may have given up on God, but HE certainly has NOT given up on you."

Kelly stares at her looking like a plug that's been disconnected from an outlet and replies, "Wow! You're as bold as my sister with a comment like that." Dawn simply responds with, "I call it straightforward and honest. A lot of people say I am too blunt. You know, a shoot from the hip type of person. That's who I am take it or leave it." Kelly has let things slide off him and changes the conversation. "I'm doing better now. Can we go back inside? I think I can handle my Dad now. Besides, you had somewhere special for me to take you to tonight, if I remember our earlier conversation." Dawn smiles and nods in agreement adding, "That's ok, we can do that another night. I am enjoying the present company." They return to the living room. Shortly thereafter, Maggie enters and invites everyone to the dining room table. They all take their appropriate places as David offers the blessing on the food, *"Lord we thank ye for the food tonight and the fellowship. Bless those who made the meal and bless this evening. We thank ye Father and ask it in the name of Jesus Christ. Amen."*

The time they share together works out better than Bethany or Momma were hoping for. Daddy and Kelly have never been so civil to each other since before Kelly attended high school. The time comes for everyone to go their separate ways. First Jon and Dawn leave, and then Kelly walks to the front door. He kisses his Momma on the cheek, and for some reason gives his Daddy a slight grin before exiting the house. Maggie closes the door behind him and leans up against it with her back. She draws a deep breath as she shares a look of mission accomplished with Bethany. The two ladies begin clean up with Bethany in the kitchen and Momma in the living room. David makes his way to the study, but makes sure he lets Maggie know. "I will be back out shortly me love. I need to get a few things from the study and come back out to help." Maggie nods to her husband and busies herself with cleaning up the dining room.

After a few minutes, David returns to the dining room. "Alright me love, how can I help you now?" Maggie turns and replies, "You can take the coffee cups to the kitchen. Bethany is waiting for them." David takes the cups to the kitchen and returns post haste. He collects the rest of the after dinner dishes and takes them to Bethany. As he enters the living room a third time, Maggie turns to speak but notices he his holding his left arm in an awkward manner. She asks, "David? What's wrong?" He looks at her and replies, "I don't know. My left arm and shoulder hurts really bad and it's getting difficult to breathe." Maggie calls out, "BETHANY!" She comes rushing out, "Momma, what's wrong?" Maggie answers, "Quickly, call the ambulance and call Kelly after that! I think Daddy's having a heart attack."

Bethany picks up the phone and dials 9-1-1. She gives out the information and paramedics are dispatched. She is instructed to stay on the line until they arrive. She pulls out her cellphone and calls Kelly, who answers, "Hey little Sis—." He is immediately cut off, "Kelly, Daddy's having a heart attack and we need you. Medics have been called, but Momma wants you here!" Kelly pulls over to do a U turn and races back to the house for Momma's sake. He arrives just as Bryant and Miller from C Shift are getting out of Medic One. Miller notices him and calls out, "Hey Ridge! Making house calls now?" Ridge replies, "Not quite. This is my Dad's house. My Sister called me right after calling you." Miller just nods as Kelly makes his way to the door before the paramedics. He rushes over to where Daddy is laying and moves Momma away telling her. "It's ok Momma I'm here and the ambulance is right behind me." Miller and Bryant enter the house and move quickly to assist Dr. Ridge.

They go ahead with their assessment and follow cardiac protocols. Momma holds on tightly to Kelly as they do their work to stabilize Dr. Ridge. He has returned to a state of consciousness but is showing signs of confusion. As they continue their work, Bethany steps up and clings to Momma on the opposite side. Kelly turns to Bethany and tells her, "I'll go with the ambulance in case they need my expertise. You take Momma with you in their car." Bethany reluctantly agrees and Momma nods in agreement. Kelly heads out to get the gurney as Bethany follows behind. At the door she states, "Kelly, it's great to see you caring for Daddy this way." He replies with certainty, "It's not about him. I'm doing it for Momma!" He turns and walks out as Bethany expresses a look of disgust, and returns to Momma. Kelly returns shortly with the gurney and helps with moving his Dad while Bethany just glares at him. As they leave the house, Kelly turns and calls to his Momma and sister, "He's in good hands. I'll see you shortly at the hospital." He turns and jumps into the ambulance just as Bryant is about to close the back doors. The ambulance speeds away with lights and siren activated.

CHAPTER 18

IT HAS BEEN TWO DAYS SINCE DR. RIDGE WAS ADMITTED TO THE ICU AT the hospital. Kelly sits in the Family Waiting Room clicking through the channels on the television not settling on a show. He can't decide on watching sports, a game show, or a crime drama, so he just sits there and clicks away. After a few minutes he tosses the remote on the chair next to him, gets up and walks over to the window and looks out. He notices a crowd standing in a circle holding hands and praying. He chuckles to himself a bit, but then notices a very familiar face in the crowd. He pulls out his cell phone and speed dials that person. The person on the other end answers, "Hello big brother. Any news on Daddy?" He replies rather sternly, "Well if you would be up here instead of down there with church members, you might find this out for yourself!" Bethany retorts, "Because I'm where I need to be right now. You and Momma are with Daddy, so I am supporting the members. Besides, I am coming up shortly to relieve you for a bit, so just deal with it."

He realizes the conversation is becoming louder so he quickly tries to put a guilt trip on his sister. "Look Miss Goodie Goodie, you've always been Momma's pet, so you need to get up here and take your faithful place next to her!" Bethany says a few inaudible words under her breath and blurts out, "Well maybe if you had stuck around all these years instead of only showing up when it benefited you, then this may never have happened to Daddy!" Kelly just brushes it off, "Yeah, whatever! Just hurry it up, I've got things to get done before I go back to work tomorrow." Bethany holds her phone up to where Kelly can see it and pushes the end call button with her thumb.

Bethany thanks some of the congregational members for their support as she makes her way to the hospital entrance. As she enters the ICU area, she speeds past the waiting room, totally ignoring Kelly who is still in there. Kelly paces the floor not even knowing that his sister has already passed by. Kelly's ire for his sister is mounting more and more until he receives a text. "I am in the room now. You are free to go." He makes his way out of the hospital without even saying goodbye to both Momma or Bethany.

As he drives away, his mind starts up again about all of the events from eight months ago up to today. He remembers the fact that in the days following the accident, he would have had his interview for Captain, and gotten the promotion he was seeking after. Who knows how long it will be until the next interviewing process? As he continues to drive, he thinks about his life with Sharon and what kind of future they might have had. He is also reminded of dealing with the likes of Tom Maxwell. All that keeps going through his mind is one of the last three nags Tom said to him. "You may have given up on God, but He hasn't given up on you."

He shrugs the thought off and remembers again, the struggles he had with all the therapies to bring him back to some level of normalcy. A means to get on with his life and career. He finds himself outside the city and up in the hills. He pulls over to the wayside scenic view and gets out. He walks over to the railing and just looks out over the city. There is something that is very compelling about this viewpoint. As he struggles for clarity on his own merits, he senses something eerie about where he is. He tries desperately to figure out what has brought him to this very spot, and still can not place it. After ingratiating himself in his sorrows for a few more minutes, he gets back into his car and drives away from the wayside. He looks in his rear view mirror and sees the location sign which reads Taylor's Ravine. Again for some reason he can't place it's significance, but he knows he had heard of that spot before. He speculates that he has responded to calls there in the past to ease his thoughts and continues driving back into Gold City.

As he enters the city limits, his cell phone rings. Instead of reaching for his phone, he pushes the Bluetooth button on his steering wheel and answers it before he checks the incoming number. "Hello?" He immediately recognizes the voice on the other end. "Kelly? It's Bethany! Momma and Daddy would like you to come back to the hospital and have a family meeting in the ICU room." Kelly replies in sarcastic form, "Why? Has Daddy somehow been miraculously healed?" smiling deviously as he finishes his questions. Bethany answers very sternly, "This is not a time for sarcasm Kelly! This is serious and he wants you here right away." Kelly replies, "Alright Miss Perfect, I will be there in about 10 minutes, goodbye." He pushes the cancel button before she can even reply.

Kelly returns to the hospital and makes his way to ICU Room 4 to meet with Momma, Bethany and Daddy. Daddy looks up at Kelly and states, "I know you haven't wanted much to do with me over the years, but I need you to do me a very important favor. Since I am in need of rest, I will let Momma explain what I am asking of you." Kelly nods and turns to Momma as she begins, "Kelly, your Dad will not be well enough to speak this Sunday, so we talked it over and..." He cuts her off, "Hold on Momma, I am NOT going to preach the sermon for him!" Bethany immediately chastises her brother, "Are you not thinking straight? You don't even come close to being as good a preacher as Daddy!" Momma quickly intercedes, "Both of you knock it off and let me finish!" She pauses to catch her breath and regain her composure, then continues, "We both agreed to call an old friend of ours and ask him to take the pulpit this Sunday. We need you to go to the airport in Capital City and pick up our guest speaker and his wife later this afternoon."

Kelly reluctantly agrees, "Ok, I guess I can do that. Do you know where they're staying?" Momma replies, "Take them to the house and they can stay in the guest room. We have also given them permission to utilize our home in whatever way they need. I will be home later tonight to fix dinner for them." Kelly looks at his watch and asks, "What time are they do in? I've got my own things to get done today too." Bethany jumps in, "Like what? Work out? Sleep?" Momma replies, "Bethany, that's enough!" She looks at her watch and turns to Kelly, "You should get going. Their flight will be landing in the next two hours and it's at least an hour's drive down there. Plus parking and finding the right gate." Kelly asks, "How will I know who I am looking for?" Maggie hands him a piece of paper and replies, "Just hold this up and they will come to you." He glances at the paper which reads Gold City Community Church with the airline and flight number on it. He then leaves for the airport thanking Momma and walks out of the room. David and Maggie look at each other and smile.

Kelly exits the hospital and gets in his car. He pulls out of the parking lot and checks his gas gauge. He stops at the gas station and fuels up before leaving the city. Halfway through his fueling, he stops the pump and thinks to himself, "Why am I taking my little car to pick this guy and his wife up when I should be using Mom and Dad's town car? After all, I'm doing this for them and not me." He gets in and goes back to the hospital and changes cars in the parking lot. Momma gave him the keys when Daddy was admitted and hadn't asked for them back yet. He looks at their gas gauge and sees they have a full tank so good call on his part.

While he drives, he thinks about the prospect of possibly running into Dawn while he is there. His heart begins to race simply at the very thought of her. He begins to realize that she may very well be the woman he has been looking for. Then again, he thought that way at one time about Sharon also. Yet in his mind, he can't help but wonder the possibilities of a serious relationship with Dawn. His only drawback is that she's a Christian, but he figures he can learn to tolerate that as long as she loves him for who he is. Before he realizes it, he is pulling into the airport complex in Capital City. He has to veer off to the left to get to the parking area. He figures he should probably park as close as he can to the terminal, since the couple is presumably close to his parents age they shouldn't have to walk too far to the car. He gets out and heads for the terminal and makes his way to the appropriate gate after checking the Arrival/Departure Screen. He looks at his watch and sees he is a bit early, so he stops at the Airspresso Coffee Shop for a drink. Then he returns to the gate and waits.

He takes a few sips and tries to go over in his mind how to greet these strangers. He figures the direct approach is best and goes with just holding up the sign and let them find him. As he looks up, he notices a plane landing that matches the airline company and looks at his watch. He is within minutes of the gate time, so his presumption is confirmed. The plane taxi's to the gate and his nerves begin to skyrocket in anticipation of seeing Dawn, if she's even working this flight. Even if he does, his mission is to pick up the guest speaker and his wife as Momma and Daddy had asked him to. Although he can at least be polite and say hello.

After a few minutes, the gate door opens and a very familiar figure is centered in the framework. Sure enough, it's Dawn Simon. The very woman he was hoping he would get to see if it was his fate. He quickly walks up behind her and opens his mouth to say hello and is stunned to hear her say, "Hello Kelly! What brings you here? How did you know that I was on this flight?" Kelly fumbles his words a bit and then replies, "Hello Dawn. Actually I am here at my parent's request to pick up the guest minister and his wife for this weekend." Dawn replies, "Oh, ok. Come to think about it, I did chat with a couple on the plane who match that description. As a matter of fact, they spoke very highly of Gold City."

Kelly smiles, confident in completing his task his parents gave him. Kelly asks, "Can I call you later?" Dawn smiles and replies, "Tell you what. If they don't mind waiting a few more minutes, I will ride back to Gold City with you. Would be kind of fun to surprise Bethany." She pauses and asks, "How's your Dad doing?" Kelly smiles and answers, "He's getting better, but not able to preach yet. Hence, the reason why I am here." Dawn turns back to the gate hallway just as passengers start to exit the plane and begin to fill the concourse area. He steps back and holds out the piece of paper as Momma had instructed him to do. He is passed by several of the passengers who meet their waiting family members and disperse around him. He looks at his watch and keeps holding the paper up, becoming frustrated at how long it's taking these people to find him. He looks down at his watch again, looks himself over from top to bottom and notices his shoe is untied. He puts the piece of paper in his mouth and squats down to tie his shoe laces.

At that moment two pairs of legs step up to him. One wore slacks and dress shoes, and the other in knee high skirt with black heels. His attention is drawn to a soft spoken and petite voice stating, "Excuse me. I believe my husband and I are looking for you. Our ride to Gold City?" Kelly finishes his laces and rises up to greet this lovely sounding female. His polite smile is quickly changed to a look of shock. He blurts out, "You have got to be kidding me! Of all the people I thought that I would never see ever again!" He just can't believe his very eyes as that familiar voice is heard, "Lieutenant Kelly Ridge! In the flesh and blood, standing before me right now." Kelly continues to embellish himself in misery, "This can't be happening. Please tell me this is a bad dream and that I need to wake up! I can't believe my dad would send me to pick up Tom Maxwell." The man is concerned and replies, "I know. I am the last person you thought you would ever see again. To tell you the truth, neither did I, but The Lord had other plans for me." This exchange has increased the curiosity of the female passenger who inquires, "Well my darling, you could have the courtesy of introducing me to your friend."

The man turns to his wife, wrapping his arm around her waist and replies, "I am so sorry dear. I would like to introduce to you the man mainly responsible for me coming home eight months ago. He is the one and only Lieutenant Kelly Ridge of Gold City Fire Department." He turns to Kelly and continues, "May I introduce my wife, Cheyenne Maxwell." She becomes a little bit embarrassed at first, then moves forward and hugs Kelly and tells him, "Thank you so much for being there when Tom needed to be rescued." Then she whispers in his ear, "The Lord knew where He wanted you that day." She then separates herself from him and steps back next to Tom.

This comment and gesture makes Kelly very uncomfortable so he does his best to deflect by changing subjects, "Well then, let's get you two down to baggage claim so we can get you to Gold City." They all turn and make their way out of the concourse and down to baggage claim. Kelly finds himself wanting to put some temporary distance between them stating, "Tell you what. You two wait for your luggage and meet me at the airport entrance. I'll bring the car around and pick you up. You're looking for a light blue town car." Tom and Cheyenne nod in agreement as Kelly turns and leaves. He increases his pace and thinks to himself, "I can't believe that Momma and Daddy would subject me to this kind of humiliation. Of all the people he could have asked, why did he have to choose Tom Maxwell? If I had only known, I would have parked at the other end of the lot and made them walk!" He has totally forgotten about waiting for Dawn as he gets to the car.

He unlocks the car and gets in, starting it before his bottom hits the seat. He makes way around to the terminal where Tom and his wife are waiting by the curb. For a fleeting moment he considers running the curb, but knows deep down that he is not that type of person. He stops the car, opens the trunk and returns to the driver's seat and waits. The Maxwell's take note of Kelly's behavior, and load their luggage into the trunk. They both get into the town car, with Cheyenne taking the back seat as Tom joins Kelly as the front seat passenger.

As much as Kelly is hoping for a quiet ride back to Gold City, he knows it's not going to happen. Maybe if it had been anybody else but Tom Maxwell, that might have been a very different experience. Of course his suspicions are confirmed as Tom asks, "So tell me, how have things been for you since your accident?" Kelly sternly replies, "Great! Considering the fact that I was up for a promotion to Captain and all that went out the window." Tom shows concern and replies, "You know Kelly, I'm not going to be sorry for saying this, but God had other plans for you. If you would just accept that fact, I believe your life would be so much better. I shared my testimony with you in that hospital room to try to help you see the necessity of God in your life, and you still haven't got the message." Kelly becomes belligerent and replies, "There you go with crediting everything to God! Have you ever thought that maybe, just maybe things are supposed to happen a certain way that God has nothing to do with?"

Tom responds directly with scripture then with chastisement, "Philippians 4:13 says, *I can do all things through Christ which strengtheneth me.*" To me, God has everything to do with it. Sounds like the world has made you weak! You grew up in the faith and lost it somewhere down the road." This infuriates Kelly to the point that he pulls immediately off the road and brakes hard, displacing the gravel as he stops the car. He turns to Tom and angrily replies, "Look here Maxwell! I've had enough of this foolishness you are feeding me. I told you months ago that God and I made an agreement, and it's worked out really good so far." Tom expresses a disheartened look and replies, "Look, I am sorry if you are being offended, but remember that I also told you that you may be finished with God, but He's not finished with you." Again Kelly snaps, "Unless you want to walk the rest of the way to Gold City, I would suggest that you keep your evangelizing to yourself!" Kelly thinks to himself, "It would have been much better if I was picking up Dawn and not Mr. and Mrs. Preacher."

Tom nods to Kelly's request and turns to look at Cheyenne in the back seat. She just looks at her husband with a distressed look on her face as she reaches for his shoulder as Tom cautiously asks, "May I ask you a question regarding your Dad?" Kelly sighs heavily and replies, "Sure. What would you like to know?" Tom continues, "Does he want me to come to the hospital directly or get lodging fir--?" Kelly rudely interrupts him, "I'm supposed to take you to my parent's house and you can stay in their guest room. Momma said she'd be home to fix supper later. You wait their for her. I AM NOT a taxi service! My instructions are to pick you up and take you to the Ridge family home." Tom nods and calmly replies, "Okay then, that will be fine, thank you." They all remain silent as they continue on to Gold City.

CHAPTER 19

As they pull into the driveway of the Ridge home, Kelly shifts the town car into park, gets out and walks to the front door. He has made it clear that the Maxwell's are supposed to fend for themselves with their own luggage. They do so and make their way to the already open front door. They enter to find Kelly leaning against the banister at the bottom of the stairs. He points up the stairs and states, "Upstairs, second door on the left across from the bathroom." Tom replies, "I'm impressed you know the house so well." Kelly answers, "I should! It's my old room when I lived here." As she starts up the stairs behind her husband, Cheyenne turns to Kelly and thanks him. "Thank you so much for going out of your way to help us." Not resisting a sweet sounding voice, Kelly's demeanor changes and he replies, "You're welcome Mrs. Maxwell and please enjoy your stay here in Gold City."

As she continues up the stairs, She turns to Kelly, smiles politely and adds, "It's Cheyenne." Kelly can't help himself as he watches Tom's wife ascend the stairs. his mind entertains a lustful thought briefly and quietly wonders, "What in the world does she see in the likes of Tom Maxwell? I just can't imagine being married to a man like that, who is constantly beating everyone he meets over the head with that God nonsense." Just as he finishes his thoughts, Bethany comes rushing in with an excited tone, "Kelly, We've been trying to reach you on your phone. Momma needs the town car back at the hospital. Looks like Daddy might be coming home tonight." Kelly holds up both hands and replies, "Well As you can see, I don't have my phone on me. I left it in the car." He begins to walk over to door, but turns to Bethany and declares, "I can't take any more of them so you watch them, I'm out of here." He slams the door behind him.

As he gets into the car, his phone rings. He answers without looking at the screen, "Hello?" A very familiar female voice is on the other end, "Hi Kelly! Did you forget to wait for me at the airport?" He quickly realizes his error and apologizes, "Dawn, hi, I am so sorry. I was so caught up in getting the Maxwells and forgot about waiting for you." Dawn replies, "That's ok, after we spoke, I ended up doing a hopper flight over to Central City. I will be back at Capital City on the return hopper soon." Kelly asks, Do you need me to come back down and get you? I am willing to do that if it will make up for earlier." Dawn smiles to herself as she senses the softness in Kelly's voice and replies, "No, that is very sweet of you, but my co-worker Candace said she will give me a ride to Gold City. Maybe we can hook up later tonight?" Kelly smiles to himself and replies, "Hey, yeah sure, that would be great. I need to get the car back to the hospital so I will see you later ok?" He pauses to hear her reply and finishes, "OK, bye bye." He hangs up and starts the car, backs out and heads for the hospital.

Meanwhile back at the hospital, Momma has been moving frantically around the ICU room, trying to gather up David's belongings to send home with Kelly. Even though Maggie had told Bethany to go to the house and find Kelly to let him know that his dad was coming home, the reality was just discovered in that time that the doctor wanted to give him one more day in the room and then send him home tomorrow. Kelly returns to the hospital parking the town car closer to the main entrance. He gets out and slowly makes his way into the hospital being sure to glance at all the pretty RN's as he walks by them. After a few more minutes he arrives at the ICU and enters Room 4. Suddenly, he senses a brief familiarity about the room as Momma turns to him, "Oh Kelly, I'm glad you're back. Did you have a good trip? Did you get our guests to the house? Did they find the accommodations to be acceptable?" Just as he starts to speak, there is a familiar voice that comes from the bed, "Aye Maggie, slow down and let the boy speak. He can't answer you if you keep asking him so many questions at once." She nods and let's Kelly speak, "Yes to all three Momma. If Daddy would mind his P's and Q's I will be just fine." David scoffs, "All these years and you still show me no respect. I find it hard to believe sometimes that you are a Ridge!"

With this, Momma chastises her husband, "Will I can certainly believe it. You both behave the same in several areas. Like father, like son it is." David tries to defend himself, "Don't listen to your mother me boy. She's been under a lot since me demise." Maggie quickly deflates her husband's comment, "Don't you be telling him that! I've had to put up with the fighting and bickering between you two for years now. I'm sick and tired of constantly being a referee. If you two can't make peace soon then I am going to end up in that bed. Please, both of you. I beg you to make peace." David nods in agreement in an ashamed manner, but Kelly must make one last cutting comment, "I will when he apologizes for all the grief he's put me through all these years." David scoffs again as Maggie touches his shoulder as a signal that she will handle this. "Now Kelly Michael Ridge, that's not fair to say. Your Dad has done more for you than you know. If you would just open your eyes to that, your perspective on everything might just change." Kelly just let's her words roll off his shoulders and replies, "Yeah maybe!" He changes the subject, "So Bethany told me to get the car back so he could go home." Maggie responds, "Well unfortunately that has changed since you got here. The doctor wants to keep him here one more night and then let him go tomorrow. Besides, I need to get home and feed our guests dinner." Kelly feigns ignorance and asks, "So what are you trying to say?"

Maggie takes a deep breath and replies, "I was hoping that maybe you'd stay with your Daddy so I can go home and be a hostess to our guests." Kelly replies with some sarcasm while respecting his Momma, "Ok, sure! As long as they give him his sedative first!" All Momma can do is look down and shake her head slowly. She is visibly discouraged by her son's comment, but chooses to remain quiet. Kelly blurts out, "Hey Momma?" Momma turns to Kelly before walking out of the room, "Yes?" Kelly asks, "Can I come home once Daddy's settled for the night and have dinner?" Momma is a bit taken back by his request, as Kelly becomes puzzled by even his own words. She asks, "Do you really? Or is this another one of those sarcastic comments?" Kelly replies, "I don't know, but something is telling me I need to be there. I can't explain it, but all I am hearing in my head is go." Momma is still stunned by his reply, but just let's it go and answers, "Alright son, dinner will be at 6:30. Don't be late getting there." Kelly nods in agreement as Momma turns and leaves the room.

Kelly looks at his watch and then stares at his Dad. He wonders if things were this way when he was the one in the bed. He concludes to himself that Daddy wasn't involved in anything about his own dilemma eight months ago. He moves over to the chair and waits for the time to go by slowly ticking away. He looks over at his Dad, who is resting from the day. Kelly reaches for the remote for the TV and starts flipping through the channels. This activity has roused his dad who calls out, "Maggie? Maggie?" Kelly gets up and puts himself in his Dad's line of sight and replies, "She went home to feed your house guests. Soon as you get your sleeper meds, I'm out of here!" David expresses a downtrodden look and replies, "Oh Son, I wish the Good Lord would soften your heart to forgiveness. It's been such a wide canyon between us." Kelly looks boldly at him and replies, "Look, let's not tall about it. We're better off this way."

Kelly looks down again at his watch. It's earlier than his expected time to leave, so he makes something up to have an excuse to leave. "You know Dad, you're in pretty good hands here and Momma is expecting me and they will be bringing your super tray soon." David scoffs a bit and replies, "Just like me when it comes to your stomach. I could never resist your Momma's cooking either." He pauses for a moment and continues with a slight chuckle, "Strange as it is, that the one person who's upset you most through this whole mess is now the one you will sit down to a meal with." Kelly just shrugs his shoulders in denial and replies, "Did you ever think it might be Momma's cooking?" He looks at his watch again adding, "Look Dad, I need to go. Someone will be back in the morning to get you. Good night Dad!" He exits the room just as the nurse enters with David's dinner tray.

Meanwhile back at the Ridge residence, Momma has been busy putting dinner together. Bethany has arrived and has jumped in to help with things. Tom and Cheyenne come down to the kitchen as Cheyenne asks, "Is there anything that I can help you with to prepare the meal?" Maggie turns to her and replies, "Good gracious no me dear. You and your husband are guests in our home. Taking care of your needs is my responsibility as the hostess." Cheyenne excepts her response and replies, "Thank you so much for your kindness Mrs. Ridge." Maggie gives her an up and down hand wave and adds, "Please call me Maggie. No reason to be formal in our home." She turns to Tom, "And that goes for you too." Tom nods and replies, "Very well then, Maggie it is." Both Tom and Cheyenne move to the living room and sit together on the couch. Cheyenne looks around at all the pictures and decor and comments, "They certainly do have several family heirlooms in here. You can definitely see the Irish Heritage in each piece of decor." Tom agrees, "Oh yes, definitely my love. All the way from Dublin to Killarney." Maggie smiles and replies, "Very good Tom. Your knowledge of Ireland is noted." Tom replies, "Thank you Maggie. Ever since I have gotten to know Dr. Ridge, Ireland has always fascinated me. Maybe Cheyenne and I can visit it some day."

About this time there is a short knock at the door. It opens and a familiar voice is heard, "Momma? Beth? I'm back for dinner!" Bethany appears in the hallway as Kelly enters through the door, she exclaims sarcastically, "Oh! Our brave hero has returned." She fakes a fainting spell then snickers as she walks away. Kelly plays this off and replies, "Funny Beth, funny." Momma enters the hallway and greets her son, "Hello Kelly. Please wait in the living room with our guests. Supper is almost ready and your sister needs to get back to the kitchen and help me finish." Kelly nods and turns to the living room and starts to enter. He comes to an immediate stop as soon as he sees the Maxwell's on the couch. He expels a heavy breath and exclaims, "I think I'll wait in Dad's study. At least I can be at more of a relaxed position in there." He moves down the hallway and enters the door to the study just behind the stairs. Feeling privileged and since his dad is still hospitalized, he sits at the desk chair and puts his feet up. Once again his mind is flooded with memories from eight months ago. Although Tom Maxwell sits in the other room, Kelly can still here the words, *"You may be done with God, but He isn't done with you."* resonating in his mind. He tries in desperation to figure things out, but he keeps returning to those same words. All of this is broken when he hears Momma call out, "Dinner is ready everyone. Please come to the dining room."

Kelly jumps up from behind the desk and makes a direct line for the dining room, just across from the study. He audaciously sits himself down at the head of the table, in Daddy's chair. Momma enters the dining room followed by Tom and Cheyenne. As she makes eye contact with Kelly, she glares at him for his audacity and chides him, "Kelly Michael Ridge, this is the second time I have had to use your full name today! You know no one sits until we are all at our places." Kelly replies to Momma in a lackluster tone, "Sorry Momma. It's not like there's anything important about this meal." Momma becomes stern with him, "Please, these people are guests in this house and I expect courtesy and respect out of you."

Kelly takes the best way out and just replies "Yes Ma'am." As the Maxwell's enter, Maggie turns to Tom and asks his to bless the food. Tom nods in agreement, bows his head and begins, *"Heavenly Father, first I want to praise You for who You are. I want to thank You for the many blessings that You have bestowed upon us. I want to thank you for the Ridge family and their hospitality to both Cheyenne and I. Father, I lift up Dr. Ridge to You and ask that You will heal him and give him a full recovery. I also want to thank You for giving me the opportunity to see Kelly again. Now Lord, I ask You to please bless this food to our bodies and to grant us a wonderful evening according to Your will? We thank you in the Name of Jesus, Your Son, Amen."*

Everyone except for Kelly repeats, "Amen." and takes their seats. Kelly looks at Tom with great disdain for what he said in his prayer. Tom is aware of what Kelly is doing and decides to ignore it. He looks at Cheyenne and smiles lovingly at her. He turns back to Maggie as she asks, "So, how long will you be staying with us? A few days? A week?" Tom replies, "Well, we are probably here for at least the weekend. The flight was planned as a one way trip, pending on Dr. Ridge's condition. We were going to just make it a one way ticket home when it was time to leave." Maggie smiles and replies, "Then you both are welcome to stay with us as long as you need to." Kelly makes a very obvious and obnoxious deep breath at this.

Kelly then mutters something under his breath making Momma ask, "What was that Kelly dear?" He is slightly embarrassed by the question, figuring he was quiet enough or so he thought answers, "Nothing Momma!" and makes up an excuse, "I was just reminding myself about something that I had to do at work tomorrow." Cheyenne interjects, "That's NOT what you really said though, is it?" Kelly becomes very offended, "Excuse me? You have no idea what I said to myself." Tom feels the need to defend his wife and cuts in, "By the way, did I ever tell you that my wife Cheyenne is an excellent lip reader? It's one of her many talents she has in working with special needs kids back home." She agrees modestly and continues, "So, do you want to tell us what you really said, or can I just translate for you?" Kelly's ire increases as she continues her blistering assault on him. "Tom told me everything about you when he was home and since I have been here, you have been nothing but downright rude to Tom and in turn, to me!"

Kelly abruptly pushes his chair back away from the table and announces, "I need to be excused please Momma? I don't need this at all right now." Maggie is utterly shocked at Kelly's outburst, but remains quiet and excuses him. He acknowledges her and leaves the dining table. As he enters the hallway, he can't decide right away if he wants to leave or hide in Daddy's study. After mere milliseconds, he opts for leaving. This way he doesn't feel like he's been cornered in one part of the house. As he exits through the front door, he makes sure the slamming of the door is loud and very obvious.

Maggie begins to apologize for his behavior, "I am so sorry for Kelly's behavior. He has been so bitter about just about anything lately." Tom Maxwell shrugs it off and replies, "Oh, you need not apologize for his behavior Maggie. Kelly has been bitter over much more than the events of eight months ago. I truly believe that it's our Lord and Savior really coming down on him to bring him back into the fold." Bethany asks, "This is what you believe is happening? Tom turns to her and replies, "I certainly do. You see your brother told me back on that ride in the ambulance with me, that he made what he felt was a deal with God." Maggie looks a bit puzzled and questions, "Made a deal with God?"

Tom nods and continues, "He claimed that as long as God wanted nothing to do with him, he wanted nothing to do with God." Maggie is stunned and replies, "He did?" Tom turns to Maggie and continues, "Yes he did, and it had reminded me of something Pastor Charles Spurgeon once said, *"The way you view God will eventually show up in the way you live your life."* The way I see it is evident in Kelly's life right now. He lives his life on his terms really and not on his Creator's terms at all. He views God as a barrier to achieving his goals and aspirations. Plain and simple, he is rebelling against God." Bethany flippantly asks, "Well, I don't really get sometimes why we have been praying for him for so long?" Cheyenne turns to Bethany and replies, "Come on Bethany. Scriptures tell us that we are to pray without ceasing. No matter how long it takes, we need to pray that he realizes his sin of falling away and repents." Bethany snaps back, "Yes, but even Paul had dusted off his sandals and walked away." To this Cheyenne answers, "Yes eventually he did, but why be like Paul? Your brother needs our prayers more than anything else right now." Tom adds, "I agree. Especially right now." To this Bethany fires back, "I get that, but, sometimes it angers me that I have been here at home helping with inside chores and helping with the lawn and gardening. Kelly has been gone for so long now, that this all this takes place and you want to just give everything back to him like it never happened."

Tom smiles at Bethany and replies, "Let me ask you a question. Do you remember the Parable about the Prodigal's son?" Bethany nods in agreement as Tom continues, "In Luke Chapter 15, it's the younger brother that takes his portion of the inheritance and leaves. After a period of time he depleted his funds and had nothing to show for it." Bethany nods and Tom continues even further, "As I am sure you know, he goes home and expects to be treated as a slave. But no, his dad welcomes him home with a celebration." Bethany looks somewhat dumbfounded and states, "I think I am on board with you, like you are comparing Kelly to being the prodigal's son." Tom agrees, "Yes, but here's where I am going with this. The older brother complains about what he does for his dad and never got a celebration party, but the younger comes home and his dad tells the older brother.." He pauses and brings up his Bible app to Luke Chapter 15 verse 31,32 and reads, *"And he said unto him, Son, thou art ever with me, and all that I have is thine. It was meet that we should make merry, and be glad: for this thy brother was dead, and is alive again; and was lost, and is found."*

Bethany's eyes begin to widen as Tom finishes, "Right now, I see you as the older sibling questioning this in the same manner as he did. But, notice again what his dad told him in that all he needed he had access to anytime he wanted it. He also told him that this was all right because his lost brother was found again and came home." Bethany realizes where she is having problems and replies, "You know, I never thought about all of this until now Mr. Maxwell. I am so sorry for my outburst. Momma, Mr. and Mrs. Maxwell will you please forgive me?" Momma and the Maxwell's nod and smile as Bethany returns the same to them. Tom then turns to Maggie and explains, "What it is and it comes down to, and I have been thinking about this a lot, is what is in Kelly's heart. In all his years in fire service he is battling a fire, an unquenchable fire that he cannot put out. It consumes him every day of his life. It is much like the fire John The Baptist refers to in Matthew 3:12 and Luke 3:17."

Maggie responds with a concerned look on her face, "Mercy!" Cheyenne adds, "Tom and I have been praying constantly for Kelly in our couples devotional time especially." This information has found Maggie in a quandary about her son. With this, Tom looks at his watch and closes the conversation, "I would love to continue with this in the morning. I think Cheyenne and I will head off to bed. It's been a long day for both of us." He turns specifically to Maggie and adds, "Thank you very much for dinner." Maggie smiles as Cheyenne rises to join Tom and they exit the dining room. Bethany gets up and starts to gather dishes. Although she is worried about Kelly, Maggie graciously rises and takes some dishes to the kitchen as well. She turns to Bethany in the kitchen and comments, "Such a lovely couple. I wish your Daddy could have been here." Bethany smiles and replies, "Oh Momma, he'll be here tomorrow and then you both can spend time with them." Momma replies, "I just hope it's not too overwhelming for him." Bethany responds with, "If I know Daddy, he'll want to get back to the ministry with Mr. Maxwell no matter how he feels." Both ladies finish their task and head off to their respective bedrooms. "Good night Momma." Bethany states before entering her room. Maggie looks at her and replies, "Good night dear one." She then looks towards the ceiling and whispers, *"Lord, grant David a peaceful nights rest and watch over Kelly wherever he may be. Thank you Jesus, Amen."* These unexpected truths she has learned about her son has really afffected her emotionally. She enters her bedroom and closes the door behind her for the night.

CHAPTER 20

THE NIGHT HAS PASSED AND IT IS EARLY MORNING. MOMMA'S ALARM sounds at 6:00 am and she is up and moving about the home accomplishing her wife and motherly responsibilities to keep the Ridge home maintained. Bethany remains upstairs on her room preparing herself for her days activities. Tom and Cheyenne have been doing the same for themselves in the guest room. After a while, Momma makes her way through the living room to the stairs. She is visibly concerned that she sees no evidence of Kelly coming back to the house after his abrupt departure last night. As she passes through, she makes a quick scan of the room to make sure everything is tidy. She takes three steps up the stairs and calls, "Breakfast is ready everyone!" As she returns to the main floor, she hears the upstairs doors open and footsteps across the upper hallway.

Bethany is first to appear and greets Momma in the living room, "Good morning Momma!" Maggie replies, "Good morning me child. How was your sleep?" Bethany answers, "I had a very good nights rest and am ready to take on today, it's just that...". She stops mid sentence as her Momma reacts, "What is it my dear?" Bethany takes a deep breath and replies, "I went to bed thinking about what Mr. Maxwell said about the Prodigal's son. I never realized how much I had been behaving like the older brother lately." Momma nods her head showing concern in her eyes as Bethany continues, "I feel like I need to apologize to Mr. Maxwell in regards to the conversation last night."

Just as she finishes her sentence, a gentle voice comes from behind her. "Apology accepted, Thank you." She turns and finds Tom and Cheyenne entering the room. She is a bit embarrassed and excuses herself quietly slightly grinning as she goes into the kitchen. Maggie smiles as Bethany passes and greets the Maxwells, "Good Morning to you both. I hope you slept well." Cheyenne replies, "Oh yes thank you Mrs. Ridge." "You're very welcome, but please call me Maggie." is her response. Maggie then asks, "May I get you both a cup of coffee?" Cheyenne smiles and replies, "Oh that would be wonderful Maggie. Thank you." She turns to her husband, "Tom? How about you?" Tom replies, "That would be great. Thank you Love." Cheyenne goes to the kitchen where Bethany is.

Tom then notices some worry on Maggie's face and asks, "Are you ok Maggie? You look preoccupied about something. I mean, I know I am not Dr. Ridge, but I can sense when there is something not right in a person." Maggie fumbles her words a bit, "I am worried about Kelly. He's been gone all night and I don't know what to think." Tom shows concern and replies, "Forgive me for being direct but, if you haven't gotten any bad news on the phone then I am sure he's alright." Maggie smiles and takes a deep breath, "Yes, I am sure you're right. I'm just a silly old woman who loves her children no matter how they've strayed." Tom smiles, "Stay strong Maggie. The Lord has everything under control." Just as he finishes his sentence, the front door opens and Kelly enters the house. Maggie quickly notices and fast walks to the door. She hugs him and exclaims, "Oh son! I have been worried sick about you."

Kelly surprises her and gives her a warm embrace. He whispers in her ear. "I'm sorry Momma for that. I've had a lot to think about that I was up all night at Taylor's Ravine." She replies, "Good gracious dear! You do look a bit worn down." They separate from the embrace as Kelly asks, "Can I join you for breakfast? I haven't eaten all night either." Momma replies, "Of course you can. Just as long as you behave yourself around the guests." She smiles that Momma smile at him as he replies. "Okay Momma, I promise you this time, but do I have a few minutes before I join you?" Momma nods as Kelly adds, Dad comes home today, right?" Again she nods and smiles at him. "Yes me son, he does." Kelly turns to use the downstairs bathroom and then returns to the dining room for breakfast.

As he sits down, he asks a question of Tom Maxwell. "So tell me about what you have been up to in your life and ministry?" This takes Tom off guard at first, so he cautiously replies, "Well, uh, I went back home after the accident, spent a couple more weeks recovering at home and then went back to work at High Mountain Ministries full force. The ministy's insurance covered the accident with the plane and there was a new one waiting for me when I fully recovered. So, it didn't take ne long to get back to flying." Kelly expresses an interest and asks more questions. "So tell me about this Ministry you are a part of. What do you do? How many of you are doing that? Do you like it?" Tom is becoming more and more puzzled by Kelly's sudden interest in him. As a matter of fact, he senses that Kelly is going to become sarcastic at some point of their talk and immediately calls him on it. "Look Kelly, I need to know if you are genuinely serious about these things or are you setting me up for a sarcastic comment?" Kelly pulls himself back a but and replies, "Mr. Maxwell, I have never been more serious in my life. I will assure you, right here in front of my mother, that I have no intention of ill will to you. I spent alot of time thinking some things over last night, I would like to discuss some things with you after breakfast privately in Dad's study." Tom replies rather suprisingly, "Sure, if that's what you really want." He smiles at Kelly and continues, "To answer your questions, Cheyenne serves as the secretary as well as handling the special needs clientele. I have two other associate evangelists that take care of music and children's ministries respectively." Kelly sits there quietly and listens intently to his answer as everyone finishes their breakfast.

Tom then turns to Kelly and asks, "Are you ready to talk privately?" Kelly nods, and the two of them leave the table and go to the study. Tom enters and heads for the couch to sit down. Kelly sits in the chair across from the couch facing him. Several minutes pass before Tom breaks the silence, "Well, Okay, what's on your mind?" Kelly takes a quick glance around the room and begins, "First off, I wanted to apologize to you for how I've been treating you." Tom very quickly replies, "That's quite alright." Kelly continues, "No, really, I mean it. Not just for my behavior last night, but for all the animosity I have shown you all these months." Tom is rather overwhelmed by what Kelly has said. He asks, "What happened last night while you were gone? You were really angry and stormed off. It's like you've gone through some sort of transformation. Kelly you have been so bitter about yoiur life that I am really caught off guard by this. I'm having trouble believing you right now." "I know." he replies and continues, "This is why I needed to talk to you one on one. But if you would please hear me out, you might be able to see that I've been wrong all this time." Tom hesitates at first, the nods in agreement. He signals him to proceed with a hand gesture.

Kelly gets up from the chair and starts pacing the room, then turns to Tom and begins, "You see, most of this issue with my dad began back 12 years ago when I was 18. I was getting ready to graduate out of High School, and I was expecting a very extravagant gift from my dad like a new car that I really had my eye on." He takes a couple of deep breaths before he continues, "You see, when he was going to present my gift, I was expecting a set of keys." He pauses briefly then continues, "Instead he gives me a box with a brand new leatherbound Bible complete with my name, Kelly Michael Ridge in goldleaf print in the lower right hand corner." He takes another deep breath and finishes with, "I became angry with him and threw the box down on the very couch you're sittiing on, walked out and never came back." Tom asks, "So instead of seeing the Spiritual value that was being shown to you, you preferred the material worldly thing." Kelly agrees, "That's right. I then told God that I wanted nothing to do with him, and He was to have nothing to do with me."

Kelly continues as Tom sits and listens, "I spent my life doing everything from working in fast foods and nursing homes. I even went as far as working for a pig farmer for a bit." Tom begins to remember what Dr. Ridge told him that night in the hospital chapel while Kelly opens himself up even more to Tom. "I harbored all those hard feelings about my dad for all these years and figured I had a pretty good handle on things. I was up for a promotion to captain on the fire department. My fiancee Sharon and I were going to get married. Everything was going really goood for me, until.." Tom repeats Kelly's last word as a question, "Until? Kelly turns and looks directly at Tom and replies, "Until I had to respond to a call for some guy that flew his plane into the treeline behind the city ballfield while trying to land at the airport." Tom asks, "Obviously you are referring to me?' Kelly nods and adds, "Exactly! Eight months ago, my life seemed to start falling apart and it all went downhill for me. Everything I had hoped and dreamed of came to literally a crashing halt." Tom asks, "So because I involved myself so much in your life, you chose me to be the one to direct your anger and frustraation at? I made an easy target for you because I am a Christian" Kelly smiles and replies, "Yeah and it felt good to stick it to you, so to speak, up until last night."

Tom asks "How so?" Kelly moves back over to the chair and sits down. He continues, "I took a drive up to Taylor's Ravine and stood outside my car, leaning against the hood. I stared down into the ravine, and contemplated ending it all right then and there. Then I looked up to the sky for a couple of minutes. Suddenly I realized, that this was the place where Sharon lost her life while I was in the hospital. Seemed to me to be quite a fitting place to die. I Thought she was everything to me." Tom interrupts. "I thought your promotion was your hope and dream." Kelly wants to answer, but gets choked up a bit as he tries to recenter himself and continues, "Sharon was a part of those dreams. Anyhow, as I was saying, All I could do was begin to cry." Kelly moves back over to the chair and sits down and continues, "I mean I really cried my heart out for Sharon, as well as for myself. It's like everything that I had bottled up inside me just started pouring out. I mean all the memories of the plane crash, you, my animosity for you, my accident, the recovery. All of it came back and hit me like a ton of bricks." Tom replies, "And you can't figure out why, right now, all this is happening." Kelly answers, "Exactly! It's like there's been some sort of unquenchable fire burning inside me for the longest time. I've been a firefighter for over 12 years now and this one keeps raging no matter how much proverbial water I douse it with. This fire just won't stop burning!"

Tom smiles brightly and begins, "Ok now, I'm going to warn you up front that I am going to go biblical on you. Are you ready?" Kelly nods, "Bring it on! You're going to eventually." Tom is elated by his response. "You made me think of the two places in scripture where it refers to an unquenchable fire specifically. In Matthew 3:12 and again in Luke 3:17 they basically say the same thing, it's just the two writers state it slightly different." Kelly replies, "Those verses do sound familiar. They both crossed my mind many times, especially when we fought a structure fire where they used cedar wood. It takes forever to put those out. I fought one of those before I worked the medic unit. It burned for hours before we got it under control"

Tom grins at Kelly, "There you go. It's the same idea there." He opens his Bible to Matthew Chapter three and Verse eleven and twelve and preempts it, this is John the Baptist preaching in the wilderness, *"I indeed baptize you with water unto repentance: but he that cometh after me is mightier than I, whose shoes I am not worthy to bear: he shall baptize you with the Holy Ghost, and with fire: Whose fan is in his hand, and he will throughly purge his floor, and gather his wheat into the garner; but he will burn up the chaff with unquenchable fire."* Both of these are references to The Lord keeping the good parts and destroying the bad parts. Essentially separating the saved from the unsaved. The wheat from the tares " Kelly looks right at Tom and tries to justify himself, "But I was saved as a teenager long before all this." Tom agrees, "I will not doubt you on that. However, you have let the pleasures of this world take over your life and chose not to include God in it. All these skills you achieved came from God, but you became so much of a worldly person that you became blinded by sin." Kelly becomes silent and just listens intently to what Tom is telling him. "The devil convinced you of a lie and you have tried for so many years to exclude and escape from God's will, but He has always been there waiting for you to call on His name." He pauses and then asks, "You know what I believe?" Kelly just shakes his head and looks down at the floor. Tom continues, "I believe now that The Lord sent me here to help you find your way back to Him." He leans in to Kelly and finishes, "The Lord has finally convicted you through the work of the Holy Spirit. That's why you are feeling this way."

Just then, there is a slight knock on the study door followed by Momma's voice, "Kelly? I'm going to go to pick up Daddy now. I will be back with him later." Kelly calls out, "Ok Momma, thank you." As she steps away from the door, Kelly turns to Tom. "You know, my Momma is one special lady." Tom smiles and agrees, "I know she is. Your dad and I have spoken quite a bit about her since the accident I had, which in turn caused our meeting." Kelly chuckles slightly before answering, "I don't know what would have happened to me if it hadn't been for Momma." Tom is curious and asks, "What makes you say that?" Kelly replies, "I'm sure my dad was more interested in his work than his own son. So, if it wasn't for momma being there those first few days, I probably would have given up." Tom is thoroughly taken off guard be Kelly's comment, "Wait! What?" Kelly repeats, "I said if it hadn't been for momma…". Tom cuts him off, "Sorry to cut you off, but it was your dad that was with you those first three days not your mom. I spoke with him in the hospital chapel the first night you were admitted. Kelly, he stayed with you at your bedside pleading with God to spare your life and bring you back. He was the one that stayed by your side from the beginning." Kelly is stunned by what Tom is telling him, "But when I came to, it was Bethany that was there and then momma stayed with me after that." He pauses to experience a moment of reality. "You mean to tell me my dad did that?" Tom replies, "Yes he did that Kelly. Your dad has been praying and fighting for you all this time."

Kelly is both suprised and shocked by this that he leaps out of his chair and runs to the front door. He opens it and calls out, "Momma! Wait for me! I need to go with you to get daddy." Maggie hears this through her open car window and stops immediately. Kelly runs up to her window and exclaims, "I want to go with you to pick up dad. I owe him the biggest apology." Maggie begins to tear up and asks, "Oh Kelly, do you really mean it?" Kelly starts to cry as well and in a very broken voice states, "Yes momma, yes! I have never been more sorry in my life then right now. Please momma, can I go with you?" Momma smiles at him very lovingly and nods her head. Kelly jumps up and dashes around to the passenger side and gets in. Momma exclaims, "I can't remember when the last time was that you were excited about seeing your daddy."

Kelly just shrugs it off with, "Yeah, well can we just get there please? I need to tell him something very important." Momma smiles and replies, "Alright son, I'm going as quickly as I can. Kelly sits in the passenger lightly drumming his knees with the palms of his hands. He glances at momma, and then looks back and forth along the roadside counting mailboxes to pass the time. It does not take long for them to get to the hospital and park the car. Kelly jumps out and runs around the car to help momma out. He exclaims, "Come on, come on! We can't keep daddy waiting." Momma is extremely puzzled by her sons behavior, but smiles and shrugs it off as they make their way to the entrance. They enter the hospital and quickly make their way to the Intensive Care Unit. As they enter, they find Dr.

Ridge already waiting for them in a wheelchair. David looks up and asks, "Aye Maggie what took you? I see you brought our son." He turns to Kelly and asks, "What now? Did you come to belittle me in front of everyone? Haven't you been hard enough on me all these years?"

Kelly squats down next to the wheelchair. He looks into his dad's eyes before speaking. "Dad, there's something very important that I need to say to you." He looks at his son and asks, "Now what would you be having to say to me? All these years you haven't shown me one lick of respect and I'm supposed just make like it never happened?" He turns to Maggie and exclaims, "Maggie, I'd like to go home now." Maggie steps up and interrupts, "Now David, wait a minute. I think that this is something that you might want to hear. Something has got him to be like this." David looks at Maggie's facial expression, then turns his focus back onto Kelly. "Alright me boy! You must have something on your mind according to your Momma. What is this important thing you wish to tell me that you've been waiting to to tell me all these years?" Kelly clears his throat and begins, "Well Dad, last night I had dinner at the house with Momma, Bethany and the Maxwells." David looks at Maggie and asks, "Look here me wife. He came down here with you just too tell me he had dinner?" Maggie sharply chastises her husband, "David Seamus Ridge for once just shut your mouth and listen to what Kelly has to say!" David is astonished by his wife's boldness towards him. He turns back to Kelly, sighs, shrugs his shoulders and listens cautiously. Kelly continues his story,"Tom and I had a heated exchange and I stormed out." Daddy sighs heavily like he expected that behavior. Kelly sees that and continues, "I know what you are thinking, but please let me get this out." Dr. Ridge nods and waves his hand for Kelly to continue, "I went up to Taylor's Ravine to clear my head. All of a sudden I realized that was the place where Sharon lost her life, I broke down completely. I just began to cry and I couldn't stop. I remembered everything that had taken place in the last year Dad, everything." As Kelly pours his heart out to his dad, momma just stands back and silently watches. She is beginning to become emotional and fights back her tears. She can't believe what is taking place at that moment right in front of her. Kelly continues, "I remembered it all dad, from the time I woke up through last night. But dad, I came with momma because I had to tell you something very important." Dr. Ridge has remained very quiet, and has not interrupted Kelly at all.

Kelly rubs his eyes to try and fight off the tears and complete his thoughts. "I came here to say that I am sorry for all the bitterness and anger that I have shown you all these years. Dad, I'm not worthy to be called your son. I want to come home and ask to be restored. I understand if you do not want me back, it's ok because of how I have been." Dr. Ridge can no longer hold his emotions inside of him and begins to cry joyfully. Kelly sees this and starts crying also. He leans in and adds, "Will you please forgive me for what I've done and take me back as your son, dad?" David gathers his emotions and replies, "I have only one question for you. "Can we pray together right here, right now?" Kelly nods as both dad and son bow their heads together for the first time in years as Kelly begins, *"Lord, Thank you for the wonderful Savior that You are. Thank you for giving me a father who has loved me far beyond anything I can imagine. A father who stayed by my bedside and prayed for me after my accident. Thank you for Tom Maxwell who helped me to see all these truths that has finally brought me to my breaking point. Thank you Lord for freeing me from these chains of sin. Lord God in heaven, I come before you and ask that you will forgive me for all my hatred and I ask that you restore me to your loving grace and mercy. I cry out to you and ask for your redemption. Thank you Lord! I ask this in the name of Jesus Christ my savior, Amen."*

The two men embrace each other for several minutes and then separate. Kelly rises and moves to the back of the wheelchair. He looks over at Momma, who has cupped both her hands over her mouth and nose, and is crying joyfully. Kelly gives her a strong hug, turns back to the wheelchair, and pushes his dad out of the room and down to the hospital's main entrance. Momma has already gone ahead of them to pull the car up. While they are waiting, David looks up at his son and asks, "Tell me son, since it's just the two of us right now, Was there anything else you wanted to share with me?" Kelly stops the wheelchair and looks down at his dad. "Well the first thing is that the Holy Spirit convicted me." David stops him, "Now you're just telling me that because I'm a minister." Kelly reassured him, "No dad, I mean every word of it. Second, I was told it was you who stayed with me for the first 3 nights. That spoke volumes to me dad. I honestly wanted nothing more to do with God at all. I never imgined any of this would ever be happening. I was expecting something big to change me when all I began to hear was a small whisper." David assures him, "Sometimes son, that's all He needs to do."

Just as Maggie brings the car up, Kelly's cell phone rings. Momma comes around the car as Kelly makes a one minute gesture with his finger and answers his phone. As he pushes the answer button, he recognizes it as the fire department main number so he is sure to identify himself with rank. "Hello? This is Lieutenant Ridge speaking." The voice on the other end begins, "Good morning Lieutenant, this is Chief Brewer. I've been trying to reach you for some time now.' Kelly looks at his phone and realizes he has had the ringer off and apologizes right away. "Sorry Chief, my phone has been on vibrate and I've been busy with a personal matter." Chief Brewer responds, "That's ok Ridge! I'm calling you because I wanted to be the first to congratulate you." Kelly replies, "Congratulate me?" Chief Brewer again states, "Yes congratulate you. The City Administrator and the Fire Commission has gone ahead and approved your promotion. So, congratulations Captain Ridge. Now, stop by the fire station and pick up your dress uniform and report to the city council chambers at 3 o'clock this afternoon for your pinning service. Oh and you're welcome to bring anyone you like with you for the ceremony. See you then Captain."

Kelly's mouth proverbially drops to the ground as he hangs up the phone. He turns and looks at his parents with awe. Momma asks, "Kelly? Is everything ok?" He looks at his parents, smiles brightly and announces, "Momma, daddy, I got my promotion to Captain. I have to stop by the department and get my dress uniform and report to city hall by 3 today." Momma gets excited and replies, "Oh Kelly, that's wonderful." She turns to David, "Isn't that wonderful news me husband?" David simply answers her with, "Aye." They get in and make their way to the fire station.

They arrive at the station and Kelly jumps out and dashes inside like he was responding to a call. After what appears to be mere seconds, he returns to the car and jumps in with dress uniform in hand. He remembers, "Oh, and they want me to invite everyone I know that I would like to be there." They get back to the family home and enter through the front door. Bethany runs up to her daddy and hugs him, "Oh daddy, I am so glad you are home again." She kisses his cheek and he smiles. He then informs her about the news. She gets excited and exclaims, "I need to call Jon and Dawn and see if they can make it." She turns and runs off to the other room with cell phone in hand. David makes his way to his study to spend some time in the scriptures and pray. Deep down inside him, he is overjoyed with Kelly's news, but did not want to let on. Kelly sits out on the back patio and just relishes in the news.

Several hours have passed and it is drawing closer to the time to leave. Kelly has fallen asleep and has to be woken up. Daddy strolls out casually and announces in a loud voice, "You can't get your promotion if you're going to waste the time on sleep!" Kelly wakes and looks at his watch. When he realizes the time, he quickly jumps up and runs into the house. David chuckles to himself as Kelly quickly vanishes. Within minutes he is dressed in his formal uniform and is ready to walk out the door. He turns to the rest of the family in the house and yells, "Hey come on, we're all going to be late for the ceremony." He closes the door and turns around only to find Momma, Daddy, and Bethany standing on the walkway clapping. He smiles and joins them all in the car.

As they pull up to the city hall, he takes notice of Engine One, Medic One, and Battalion One's response vehicle parked outside. As they approach the council chambers, Dr. Ridge looks at Kelly and suggests, "Son, why don't you go in first and we will follow behind." Kelly smiles and nods in approval of his dad's idea. Kelly reaches for the chamber doors. He takes a couple of breaths of confidence then opens the doors. He has a greeted with a round of applause as he takes note of all those who have been involved in his life. Everyone from A shift is present along with Chief Brewer, Captain Becker, Rick and Annie, Jon and Dawn, Tom and Cheyenne Maxwell. Linda Barnett and nurse Erin who cared for him in ICU was even there.

Chief Brewer says a few words of gratitude and then turns things over to Captain Becker. The Captain rises and calls Rick forward. "First, I would like paramedic Schmidt to come forward first." Rick rises and makes his way to the front of the chambers. Captain Becker steps up to Rick and states, "Paramedic Schmidt, I hereby promote you to the rank of Lieutenant." Chief Brewer shakes his hand after Captain Brewer. Annie steps up and pins the Lieutenant bars on his collar. They share a brief smile and Annie returns to her seat. The Captain then turns to Kelly, "Lieutenant Ridge, would you please step forward?" Kelly gets up and stands in front, turning to the chamber gallery. Captain Becker begins, "Now that I am retiring from fire service, it gives me great pleasure to hand over the role and responsibilities to someone who I believe exemplifies Gold City Fire Department. Kelly Michael Ridge I hereby officially promote you to Shift Captain with all rights and privileges included. You may pick one person to get the honor of pinning your Captain's bars on your collar." Kelly looks around the room as everyone stands quietly and anxiously awaiting his choice. Kelly takes another deep breath and states, "When I was promoted to Lieutenant, my mom had the honor of pinning me then. I think this time, it should be my dad, Dr. David Ridge." Dr. Ridge slowly rises from his chair and receives the pin from Captain Becker. He turns and begins to pin the Captain's bars on his collar and tells him, "This is a proud moment for all of us son. I will tell you, May the sun always shine warmly on your face. Congratulations Kelly!"

Dr. Ridge turns and stands next to his son. The room erupts in applause as Kelly looks around the gallery. His looking stops at Dawn who gives him a big smile. He returns the smile and shakes hands with the Chief, retired Captain Becker and then turns to his dad. They embrace with Dr. Ridge lightly tapping Kelly's back. He then turns to the gallery and makes the announcement, "To celebrate this day where not only did Kelly receive his promotion, but also in turn has given himself back to our Savior Jesus Christ. I want to invite all of you back to the Ridge Family home to celebrate this day with us." Everyone claps and cheers for Kelly. Rick shakes Kelly's hand stating, "I wanted to find just the right moment to tell you this and I think no is the time. Kelly, Annie and I gave our lives to the Lord about two weeks ago. I haven't said anything because I didn't want to offend my best friend." Kelly smiles and embraces Rick, replying, "Nothing will keep us from our friendship."

A few hours later, everyone has gathered at the Ridge home as invited. Kelly walks over to Dawn and asks, "Now that I got my life right with God and my family, how would you feel about becoming Mrs. Kelly Ridge?" Dawn cups her hands over her mouth and begins to cry. She looks at Kelly and nods saying, "Yes!" Just as they hug, there is a knock on the front door. Dr. Ridge steps away to answer it and is away for several minutes. He returns to the living room and announces, "Friends and family, We just got a visit from the Smith family who has the farm just outside of town. They wanted to thank me for helping to bring their twin boys to The Lord. You'll never guess how they wanted to repay me." Everyone stares at Dr. Ridge and waits for his answer. He proceeds to ask, "How long do you think it would take for a full side of beef to cook?" There is a moment of silence before everyone bursts out in laughter. Jon raises his hand and replies, "Why don't you save it for the double wedding of Kelly and Dawn and Bethany and I." Everyone huddles around the two couples congratuling them.

From that point on, the Ridge Family was restored and Kelly never started his day without spending time in Bible study with Dawn. They married in that double wedding with Bethany and Jon. Kelly had found a new life in Christ serving Him in whatever capacity he could. Jesus Christ became his personal Lord and Savior. He was certain of his salvation and didn't want to miss a thing.

FINAL THOUGHTS

Dear Friend,

Do you know Christ as your personal Savior?

Have you asked Him to forgive you of your sins?

Have you accepted the free gift of Salvation?

Are you certain of your place in eternity after you die?

In Romans 3:23 KJV, the scriptures clearly state that *"For all have sinned and come short of the glory of God."*

In John 3:16,17 KJV Christ declares; *"For God so loved the world, that he gave his only begotten Son, that whosoever believeth in him should not perish, but have everlasting life. For God sent not his Son into the world to condemn the world; but that the world through him might be saved."*

Good deeds and works WILL NOT save you. God's grace is all you need. Ephesians 2:8,9 KJV tells us: *"For by grace are ye saved through faith; and that not of yourselves: it is the gift of God: Not of works, lest any man should boast."*

Jesus Christ is waiting for you to call out to Him just like He was waiting for Linda Barnett in this story. Romans 10:9-13 KJV scripture also tells us *"That if thou shalt confess with thy mouth the Lord Jesus, and shalt believe in thine heart that God hath raised him from the dead, thou shalt be saved. For with the heart man believeth unto righteousness; and with the mouth confession is made unto salvation. For the scripture saith, Whosoever believeth on him shall not be ashamed. For there is no difference between the Jew and the Greek: for the same Lord over all is rich unto all that call upon him. For whosoever shall call upon the name of the Lord shall be saved."*

"Finally. Christ calls out to you in Revelation 3:20 KJV, *"Behold, I stand at the door, and knock: if any man hear my voice, and open the door, I will come in to him, and will sup with him, and he with me."*

So what will your answer be? I sincerely hope that you make the right decision, right now. It's as simple as 1,2,3:

1. Ask Jesus to forgive you of your sins.
2. Believe in The Lord Jesus Christ that died on a cross as payment for your sins and rose the third day according to the scriptures.
3. Ask Him to come into your life and save you.

If you have done this sincerely in your heart then you can be assured of your salvation from Jesus Christ.

All the best to you as you begin this new chapter of your life.

Blessings,
Michael C. Jones

Printed in the United States
by Baker & Taylor Publisher Services